A Sweethaven HOMECOMING

COURTNEY WALSH

New York, New York

A Sweethaven Homecoming

ISBN-10: 0-8249-3171-8
ISBN-13: 978-0-8249-3171-1

Published by Guideposts
16 East 34th Street
New York, New York 10016
Guideposts.org

Distributed by Ideals Publications, a division of Guideposts
2636 Elm Hill Pike, Suite 120
Nashville, Tennessee 37214

The characters and events in this book are fictional, and any resemblance to actual persons or events is coincidental.

Every attempt has been made to credit the sources of copyrighted material used in this book. If any such acknowledgment has been inadvertently omitted or miscredited, receipt of such information would be appreciated.

Cover and interior design by Müllerhaus
Typeset by Aptara, Inc.

Printed and bound in the United States of America
10 9 8 7 6 5 4 3 2 1

DEDICATION

For Sandra Bishop—first and foremost my friend, but also my champion and my cheerleader. Thank you for believing in me. Always.

ACKNOWLEDGMENTS

I don't consider myself a sappy person, but there are sometimes reasons to gush a little bit. One of those reasons is when you're thanking people who made it possible for you to write your second novel. If there's one thing I've learned, it's that none of this is easy…and that's what makes it worth it.

But I could never do it without the support and friendship of the following:

Adam. You may hate it, but you still manage to build me up daily. You love me just the way I need to be loved, and I'm so thankful for you. I'm so fortunate to be married to a fellow Creative who understands why I talk to myself and who isn't afraid to roll up his sleeves and man the house while I'm on deadline (and because I'm a terrible cook). You are truly my favorite person in all the world.

Sophia. My beautiful, talented daughter. You can be whatever you want. I hope you dream big. I'm so proud of your conviction, your integrity, and your kindness. You make me proud every day.

Ethan. My sweet, spiritual boy. Thank you for all your prayers as I worked on this book. They helped me every step of the way. I'm so happy to be the mom of such a kind, creative boy.

Sam. My baby who just isn't a baby anymore. Thank you for the constant interruptions that remind me to take breaks…and for making me laugh. You are such a bright light to me.

My sister, Carrie Erikson. How did the little girl who used to steal my clothes without asking grow up to become such a wise woman and faithful friend? Thank you for helping me muddle through the spiritual side of my life, reminding me what God really says as opposed to what I feel like He said. Oh, and thank you for always being the loudest person in the movie theater... it's not only embarrassing how loud your laugh is, it's infectious. And then we both end up looking like fools. Love you!

Melody Ross. Years ago when I first met you, I had no idea what an amazing, supportive, kindred friend you'd turn out to be. Thank you for being so generous with your encouragement, your experiences, and your love. They mean the world to me.

Jessica Goldklang. In my mind, Suzanne had your handwriting, but that's just one of the many things I love about you. You've always understood me when people often don't, and it feels good to be "gotten." Thank you for that.

Deb Raney. My very good friend and mentor. Thank you for answering all my questions, for your invaluable advice, and for being one of the kindest (and most genuine) people I know.

Mindy Rogers. I'm so thankful that our friendship has withstood the test of time... and all those other tests too. You're the real deal, and I love you for that.

Those brave enough to read the earliest drafts of my books: Carla Stewart, Gwen Stewart, Ronnie Johnson, and my mom, Cindy Fassler. Your feedback and encouragement were and are invaluable to me.

My editors, Lindsay Guzzardo and Beth Adams, whose insights improved this story one draft at a time. Thank you for your wisdom and for all the hard work in helping me bring Sweethaven to life.

My parents, who believe in me, keep me on track, and help me stay grounded in the real world.

And, of course, to my Lord and Savior, Jesus Christ. Thank You for putting this dream inside me and then helping make it come true. Discovering my purpose and Your plan for my life has been among my greatest joys. I am most blessed to be Your daughter.

The ache for home lives in all of us. The safe place where we can go as we are and not be questioned.

—Maya Angelou

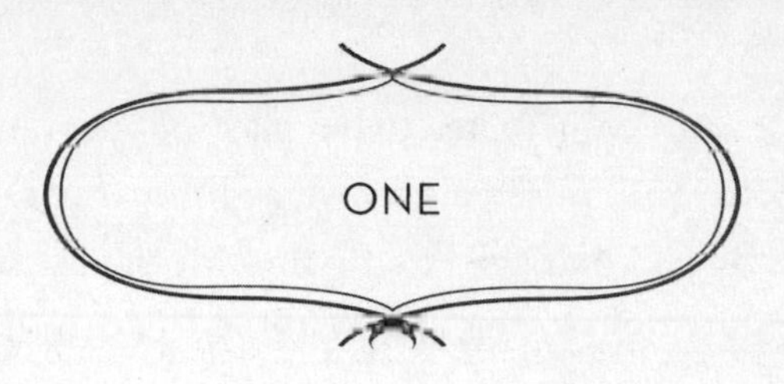

ONE

Meghan

"Care to explain this?"

A bead of sweat gathered just above Meghan's upper lip as the television lights radiated down like scorching sun in the middle of the desert in July. She glared at Shandy Shore, who'd just posed a question that hadn't been on the list during rehearsal. In her hand, the talk show host held a photo of nineteen-year-old Meghan. A photo Meghan had worked hard to bury. A photo she never thought she'd see again.

Meghan couldn't look at the picture. She stared at the floor as humiliation wormed its way through her stomach. The only thought in her mind: *Someone is gonna pay for this.*

Across the stage, a microphone waited for her and the four guys in her band, but as she stared at the photos in Shandy's hand, Meghan couldn't muster the courage—or the desire—to perform. In the wings, Duncan skulked in a circle around the show's producer, a small, pudgy man wearing a headset and carrying a clipboard. Her manager pulled the clipboard from the man and ordered his attention. Duncan wouldn't stop till he'd made his point.

We approve all questions ahead of time, he would tell the producer. They'd had an agreement.

They hadn't held up their end of the bargain.

"Ms. Rhodes?" Shandy pulled Meghan's attention. Underneath a tousle of blonde hair, Shandy's makeup looked an inch thick. Dark eyeliner and lipstick contributed to her plastic appearance. Now, she stared at Meghan with raised eyebrows, a glimmer of satisfaction on her face. Shandy had managed to dig into Meghan's past with such fervor, she'd uncovered her most horrifying secret, and worse, she'd done so on national television.

"Some mistakes are better left buried, don't you think, Ms. Shore?" Meghan narrowed her eyes, studying the heavily lined lids of Shandy's eyes.

"Especially ones that could cost you your children." Shandy's expression turned smug as she pulled a packet of papers out of a file folder.

Meghan glanced at Duncan, who stared back, a clueless expression on his face.

"What are you talking about?"

Shandy handed Meghan the papers. "Our top-notch researchers recently discovered your ex-husband is taking you back to court. He wants full custody of your four-year-old twins."

Meghan swallowed around the dryness in her throat. Her breath came quicker. She clenched her fists on the armrests of the plush sofa, the lights feeling more like an interrogation tactic with every second that ticked past. Meghan inhaled and shut out the sounds of the crowd. She focused on staying calm, otherwise she'd see her meltdown replayed on late night television for weeks. Duncan had his cell phone to his ear—probably hunting down whoever was to blame.

Shandy seemed to revel in watching Meghan squirm. "You look surprised. Do you mean to tell me you didn't know he was fighting you for custody?"

Meghan stuttered an unrecognizable response.

Shandy Shore turned to the camera. "Your bitter divorce made headlines only a few short years ago, and now it looks like your personal life is creating more competition for your professional life. Seems to be a trend."

Meghan shook her head. "I don't know what you want me to say."

"Do you have anything at all to say about these photos? Seems the timing for their release is rather suspect, don't you think?"

A deep breath steadied her voice. "I was young." Had she disguised her anger or did she come across the way she felt—like a teapot ready to blow?

"And desperate to make it."

"Aren't all nineteen-year-olds desperate to make it?" Meghan looked away, her face flushed as the heat of embarrassment rose. "It was a stupid thing to do."

"And your ex-husband covered them up for you, isn't that right?" Shandy's tone almost radiated glee.

Meghan pursed her lips. "Let's leave him out of this."

Let me be the one to handle Nick.

"I don't see how we can. The way I heard the story, you and your ex were on the rocks, he caught you posing for these photos and it nearly destroyed you. Didn't he almost go to jail for beating up the man who took these pictures?" Shandy's expression intensified.

Nick's face flashed in Meghan's memory. The couch. The slimy photographer who'd tricked her into posing for those ridiculous pictures. Said it'd make her a star. Nick's fury as he broke through the door. The only time she'd seen him lose his temper.

Because of her.

Just more damage she'd left in her wake.

But Nick said he destroyed them. Did he hate her that much? Had he held on to them all these years, intending to harm her if things went south?

"You know these photos are on the Internet? Do you worry this will tarnish your career? In the past few years you've reinvented yourself. Cleaned up. You even sing hymns at your concerts these days, is that right?"

Meghan's breath shook inside her as she inhaled. "Are you saying I shouldn't sing hymns if I've done things in the past I'm not proud of?"

Meghan had thought the same thing more than once. As if singing hymns could rid her of all the guilt. She'd never been clean enough—no matter how hard she tried.

Shandy laughed. "Of course I'm not. But you aren't exactly a good role model, now, are you? Having done a stint in rehab after your friend's son drowned in Lake Michigan under your supervision—then walking out on your own husband and twins."

Meghan's mind turned to Alex. How many years she'd tried to forgive herself for his death. She'd been unsuccessful. The journalist homed in on her like a missile on a target. "Seems this custody battle is long overdue."

"I think I'm done, Ms. Shore." Meghan stood and took off the microphone. Her hands shook and she couldn't swallow for the rawness in her throat.

Shandy quickly looked at the camera, then, like a pro, she smiled. "We'll be right back with more of the Shandy Shore Show."

Meghan met Duncan in the wings. "Do something," she said. "I am not going back out there."

"I'm trying, Meg," Duncan snapped.

Meghan glanced back at the show's host. A makeup woman powdered Shandy's nose, and the producer stood at her side, perusing a clipboard. She fought the urge to tackle her to the ground. But any physical pain she could inflict didn't compare to the emotional angst Meghan felt at that moment.

On the stage, her musicians had disappeared and another band had taken their place. After two minutes passed, the audience quieted and Shandy went live again.

"Ladies and gentlemen, as you've seen, we've had an unexpected turn on this show. You've gotta love live TV. But have no fear, Shandy Shore will never let you down."

Meghan paced. Her bandmates came around the corner, confusion on all of their faces.

"What's going on?" her bassist asked.

Meghan put her hand to her forehead. "I don't even want to know."

Shandy perched on the couch like a bird on a wire looking for smaller animals to pounce on. "I've always got a Plan B in my back pocket. So while Meghan Rhodes wasn't willing to tell us the truth about the scandalous pictures that are circulating the Internet or her ex-husband's plan to keep her from seeing her own children, we will still enjoy a little country music this afternoon. Please welcome my special surprise guest, Kingston Court."

The audience erupted in cheers and applause as the lights came up on the stage where her band had stood only moments before. Meghan glanced at Duncan, who had stopped midsentence, his mouth agape.

"They set us up," Duncan said. "They never intended for you to play."

"No, they intended to humiliate me." Meghan stared at Shandy Shore, who glanced in her direction, a smile on her face. Shandy had nothing against her personally—she was just a fading star and needed a big scoop.

She got it.

"This was a setup?" her lead guitar player said, shaking his head. "They dragged us all the way to New York for nothing?" The guys in the band wouldn't be nearly as collected as Meghan had been, and at this point it didn't matter. Let them tear up the soundstage for all she cared.

Meghan had too much on her mind to worry about damage to Shandy's set, namely, a supposed custody fight. Would Nick really take the kids away from her? Why now?

Meghan grabbed her cell phone and disappeared into the alley outside the New York studio and faced the back wall to avoid being recognized by the people passing by. She grimaced as the stench of urine and garbage accosted her. She had to make this quick, before she lost her lunch right there in the alley.

She hit the number one on her speed dial and waited for Nick to answer. Her ex-husband didn't deserve the first position in her contact list, but she'd never bothered to change it.

What does that tell you?

"Hey, it's Nick. Leave a message."

She couldn't say what she needed to say on a voice message. Her hands shook as she turned the phone off and leaned against the brick exterior of the building.

When she closed her eyes, the image of the photo flashed in her mind. Like the scene of an accident, she couldn't erase it, no matter how hard she tried. Those photos had nearly torn the two of them apart all those years ago, and now he was using them as leverage with the kids? Why would he do that? Nick had never threatened to keep her from the kids before. Maybe Shandy made it all up.

But her evidence was pretty convincing.

The door swung open and Duncan appeared in the alley. "What are you doing out here?"

"Fuming," she said. Just when people were starting to forget about Alex. About the tragedy that continued to haunt her, that had cost her everything. Just when she'd turned a corner and started a new chapter. Just when her new album had been released. "You said this was a Fourth of July appearance. An interview about my down-home Sweethaven upbringing. 'Capitalizing on that ridiculously small town' I came from. That's what you said."

Duncan shook his head. "Believe me, I don't intend to let her get away with this."

"Forget it, Duncan," Meghan said. "There's nothing we can do. She has every right to be a wretched woman and you know it." Meghan and the media had never really seen eye to eye.

She walked past Duncan toward the sidewalk.

"Meghan, wait."

She spun around. "What now?"

"The custody stuff it's legit. He's taking you to court."

He reached into his jacket pocket and pulled out an envelope, his face somber.

She took the envelope. "How long have you known about this?"

Her manager's face fell. She knew that look.

"You knew before we went out there and you didn't tell me?"

"I was waiting until after the show. I didn't want you to be distracted."

"Great plan."

Duncan sighed. "This is all coming at a really bad time, Meghan. You've got to stay focused on the album."

She shook her head, staring at the envelope. "He already has them. All the time. I've seen them once in two years—and he wants custody?" Her mind raced back to the weekend Nick had brought them to her house in Nashville on the spur of the moment. She'd gotten upset that he hadn't called first—if they were coming, she needed time to prepare. As soon as they left, regret seeped in. Why hadn't she seen their visit as a gift?

The regret returned, as strong as it had been the day she waved good-bye to her babies.

"I think that's part of his argument. Might as well make it legal if you've walked away from them. It's confusing to the kids. And this photo garbage pretty much made his case for him."

She exhaled as the fog lifted and it began to make sense.

"I haven't *walked away* from them. I just…" Meghan turned around and started back toward the sidewalk.

"Where are you going?" Duncan called after her.

"I'm going home, Duncan. I'll send for my things. Can you have someone bring my purse to the car?"

"I've got to get back to Nashville too."

"I'm not going to Nashville. I'm going *home*."

Her driver Maurice waited for her on the curb outside the studio in a black car with dark windows—the perfect place to hide. After a mousy intern thrust her purse through the partially cracked window, Meghan instructed Maurice not to go back to the hotel. "Straight to JFK, please," she said. "Unless you feel like driving me to Michigan."

"What's in Michigan?" Maurice asked.

Meghan watched as they drove past skyscrapers and yellow taxi cabs, the smell of baked cement invading the car. Pedestrians hurried from one place to another, each with their own story—their own life. A busyness that had always appealed to her—until now.

"Everything that matters."

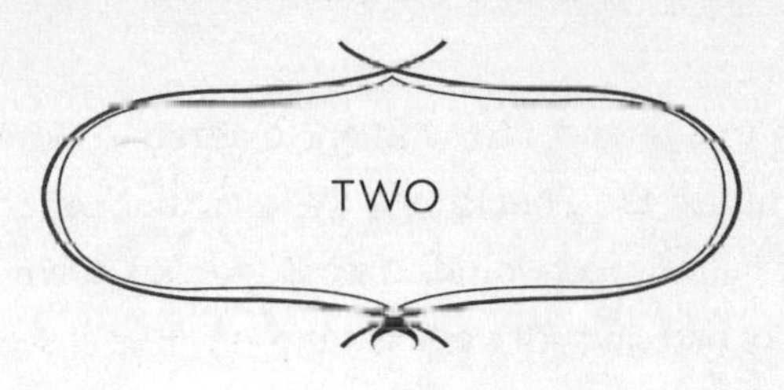

Campbell

"That's a lot of stuff."

Campbell spun around. Her suitcase had been crammed to capacity—so full, in fact, that she'd had to sit on it to get it zipped. She'd hauled it off the bed and found Tilly Watkins standing in the doorway. "You scared me."

Tilly laughed. "I'm sorry. I still have the key your mother gave me."

"Well, you'll need it if you're going to check on the house for me for the rest of the summer." Campbell dumped the morning's coffee down the drain and met Tilly's eyes. A look of disapproval waited for her there. "If you don't have time to check on the house, I understand."

Tilly had never hidden her true feelings about the little cottage town where Campbell planned to spend the rest of the summer. After Campbell's mother died and she found an old scrapbook full of memories about a place called Sweethaven, she had hopped in the car and headed to Sweethaven on a hunt to find her father. What she found was a family of old friends who'd loved her mother her whole life. Why couldn't Tilly see how important that was?

"It's not that and you know it. Your mother was my best friend—I'd do anything for her—and you." Tilly walked across the kitchen and leaned against the counter.

"Then what is it?" Campbell had known Tilly would fight her on her decision to go back to Sweethaven. It had taken her almost an entire month to convince the woman to agree to watch the house. Now, she'd missed the Fourth of July festivities on account of the guilt. "I can't believe you wouldn't want to head down to Navy Pier with me," Tilly had said. "It's our tradition."

Tilly had tried to convince Campbell, but her mind was made up. She'd stay through the Fourth and then she'd go. Reluctantly, Tilly finally agreed.

"I'm just not sold on the idea of your leaving home to spend the summer *up there*." She said it like Sweethaven was condemned. "Do you really think your mom would've wanted you to leave the house for that place? And those people?" She stared at Campbell.

No, Mom wouldn't have wanted her there. If she would've, Mom would've told her about Sweethaven instead of leaving her to piece together the remnants of her childhood through an old scrapbook and a box of art. She couldn't tell Tilly that, though.

"Those people were my mom's friends, Tilly," Campbell said.

"*I* was your mom's friend." Tilly looked away and Campbell's heart sank. In her rush to discover her father's identity, Campbell had abandoned her life in Chicago—and that included Tilly.

"Why don't you come with me? Or join me for a week?" Campbell took a step closer to her.

Tilly shook her head. "I can't leave."

"Why not?"

"My life is here. I belong here. And so do you."

"Do I, though?" Campbell crossed her arms over her chest. "What if there's more than this? More than taking pictures for a Web site? Mom wanted what was best for me, Tilly. I don't think this is it."

Tilly opened her mouth to say something and then closed it, as if she'd thought better of it.

"What?"

She shook her head again.

"You were going to say something. Don't pretend you weren't."

Tilly stared at her. "Is *he* going to be there?"

Campbell felt her shoulders tense. "Who?"

"Your grandfather." Tilly's jaw tightened and Campbell felt like she'd just been challenged.

"He does live there."

"Can you honestly tell me your mom would've wanted you to spend time with that man? The man who abandoned you both?"

Campbell turned away from her and grabbed a sponge. She began wiping down the counters, even though she'd cleared and cleaned them the night before.

"You can't tell me your mother wanted you to have a relationship with him."

"He's my grandfather." The words slipped out, almost a whisper.

"And your new daddy, will he be there?" Tilly's tone had gotten short, and Campbell tried to remind herself that her mom's friend spoke out of hurt—nothing else. She'd been anything but excited when Campbell told her she'd uncovered her father's identity.

Campbell returned the sponge to the back of the sink and faced Tilly. "I know it hurts that Mom's gone, but I don't think she wanted to let the past dictate the way I live today. Those people are family. I need to get to know them, Tilly. I want to know them."

Tilly looked away, her eyes cast upward as if she were trying to hold back tears. "I'm your family, Cam."

Campbell stared at her for a long moment and then walked toward her. She stood several inches taller than Tilly, and when she pulled her into a hug, she wondered if Mom's old friend might collapse from the grief she'd been holding inside.

"You will always be my family and you know it. But my family's getting bigger now. There's room for everyone."

Tilly pulled back and looked at her. "Not him, Campbell. How can you forgive a man who didn't even want you to begin with?"

The words stung, but Campbell reminded herself that she'd already begun to make her peace with her grandfather—and her father, for that matter. Both men had made foolish choices and they'd hurt both her and her mom, but holding on to that pain wouldn't do her a bit of good and she knew it. And Mom wouldn't want her to. She had a chance to salvage the relationships that should've been there all along. She needed to at least see if she could make it work.

"I know it doesn't make sense, Tilly, but I need to do this. For me. Mom forgave my grandfather—she went to see him before she died."

"But she didn't take you with her. That means something, doesn't it?"

"I think it means she thought she needed to protect me. But I'm an adult now. I have to make my own choices."

"I just don't want you to get hurt. People say things they don't mean all the time."

Campbell grabbed her small suitcase and dragged it toward the front door. Tilly followed her.

"I know, Til, but I'm fine. I'll be fine. I'm going to go up there and get to know these people better—my father, my grandfather and the women my mom grew up with."

"And that guy." She smiled, finally releasing some of the tension between them.

"Yes, and that guy." Campbell turned away to hide her own smile as she thought about Luke. She propped the suitcase against the wall. She wouldn't tell her mom's friend that she'd already imagined perfect days relaxing on the beach with Luke at her side. Or evenings spent together on the Boardwalk watching the sun go down. "It's going to be the perfect summer to figure out what I want to do with the rest of my life." She turned and saw Tilly staring at her, arms crossed and leaning against the doorjamb.

"You're going to figure that out in a tiny little beach town in Michigan?"

Campbell walked past her into the kitchen and grabbed another suitcase. "It's as good a place as any. I'm hoping I can work at the art gallery—get to know how Deb runs the business a little better. I think it'll be good for me." Perhaps she should've called Deb to see how she felt about that idea. She'd made arrangements to stay in Adele's guest room, but if she couldn't find a job, she'd be no better than a freeloader.

"Just be careful, okay? Don't get your hopes up that these people are all going to stop their lives just because you're in town."

Campbell watched as Tilly grabbed the small suitcase by the front door, picked it up and headed out to the car with it.

She was going to Sweethaven to leave reality behind for a little while. Tilly didn't understand. It was the perfect time for new beginnings.

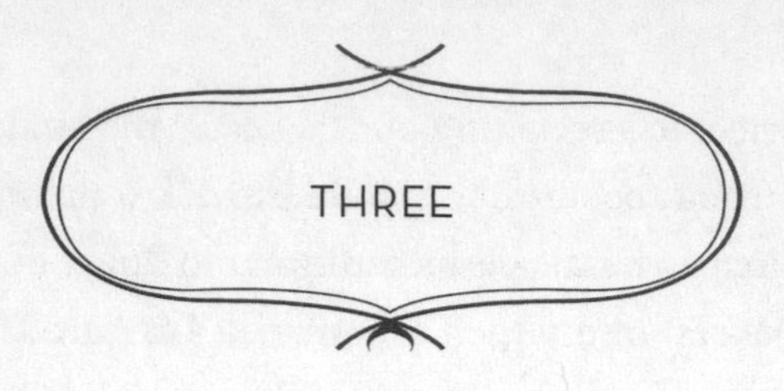

THREE

Lila

Summer in Michigan. Just like old times.

Lila had arrived just in time to see downtown Sweethaven transform from an Independence Day showcase back to its normal, charming self.

She'd missed Blue Freedom Days—something she'd looked forward to every year growing up. She'd even been "Miss Blue Freedom" three years in a row. She'd ridden on a float and waved to a crowd of admirers.

She'd tried to return in time again this year, but things back home in Georgia had been crazy. But she'd promised Mama she'd chair the Junior League Fourth of July fund-raiser, and she'd done it, even though seeing the sprays of red, white and blue covering the old-fashioned lampposts made Lila regret her choice.

Now she sat on the back porch at the lake house and stared out over the water. In the distance, small children toddled on the shore while older ones dove into the waves. From her hiding spot in the trees, she imagined they were hers. She pretended to have a daughter in a pink-and-white gingham bathing suit with a wide-brimmed sun hat to protect her baby-soft skin. She pretended, but even in the pretending, the pain, like the roots of a tree, twisted its way in.

To prevent her thoughts from meandering down a path of regret, Lila called Jane's cell, but when she didn't answer, she found herself thinking, as usual, about her husband Tom.

Since he'd admitted to being Campbell's father, Tom had given her the space she'd asked for back home, but he still came by on Thursdays to take the garbage to the curb. He didn't hound her in the evenings, but he had come over a week ago to change the oil in her car.

He took care of all the little things she'd have to handle on her own once their divorce was final.

He did it because he still loved her. He didn't want her to leave and she knew it. But the pain and humiliation of his betrayal had woven its way into her belly and rooted itself there. Fathering a daughter with her best friend and hiding it from her for twenty-five years had been the push she needed to walk away for good.

She realized her eyes had filled with tears as she recalled the moment she discovered the truth only a month before. They'd been sitting outside the art gallery and he had finally come clean. His words had devastated her, stealing her breath and rendering her useless. When she finally grasped what he'd told her, she went numb, but at home, in the dark nights, alone in their room, she felt every shred of disloyalty, of pain, of hurt. And those things kept her from taking him back.

She deserved better.

When he found out she planned to return to Sweethaven for the better part of the summer, he begged her not to go.

"We can work this out if you stay, Lila. Just give us a chance," he'd said.

His insistence—the kind of passion she'd waited to see in him for so many years—haunted her now. Had she chosen wrong, coming back to Sweethaven?

Thoughts turned to Tom and Suzanne. When she closed her eyes, she could see them on the dock together—spending all that time, getting closer—right under her nose.

How could she have been so stupid?

And just like that, the pain had returned. It carved out a hollowness in her belly, raw and exposed. Just like she felt.

She pushed the thoughts aside and stared across the water. The heat of a Michigan summer paled in comparison to Georgia's sweltering inferno, and she intended to enjoy her time away. Even if it reminded her how lonely she really was.

The rest of this summer was hers for the taking. She could do anything she wanted. In her mind, she and Tom were already separated. She could have an adventure or reinvent herself. People did that all the time, though more often than not, the people she knew did that by way of a plastic surgeon. After one last glimpse at the shoreline, Lila stood, determined not to dwell on her loneliness. She glanced at her watch. She couldn't sit in haunting solitude for one more second.

As she parked the car in a spot near the square, Lila admired the trees that flanked Main Street, old-fashioned streetlamps between each one. Sprays of pink and purple flowers decorated the town's center, planted in dark, rich soil along either side of the road. The town looked exquisite, rich enough even for Cilla Adler. Mama had always loved Sweethaven's beauty. She'd been part of the cosmetic overhaul the town had received several years ago. Lila found that appropriate. Mama liked beautiful things. No town of hers was going to turn into a dump.

Lila got out of the car and decided a stroll around town would do her good. She headed off, walking alongside the old buildings of downtown, most of which had been renovated to their original glory, preserving the historical aspect of Old Town Sweethaven.

Her stomach flip-flopped as she mentally ran through the summer's plans. Lila imagined long days with her friends, talking, relaxing and pretending their real lives didn't exist. She couldn't think of a better way to deal with the Tom mess than to walk away from it for a little while. If Mama had taught her one thing, it was the art of pretending. And she'd mastered it.

Never mind that there seemed to be an aching hole in her stomach the size of the Grand Canyon. She'd push that away, fill it with scrapbooking and laughter and memories of simpler times. Even as the thought entered her mind, Lila had to laugh. She never would've considered herself a scrapbooker, but here she was, looking forward to doing it with her friends. She'd spend the summer snapping photos, and then they'd get together and assemble them in a new album before they all went back to reality.

Just like old times.

As Lila reached the town square, she remembered she'd turned off her cell phone. She fished it from her purse and turned it back on. The display on the screen told her she'd missed a call from Tom. Her heart leaped, then sank. He'd be heartbroken when he realized she'd gone. She hadn't even said good-bye. She forced the guilt away and shoved the phone in her purse without listening to his voice mail.

She walked into the gazebo, sat down and watched the small town as it buzzed with activity. The last time she'd been in town, Sweethaven had been sleepy, but now, in early July, the pace had picked up. Tourists flittered across the brick roads, riding their bikes to the farmer's market or the beach. Families strolled downtown, while teenagers skateboarded down the sidewalk. Sweethaven had changed over the years, yet something about it seemed exactly the same.

In the distance, on Snapdragon Street, a man caught her eye. Tall and muscular, he wore a pair of khakis and a lightweight white cotton button-down. His untucked shirt and rolled-to-the-elbow sleeves were slightly out of character, but she knew that walk.

Tom.

Lila squinted as he turned the corner and headed in the opposite direction.

What on earth was he doing here? He was supposed to be home in Georgia.

Her heart raced and she wasn't sure if it was from excitement or fear. Her perfect summer would go straight out the window if she had to constantly worry about Tom. She'd come here to get away from him. But if he'd followed her—well, she couldn't deny the thought intrigued her.

She stood and followed him from the other side of the street, struggling to keep up with his pace. He disappeared into the farmer's market and left her standing there, unsure if she should follow.

Who was she kidding? She had every right to be here. But he had some explaining to do.

She crossed the street and went inside. When she didn't spot him on the perimeter, she began to search the aisles. Nothing.

"Looking for someone?" Tom's voice from behind startled her and she nearly fell into the bananas.

She regained her composure, ran a hand over her hair and stared at him. "What are you doing here?"

"You didn't get my message?"

Guilt skittered through her mind and she didn't want to admit she'd put the phone away without listening to it. "No. I didn't."

He looked away.

"What are you doing here?"

"I'm *from* here, Lila."

She raised an eyebrow. "And you haven't been back in years. Over twenty. Did you follow me?" Tom's parents had moved from Sweethaven years ago, and he hadn't wanted the burden of caring for their cottage. After all, they had the Adler lake house if they wanted to get away.

He leveled her gaze. "You are my wife."

She stared at him. *Not for long.* But as the words entered her mind, sadness joined them. She hated what they'd become.

She fidgeted with an apple on the top of the pile. "I asked for some space."

"And I've given it to you. But it's been over a month." He looked away. "I thought maybe a fresh start would be good for us."

She frowned. "I called Ginny." Their lawyer had agreed to draw up the papers to finalize their divorce.

His face fell.

An old woman scooted by, pushing a cart with a loaf of bread in it.

"Maybe we should go outside." Lila took a few steps toward the door.

"You called Ginny?"

She stared at him. The intensity behind his eyes startled her. It knocked her off-kilter and she struggled to right herself. But he'd hurt her. He'd betrayed her. What other choice did she have?

"I'll give you space, Lila, as much as you need. But I don't want us to be over."

She bit back a snide remark about how he should've thought of that before. In a moment of weakness, she'd told herself he was just a kid back then. They'd both made stupid mistakes, but he'd forgiven all of hers. Every time the idea popped into her head, though, she quickly pushed it aside. She'd made up her mind. Staying would make her weak.

Like Mama. And that was the last thing she wanted to be. All those years of looking the other way while Daddy made a fool of her—Lila swore she'd never do that.

"I don't know what to say, Tom." Lila smoothed her khaki shorts.

"At least have dinner with me. Let's talk about this. Let me attempt to change your mind."

"What if I don't want my mind changed?" She stiffened her shoulders as she met his eyes.

He reached up and touched the side of her face. "I have to at least try. Tell me you'll think about it. One dinner."

She hesitated. He wouldn't convince her, she already knew that.

"Don't give me an answer now. I'm staying at the Whitmore. Call me, okay?" He touched her hand.

A tingle shot down her spine. How long had it been since she'd felt that spark?

She pulled her hand away and met his eyes. It had been days since she'd seen him. Many days. She'd never admit it, but she missed him. And this new intensity in their relationship sparked something that had been missing for years.

Passion.

"I should go. I'm meeting Jane at the café."

Lila walked away, aware that he watched her until she disappeared behind the door. Outside, she let out the breath she'd been holding and wiped her moist palms on the seat of her shorts. Her nerves had kicked up like a gust of wind just before a storm. How ridiculous.

She hurried across the street to the café. Early to meet Jane, but in desperate need of solace. She slipped into a booth and prayed Tom didn't feel the sudden need for a cup of coffee.

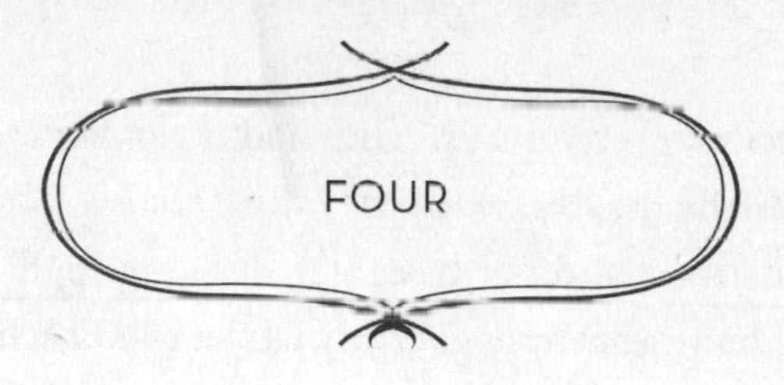

FOUR

Adele

"Me-maw, can we go out back and play?" Finn's plea came at the perfect time.

Adele had baked cookies, played baby dolls, and hidden quarters, and the twins had destroyed the house in the process. A few minutes of alone time would do her some good. She'd been eyeing the apple pie on the counter for over an hour—this way she could sneak a piece when the kids weren't looking.

"Go ahead, kids, just stay in the yard." Adele followed them out and locked the gate of the fenced in yard. "Play with Mugsy. That old mutt needs some exercise."

Mugsy perked up at the mention of her name but lay right back down.

Inside, Adele hummed to herself as she tidied the mess.

The knock on the door surprised her. She glanced at the clock. Too early for Nick to be home from work, though if he was planning to pick the kids up ahead of schedule, she'd be the last to know. He'd barely made eye contact with her when he dropped the kids off that morning. Was it still too painful for him to be in the house where Meghan grew up?

Adele wished she could ask him what had happened between the two of them, but she didn't dare insert herself into their business.

Her own kept her plenty busy. And it had taken her long enough to get Nick to finally trust her with the kids.

After Adele accused her daughter of being high the day Alex died—Adele had been wrong, it turned out—Nick had given his mother-in-law the silent treatment for years, never wavering in his support of Meghan. He'd done his best to make Adele pay for what she'd done. And had she ever paid—the accusation had destroyed her family.

She grabbed a dish towel and dried her hands as she walked to the door. When she opened it, her heart leaped.

Meghan.

"Hey, Mama," she said. "Can we try this again?"

Adele gasped, covered her mouth with her hands and stared at her daughter. Just a month before, she'd found Meghan on her porch, but her big mouth had driven her away before she'd even had a chance to ask how she'd been.

Adele's mind had replayed her biting reaction to Meghan's arrival every day since.

"It's about time, darlin', your kids won't even know who you are anymore," she'd said. Instant regret had washed over her, but no amount of apologizing mattered. The look on Meghan's face told Adele all she'd needed to know. Once again, she'd gone too far.

Not this time.

The Lord had heard her prayers and given her another chance. She desperately wanted to pull Meghan into a hug, to explain herself, but didn't dare. She didn't know what would send Meghan running again.

"Aren't you gonna say anything?" Meghan stared at her.

Adele took in the sight of her daughter. Wearing skinny jeans, boots and a V-neck T-shirt, the girl looked like she needed some food. A good home-cooked meal would do her good. "You're too thin."

Meghan laughed and looked away.

"I'm not kiddin', young lady. Get in here and I'll get you some pie."

"Peach pie?"

Adele smiled. "If only I'd known you were coming. This one's plain ol' apple. I can make a peach one later—if you're stayin'?" She tried to conceal the hopefulness in her voice. If she came across too eager, it could scare Meghan away. The girl didn't like to be anyone's source of happiness.

Meghan followed her into the kitchen. "I'm thinking about it. Rented a house out on the edge of town."

"That big one, I'll bet?"

Meghan nodded. "Huge. It's kinda lonely out there." She glanced down at the table where Adele had a scrapbook page in progress. "What's this?"

Adele looked at the page, an enlarged photo of the twins at its center and a few embellishments waiting to be glued down.

Meghan picked up the photo and stared at it. "They're so big." She looked at Adele, then ran a hand across the photo. Adele's heart clenched at the pain in her daughter's eyes. When Meghan set the photo down and looked away, Adele quickly gathered the photos and cardstock and set them aside on the counter.

"I'm sorry, darlin'." She paused for a moment. "The girls are getting together to start The Circle up again if you want to come. We haven't worked out the details, but Campbell's sittin' in for Suzanne, and I . . ." She snapped her mouth closed. *Stupid.*

"You're sitting in for me."

"No, of course not. The girls are just kind enough to let me be a part of it since I love to scrapbook and all."

Meghan waved her off and Adele took the opportunity to attempt a mood change. "I can't believe you're sittin' here in my kitchen. You know you could've stayed here."

Meghan didn't respond.

Adele looked at her old house with a fresh pair of eyes and regretted the offer. Why would her famous daughter want to stay in a beat-up old cottage with floral print curtains and one too many rocking chairs?

She cut a slice of pie, covered it with whipped cream, and set it in front of her daughter. "Here's that pie. I just made it this morning. Would you like some coffee?"

"Only if you have some made."

"I always have some made." Adele poured two cups and sat down with her own piece of pie. After a long moment she realized she'd been staring. "Pie okay?"

"It's good, Mama. Of course." Meghan took another bite. "I'm sorry to drop in on you like this. I guess I needed to get away for a little bit."

"Don't you go apologizing for comin' home, darlin'. I'm just wondering what took ya so long." Adele scooped up a bite of pie and savored the flavors. Maybe the company made it taste better than usual.

Adele assumed Meghan would come back after she got the invitation from Suzanne—Campbell's mom—but even her dying friend's last request this past spring hadn't been enough to convince her. So what *had* changed her stubborn daughter's mind?

Meghan pushed the pie around on the plate in front of her.

"I can't tell you how happy I am to see you sittin' here. I thought I'd run you off for good." Adele's stomach turned at the regret. Where Meghan was concerned, it seemed she made one mistake after another. And after six years with hardly a word, Adele was ready to stop that cycle.

"I'm sorry. I shouldn't have run off. Everything here feels so messed up. I'm not sure I should even be here now."

"Does Nick know you're here?" Adele thought about the twins in the backyard. She should check on them, but she didn't know how Meghan would react when she found out they were there—only yards away. She guessed it had been nearly a year—or was it two?—since she'd seen them. Nick hadn't said much, but she knew his surprise visit to Nashville hadn't gone the way he'd planned. Adele suspected her son-in-law had hoped for a reunion. Obviously, that hadn't happened. She pushed judgmental thoughts aside and reminded herself that's what had caused their estrangement in the first place.

Meghan shook her head, but the look on her face told Adele something wasn't right.

Adele raised an eyebrow. "After all this time you two still have bad blood?"

"I guess."

"You can't blame him for being upset, I suppose." Adele took a drink of her coffee, but when she met Meghan's eyes, her words rushed back at her like bullets from a hunter's rifle. "I didn't mean that the way it sounded."

Meghan pushed her plate away and shook her head. "Sure you did, Mama. Still siding with everyone else, I see."

"No, that's not what I'm doing. I am not takin' sides here." Adele grabbed Meghan's hand, but her daughter recoiled. "Darlin', I just want you to be happy. And I can tell by the look on your face and what I've seen on Nick's face that when you're not together—you're not happy."

Meghan's brow puckered. "Nick is fine without me, Mama. Better off without me, in fact."

"Is that so?" Adele watched as her daughter clenched her teeth—an old habit she'd had since she was a girl.

She shrugged. "If you say so."

She could see Meghan's wall go up. No sense telling her that Nick most certainly was not okay without her. Meghan would never believe that the love of her life had turned into a shell of a person. Just going through the motions, that one.

Adele fidgeted and searched for some common ground as she mentally chastised herself for putting Meghan on the defensive. Again. "Tell me about your music."

Meghan inhaled, then shifted in her seat. "It's good."

Adele laughed, trying to air out the tension between them. "You're one of the most famous country singers in the world and all you can tell me is 'It's good'?"

"It's work. A lot of work. And some not great things too."

Adele frowned. "Is everything okay?"

Meghan took a drink.

Adele leveled her eyes with Meghan's. "What aren't you tellin' me, Meghan?"

She sighed. "There's just a lot going on that you wouldn't understand is all."

"I understand more than you think, darlin'. I'm old but I'm not dead." Adele could see pain behind her daughter's eyes. She'd been through so much in her life, and Adele knew better than anyone how the wounds of the past could eat away at the soul. She put a hand over Meghan's. "I'm glad you're back."

Meghan tossed away the sentiment. "How's Luke?"

Adele stared at her for a long moment and realized Meghan had no intention of confiding in her. It stung, but she couldn't rush things. At least her daughter had come home. She willed herself to focus on that. "He's good. You should stop by and see him." She wouldn't tell her that her brother and her ex-husband were practically like brothers these days.

"I will. I've missed him."

Adele smiled and forced herself not to ask if Luke was the only one she'd missed. What about her? What about the kids?

A scream from the backyard drifted in through the windows, and Meghan's eyes widened. "What was that?"

Adele stood over the sink and peered out the window. "Nadia. It's just a fly, honey, it's not going to hurt you," she called.

"Nadia?" Meghan's voice from behind her went off like an alarm.

"It's gonna get me, Me-maw!" Nadia's voice trailed inside.

"No, honey. It's not. I promise." Adele watched her granddaughter recover from her near heart attack and then begged her own heart to stop racing. "She's a little dramatic." She laughed and turned around, pretending not to notice the nerves bubbling in her belly, but the kitchen was empty.

She walked toward the entryway and found the front door open. On the porch, she found Meghan leaning against the pillar of the house and staring out across the park. Adele inched her way toward her daughter.

"Meghan, I—"

"You should've told me they were here."

Adele pressed her lips together. "I didn't want to scare you off. Do you want to see them?"

Meghan looked away. Despite what Adele thought, maybe being away from her family had taken its toll on Meghan. Had she come home to make things right?

If so, she had a lot of ground to cover.

The front door popped open and Nadia stared at them. Adele glanced at her, then back at Meghan, who looked shell-shocked as she swiped the tears from her cheeks.

"Me-maw, I want some juice." Nadia barely looked at Meghan.

"Sweetie, don't you want to say hello?" Adele knelt in front of her granddaughter.

Nadia looked at Meghan and raised her hand in a slight wave, then turned back to Adele. She cupped her mouth, but her attempt at whispering was hardly quieter than her regular voice. "Who's that lady?"

Adele's jaw went slack and she fumbled through a litany of incoherent words. Meghan turned away and faced the street, and in that moment, Adele was sure, Nadia had broken her mama's heart.

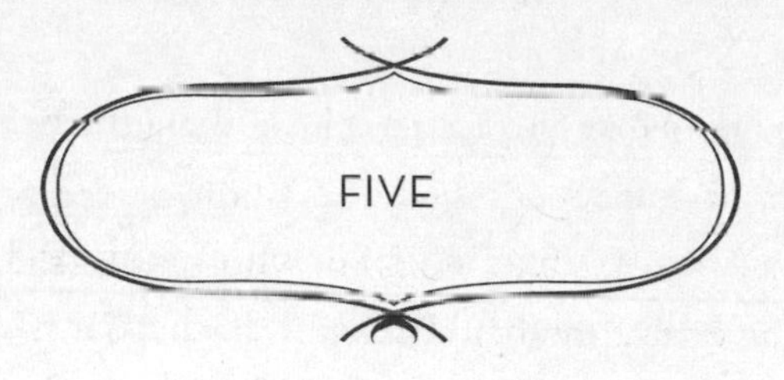

Meghan

The tires of the rental car spun on the wet pavement as Meghan sped away from her mom's house. Rain. Great. In a matter of minutes, a storm had rolled in, dark clouds hovering over Sweethaven, dropping water like a heavenly sprinkler. Rather than cool things down, this rain would release a thick cloud of unmoving air over the town, coating it with the sticky humidity typical of July

Meghan flicked the AC on in the car.

How could Mama feed her pie and coffee and not tell her Finn and Nadia were in the backyard? With a little warning, Meghan could've prepared herself to see the twins, prepared herself for the discovery that her own daughter didn't remember who she was.

Who was she kidding? Nothing could've prepared her for that.

Her muscles tightened as she drove toward the lake house she'd rented, but the thought of going back twisted her insides. Maybe the turbulent flight on a chartered six-passenger plane had turned her insides to mush, but the oversized lake house had lost its appeal.

Charcoal gray with thick white trim, an ample yard, and a tree house peeking out of the old oak in the back, the lake house should have charmed her from the start. A hammock hung between two trees that were likely over a hundred years old, and at the edge of the yard were wooden stairs built into the sand dune that led straight down to the beach. And, like something out of a brochure, four

Adirondack chairs overlooked the lake—likely the best place in the village to watch a sunset.

No, only a truly ungrateful person would find a reason to complain about the beautiful house, but the truth was, Meghan longed for something no house could offer. The comfort and familiarity she'd always clung to when she drove past the Welcome to Sweethaven sign.

She wanted to go *home.* And she didn't even know where that was anymore, only that it wasn't in a rented lake house full of empty rooms.

She pushed away the lingering hurt, the angst she felt over having lost her safe place, the jealousy of knowing her own mother probably sang her children to sleep at night.

Why hadn't Mama showed them her picture? Kept her in their lives?

Rain hit the windshield with more force now, and Meghan blinked back tears.

Mama hadn't done anything wrong—Meghan was the one who chose to leave her kids. That didn't mean her mother had to cut them off too.

Her phone rang. She fumbled through her bag and finally found it.

"Hello, Duncan."

"Meghan, where are you? I thought you said you were coming home?" He sounded annoyed.

"I did. Home to Michigan. I need to figure this thing out with my kids." Great. She'd only been gone a day and he was already having a coronary.

He let out a heavy sigh. "Can't this wait until after the publicity tour? You're releasing a new album, or have you forgotten that?"

"How could I forget that?" She'd worked nonstop to make the album perfect. The timing on this custody issue couldn't be worse.

"It's gotten some great press, Meg, but you have to ride this wave before everyone forgets about you. You know how important this is."

Her comeback. That's what they were saying. It meant everything.

Nadia's words rushed back like a slap across the face. *Who's that lady?* And Meghan realized the album didn't mean everything. Not anymore.

"Can we postpone the release?"

"If you want to kill your career."

"Duncan, this is my family." She drummed her thumb on the steering wheel.

He scoffed. "Nick's basically had full custody all along. Let him have it. More time for you to focus on what you do best—performing."

She blinked back tears and tried to see the rain coated gray-blue road that stretched out in front of her. "You don't understand."

"I understand you've got a job to do, and I need you back here. Like, yesterday. You've got *Good Morning America* this week."

She shook her head. She couldn't think about *Good Morning America* right now.

"Meghan, did you hear me?"

"I heard you."

"Get back to Nashville. Then we'll head to New York together."

"I'll call you tomorrow."

"Meghan, your career depends on it."

She hung up before he could say anything else. She didn't need him droning in her ear. Duncan didn't have kids and only saw them as a nuisance. How could he possibly understand?

Meghan turned onto Lilac Lane but drove right past the driveway to her rental house.

At this rate the twins would know her mom—and Nick's mom—better than they knew her. The thought of it assaulted Meghan like a sucker punch to the gut. What had she been doing the past two years?

The answer came as quickly as the question. Protecting them—from herself.

Her thoughts spun back two years. Her last album had just been released. Songs she'd written in rehab before the twins were even born. She'd been clean four years by that point, ever since the summer of Alex's accident, but the pressure broke her. Just like that, she lay on the cold tile floor of the bathroom, her sweaty hair matted to her head and Nick standing over her, trying to figure out why she'd throw it all away so thoughtlessly. All that rehab, all that therapy, years of sponsors and walking the straight and narrow. How could she?

"Meghan, why?"

"It's too much, and I told you. I told you this would happen. I never should've had kids. I'm like poison to them."

The look on Nick's face shamed her. "How can you say that?"

"Look at me." She collapsed into a heap then, the weight of her own body too much to hold upright. "I can't do this to them."

"What are you saying?"

Nick's face was the last thing she remembered seeing before she passed out. When she woke up the next morning, she knew what she had to do.

A life with her was toxic to her children. If she loved them at all, she had to leave.

Meghan slowed the car as she rounded the bend leading to the house where Nick grew up. The house where her children now lived. As she realized it, the thought turned her stomach. She remembered the stories Nick told about the way his dad treated them. How he'd come home drunk and use his mother—and, later, Nick—as a punching bag. How one time he got so angry at Nick for not mowing the lawn that he locked his own son out of the house and Nick had to sleep in the garage. How his dad threw him down the back stairs and broke his arm. Meghan shuddered at the thought.

Was there a remnant of that abuse still hanging in the air?

She shut off the engine and stared at the house, wondering what had happened to her ex-husband to warrant his hatred—to push him to file for custody. She couldn't spend another moment in the dark.

Her mind whirled with possibilities. What if he'd fallen in love? What if he planned to get married and raise the kids with another woman?

A wave of nausea washed over her.

She'd always been able to count on Nick's love—but this time, she'd pushed him too far. He'd gotten tired of waiting. That's why he leaked the photos. That's why he filed for sole custody. He wanted to be rid of her. And he deserved that. He deserved to move on with someone better. She wanted that for him.

Didn't she?

Meghan forced the uninvited thoughts out of her mind and focused on the white farmhouse in front of her.

The house had changed. Nick must've renovated it after he moved back. Maybe changing its exterior had enabled him to sleep under that roof and not hear the sound of his father's rage when he closed his eyes.

Could she find a way to exist in Sweethaven and not relive that day on the beach or its aftermath? Or all the sweet moments she and Nick had shared—the ones that still kept her from moving on?

She turned off the car and exhaled. The rain had let up, only scattered droplets falling now. Meghan found an umbrella in the back seat and hurried out into the damp summer air before she lost her nerve.

She walked up onto the porch and knocked, then took a few steps back.

In her mind, she planned the confrontation. It started with "What were you thinking?" and ended with "I never want to see you again." Somewhere in the middle, she'd thrown in a "There's no way you're taking the kids away from me" for good measure. But she prepared herself for Nick's glare, his green eyes searing. They'd always had a way of setting her off-kilter.

When she heard shuffling behind the door, she nearly darted off the porch, but she'd never get away in time.

The door opened, and Meghan closed her eyes for a second, gathering her nerve.

But when she opened them, Nick's eyes became the least of her worries.

Violet Rhodes, Nick's mother, stood behind the glass, and as she stared at Meghan, disgust skittered across her face. "What are *you* doing here?" Gravel churned inside Violet's vocal cords; the years of smoking had turned her voice rough like sandpaper.

Did she smoke around the kids?

"Is Nick here?" *Stupid.* She should've known he wasn't home—why else would the twins be with her mom?

Unmistakable contempt crossed the old woman's face and she shook her head. "What are you doing here, Meghan?"

"I came to talk to Nick."

"He's at work. Us poor folks have to work for a living." She took a drag on her cigarette and blew the smoke in Meghan's face.

Meghan fanned it away.

"Don't even think about trying to come back in and ruin everything again. He's just now getting over you."

Is he ever.

Meghan looked away. "Can you tell him I stopped by?"

She flicked her cigarette into the yard and put her hands on her hips. "No. I can't. You have no idea what he's been through." Violet's eyes went black.

"I think he's paid me back plenty for what I did, Vi."

Knowing washed over her face. "Oh, right. The papers." Violet wore a tight-lipped grin.

Meghan took a calming breath and swallowed her pride, walking toward the car but aware of the old woman's glare burrowing a hole into her back. Once safe inside, she realized she'd been holding her breath. She glanced up and saw the hate in Violet's eyes, still fixated on her as she slammed the car into reverse and backed out.

Tears stung her eyes and she blinked them back, trying to focus on the wet pavement. The sky had clouded over again and she squinted to see the street through the fog. She accelerated down the winding road and wiped her cheeks dry.

Duncan's words rushed back to her. *Nick's basically had full custody all along. Let him have it.* It was as if he'd said "Who cares?"

But she cared. She'd always cared. That's why she'd had to run away in the first place.

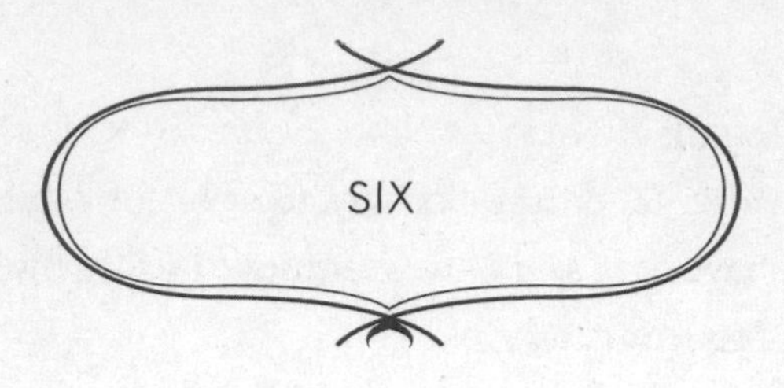

Campbell

The sign for Sweethaven welcomed Campbell back as she pulled onto Main Street. With the windows down, the warm July air blew across her face, bringing with it the undeniable fragrance of the lake. It was almost too warm not to have the air on, but Campbell had dreamed of the smell of Sweethaven for weeks. She took it all in.

Nervous anticipation welled within her. She'd been thinking about her return to this little town ever since the day she left almost two months ago. She'd gone searching for answers after Mom died, and while she'd gotten more than she bargained for, she'd come to terms with the fact that she wanted to know her father—and her grandfather for that matter. And she wanted to know the women who had welcomed her with such wide-open arms. She couldn't tell Tilly, but they were all family now.

And this summer would be about finding her place and fitting in. Finally. There had always been something important missing, and she was sure she'd found it when she discovered the old scrapbook Mom and her friends had kept when they were kids. It had led her here and told of a version of her mom she'd never known.

She entered the downtown section of town and her heart jumped. In just a few minutes, she'd see Luke again. After weeks of phone calls and late nights falling asleep with his voice in her ear, she'd finally get to see him again. And it wouldn't be like the couple of times he'd come to the city for work. Both times, he'd gotten called away, and they'd barely had time to share a quiet meal. Now, they'd have the rest of the summer to really figure out where this relationship was heading.

She smiled at the thought.

As she drove down Main Street, she glanced over at the Sweethaven Gallery off to the right, the memory of her first successful art show rushing back. Her joy, though, was short-lived when she spotted Deb, the gallery's owner, standing outside affixing a For Sale sign to the front window.

What on earth? Why would Deb sell the gallery? Why now, when Campbell had already planned to spend the better part of the summer there?

Without thinking, Campbell pulled into a parking space near the gallery and kept her eyes fixed on the older woman who had taught her mother to paint. How many other artists had Deb encouraged with her generous spirit and willingness to share her talent?

As Campbell approached, Deb turned and spotted her. She covered her mouth with her hands and concealed a squeal. "You're back!" She ran over to Campbell and pulled her into a tight hug.

Was it possible Campbell had only known her a short two months? Deb, like so many other people she'd met in Sweethaven, had captured her heart. It was almost as if they'd known each other their whole lives.

"It's so good to see you. Come in, come in." Deb ushered Campbell into the gallery, where she was met by her own photographs mixed with her mom's artwork. They were all places and faces of Sweethaven, the remnant of their first and only joint art show.

"You look good, hon." Deb stood near the front counter, and Campbell remembered the day Luke had first introduced them.

"You're beaming." Campbell didn't begrudge the woman her happiness, but her own hung in the balance. "What's with the sign in the window?"

Deb's smile fell slightly, replaced with a contemplative expression. "It's bittersweet," she said. "But necessary. I'm going to sell the gallery. I'm going to Italy."

"For good?" Campbell's spirit collapsed. All her plans were circling the drain.

"No, but when you told me about your mom, I realized time is short. I want to stop saying 'Someday I'll go to Italy' and just do it."

Campbell's heart clenched. "You're not sick, are you?"

God, please, no.

"Oh no, honey, nothing like that. I'm just antsy. I've been here my whole life. I'm an artist. I should see Rome. And Venice. And Tuscany."

Campbell sensed excitement in her voice, in spite of an overtone of sadness. "Well, then I'm happy for you. Very happy." Campbell turned and scanned the artwork they'd hung with such care in preparation for the art show.

"You've sold a few more pieces," Deb said. "Tourists love your work. It's a way for them to take a little bit of Sweethaven home with them when they leave."

Campbell turned and faced her. "What will you do when you get tired of Rome and Venice and Tuscany?"

Deb swept her arms as if she were about to twirl. "Anything I want, I suppose."

Campbell smiled. "It sounds heavenly. You'll send me postcards, won't you?"

"Of course, hon."

Campbell nodded, took one last look at the gallery, and hugged Deb good-bye. As she walked across the street and down a block to the Main Street Café, she tried to process the mix of emotions bubbling inside her. Sadness that Deb was leaving and they wouldn't have time to get to know one another, but excitement that her new friend was doing something she'd always wanted to do.

She'd shoved aside the things she'd always wanted to do out of what—fear?

Campbell crossed the street and walked inside the Main Street Café. The Sweethaven staple buzzed with activity. Businessmen lined the back wall at the bar seating, and a mix of tourists and locals occupied every table. Campbell scanned the workers behind the counter but didn't see Luke.

That's odd. He wouldn't leave the front counter at the busiest time of day. He wasn't the kind of business owner who let other people man the store. He had his hands in everything.

Delcy stood behind the counter making a drink, and Campbell smiled when they made eye contact.

Delcy's eyes lit up. "You're back!"

Campbell warmed at the idea that someone was happy to see her. Hopefully Luke would be so happy.

"Looking for the boss?" Delcy grinned.

"Is he here?"

"In the kitchen. Had some issues with the chicken salad. He's trying to work it out with the supplier. Be careful, he's in a bad mood."

Campbell had never seen Luke in a bad mood. In fact, every time they spoke, she marveled at his upbeat attitude. Maybe he'd been putting it on for her. "Is it okay if I go back there?"

Delcy nodded. "Right over there."

Campbell pushed the swinging double doors open and walked into the kitchen. A man and a woman wearing white aprons stood at a tall counter making sandwiches. The woman glanced up and frowned. "Can I help you?" she asked.

"I'm looking for Luke." Campbell suddenly felt like an intruder who'd just been caught.

"He's back in his office."

She'd never been in the kitchen and didn't even know Luke had an office. Every time she'd been there, he'd been out front serving up drinks with an extra helping of charm. Suddenly it felt like there was a lot about Luke that she didn't know.

She walked around the corner and found Luke's office door open. His familiar voice carried into the hallway. She stood outside for a moment listening.

"But this isn't what I ordered, and I need you to fix it now." Luke paused. "I have customers, Dean. More this weekend than usual. That's why I changed the order."

Maybe she should come back later.

"Just please make it right. This is the busiest time of year, and I need the order I placed by tomorrow morning or I'm going to shut down."

She heard him groan and then throw the phone on the desk. She peeked around the doorway and saw him, hands over his face, sitting in the chair.

"Luke?"

He glanced up at her and his eyes widened. "Hey. You're here." His demeanor changed and he moved around the desk and pulled her into a tight hug. "It's so good to see you."

He pulled back and looked at her. "I missed you."

He welcomed her with a kiss, and while he seemed distracted, Campbell was thankful their nightly conversations could now take place over a cup of coffee rather than over the phone.

"What was that all about?" Campbell noted the tension in his face.

"Incompetence, mostly." He shook his head. "But I don't want to talk about work. How was your drive?"

"Good. I stopped across the street to see Deb. Did you know she's selling the gallery?"

"No, I hadn't heard." He sorted through some papers on his desk, folding what looked like building plans and shoving them in a drawer. Was that something she wasn't supposed to see? Luke had been an architect before he opened the café, but Campbell wasn't sure why he would be working on plans now.

"Are you okay?"

"Just busy. I'm sorry. I want to sit and talk to you, but it's crazy out there."

"No, it's fine. I understand. Go."

He gave her a quick kiss on the cheek. "We'll catch up later?"

She nodded and in seconds, she sat alone in his office pushing away feelings of disappointment.

So far, nothing about her trip was going according to plan.

SEVEN

Jane

Jane pulled into the gravel parking lot of the Sweethaven Chapel, parking her van next to Graham's car. Emily and Jenna had gone down to the Boardwalk for the day, against Jane's wishes. She reminded herself that she couldn't shelter them from every ounce of potential danger, but that didn't stop her from worrying. She'd had to promise the girls an hour later curfew, but they'd agreed to take their bored brother down to the Boardwalk for the morning, leaving Jane alone with little to do.

Worry is faith in the enemy.

The words rushed at Jane from nowhere, and she let them settle in her spirit. She had to *choose* not to worry about the girls.

Since they'd arrived at the beginning of summer, Jane had been feeling unusually restless. When Graham had taken the role of pastor at Sweethaven Chapel for the summer, she imagined spending the time with her childhood friends. They were all getting back into town this weekend, but she'd had many long weeks of feeling useless. As a pastor's wife, she'd never gotten used to sitting on the sidelines, but being out of her comfort zone stopped her from diving in.

Still, she didn't feel right if she wasn't helping someone.

Jane walked inside the little building, much different than the large church they pastored during the year in Cedar Rapids. The chapel had been one of the first buildings in the small town, but it had been well-built and taken care of. While the lobby could use some tidying, the original wood floors gleamed in the sunlight that poured in through the windows. Maybe that's what she could do with her time—make the chapel prettier?

She walked through the small sanctuary, inhaling the scent of the old building and admiring the handmade pews. Through the back door and down a small hallway, she found Graham's office door half-opened. She peeked inside and saw him sitting at his desk, Bible open in front of him and his laptop off to the side.

She knocked gently, pulling his attention. He smiled.

"Thought I'd stop by and say hello. Maybe clean things up a little out in the foyer." She walked in and sat down across from him.

He closed his Bible and gave her his full attention. "Sounds like you."

Jane grinned. "I want to be helpful is all. I'd like our time here to make an impact."

"You know, I've been thinking a lot about our talk, how you're feeling restless." Graham leaned back. "What we could really use is a women's Bible study leader. Mrs. Anderson can't do it anymore. She's left town to take care of her sister."

Jane frowned. The kind of help she had been imagining was more along the lines of decorating the hallway. Teaching a class? That was something else entirely.

"Can you think of a better way to make an impact?" He leaned back in his chair. "Maybe you could make it a scrapbooking thing."

"I already have friends to scrapbook with," she said. But even as she spoke the words, an image of the small blue scrapbook she'd made after Alex's death rushed back to her. She could conjure every page, each one instrumental in helping her work through the grief of losing Alex.

She'd started that little prayer book to help her process her feelings—what if a journal could do the same for someone else?

"Is it for women who need help?"

"It can be whatever you want it to be. I just know it's a great asset for the community and I'd hate to see it disband."

"I suppose I could help the women journal."

"I think it's a great idea. Journaling has helped you so much—you'll be a great leader."

"You really think so?" Since losing Alex, Jane had done her best to avoid social situations at church, focusing instead on things like organization and administration. She found it much easier than coping with sympathetic stares.

"Of course. The women back home all look up to you, hon. Why would it be any different here?"

Because this was Sweethaven—the place where Jane couldn't pretend to have it all together. Did she really have any business leading these women? What if they had to broach the topic of grief? She was hardly an expert, and she knew she couldn't speak about it without crying.

"Jane, don't." Graham's voice startled her back to reality.

"Don't what?"

"Don't start second-guessing yourself. You do that, you know."

He knew her too well.

"You should do this. Absolutely. Write up a blurb for it and I'll put it in the bulletin Sunday."

"This Sunday?"

"It's already July, we can't really sit on it. You said you wanted to make an impact, didn't you?"

She nodded and then jotted down an announcement to let the women who attended the Sweethaven Chapel know when and where they could come for a Bible study—a chance to get together and learn more about God's forgiveness and love. As she thought through the words, Jane felt like an impostor. She hadn't learned these things for herself, had she?

Still, something pushed her pen across the paper and she handed Graham the facts. Next Monday, she'd meet the women as their leader—a role she hadn't planned to play in Sweethaven.

She'd settled into her maternal instincts, finding it easy to mother just about anyone, but at the word *leader*, she balked.

Could she do this?

Graham read over her words and smiled. "You seem happy."

She inhaled, his words swirling around her. "I am happy. Really happy. You were right—it's good we came back for the summer."

He grinned. "Can you repeat that?"

"I'm happy?"

"No, the part about my being right."

"I don't want you to get a big head," she said, standing. "See ya at home."

They said good-bye and Jane walked back the way she came, stopping in the sanctuary to admire the carving of Jesus on the cross that hung on the wall above the pulpit. For a brief moment, she drank in the amount of love it had taken to sacrifice Himself that way, and she said a silent prayer of thanks. Then she walked outside, glimpsed the lake, and inhaled.

She *was* happy.

She'd finally found a way to make peace with what had happened to Alex. She'd never be the same, of course, but she was happy. Truly happy.

And excited at the thought that she'd grown to a place where God could use her once again.

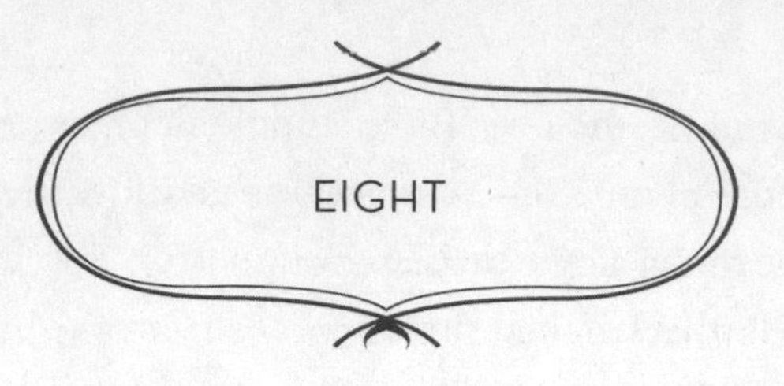

Meghan

Several warm summer days passed, and Meghan spent each one in the same place. The rental house loomed behind her, and from her spot under the shade trees in the weathered Adirondack chair, Meghan gazed out over the lake that had been the backdrop of so many of her memories.

She reached into the bag at her feet and pulled out a stack of scrapbook pages. She'd been carrying them around ever since Suzanne's letter came, as if some part of her knew she'd end up back here, and she didn't want to be in Sweethaven without the pages. All those old memories had done, though, was add chaos to her confusion.

So many of the pages had been created with her friends—her dearest friends. The same friends who'd given her spot in The Circle to her mother.

Jane and Lila would be surprised to discover how many pages Meghan had made without them. While she pretended the scrapbooking was nothing but a bother, Meghan had found solace in the quiet of journaling through her feelings. She'd filled albums with secrets and dreams and thoughts of Nick, of the twins. She'd poured her soul onto those pages, and to this day, she'd never shared them with anyone.

Now, it seemed foolish to cling to them like she did. She'd been replaced and her own children didn't recognize her. She watched as the life she'd been clinging to spun further and further away.

Meghan ran her fingers over the pages, her memory spinning at the sight of her own handwriting. Photos she'd taken such care to select, to glue down in the perfect spot.

The top layout held a series of photos from the booth down on the Boardwalk. She and Nick in one frame after the other. Smiling. Laughing. Happy. The day she admitted her feelings for him had moved past friendship into the realm of something unrecognizable to her. She'd sworn off boys, but Nick . . .

She touched the photo strip, and the angry feelings she'd carried with her from New York melted away as she studied the faces of their younger selves staring back at her. How had all those feelings of excitement and attraction deepened into true, unconditional love and then vanished into anger and bitterness?

How had someone she loved so much become her worst enemy?

Her mind wandered back to that first day, before either of them knew what they'd become. The Boardwalk stretched out in front of her like a road leading to the Promised Land. On it, somewhere, she knew she'd find him. Her guitar, slung over her shoulder, bounced a little on her back as she walked, and she began to question her decision to come.

The Ferris wheel spun, nearly empty on the blustery fall day, and she waved at Motor, Ferris wheel operator and permanent fixture in Sweethaven.

Nick sat on a bench under an old lamppost. Day had begun to fade and the hazy hint of sunset cast a golden shadow across his face. Meghan tried not to stare. When Nick Rhodes had infiltrated her thoughts she couldn't say, but he seemed to have taken up residence there. Somehow he'd stopped being that goofy kid who put bugs in her hair and become mysterious—and off-limits.

Most of the boys Meghan knew were preppy and full of themselves. Nick was neither of those things. Worse, his lack of supervision had turned him into something of a liability—he'd been arrested last month for vandalizing school property. Not the first sign of his rebellious side.

His long legs stretched out in front of him and the wind tousled his hair as a breeze picked up off the water. His army-green jacket hung loosely around his sinewy frame, and he watched her as she approached.

Nick's eyes narrowed, taking her in, making her feel awkward and self-conscious under his watchful eye.

"Barber," he said. "What're you doing down here?"

She shrugged. "Nothing better to do." She tried to stay cool. Had he forgotten that he'd told her to meet him here? "What're you doing down here?"

"Waiting for you." He watched her for a long moment, and she imagined he could see the red as it crawled up her face. She tried to be discreet as she wiped the sweat from her hands.

She played it cool. "How'd you know I'd actually show up?"

He shrugged and leaned forward on his knees. "I didn't. Just hoped."

She inhaled, then looked away. Her heart raced and she tried to stay calm.

Nick's quiet confidence unnerved her. He seemed to know exactly what he wanted, and the thought that what he wanted was *her* excited and scared her at the same time.

"You gonna sit down?" He leaned back against the bench at the end of the Boardwalk. They were alone now. More reason to be nervous. She didn't respond, simply slipped her guitar off and sat next to him. They stared out across the lake in silence, and she searched her mind for something—anything—to say. Something that didn't make her sound like a complete idiot.

She came up empty.

"Come to play me a song?" Nick's words broke the silence.

She laughed and shook her head. "I only brought it because I had to get it home from my lesson."

"You write, don't you?"

She nodded.

"Play me something you've written."

She didn't dare. Her most recent song would be too familiar. All about him. He'd know it the second she started singing.

"All right, you don't want to share, that's fine." He grinned. "I can wait."

She shifted in her seat, her mind running through possible songs she could strum. Short songs and ones she hadn't written. Her songs were like a scrapbook—markers of the memories at given points in her life. The point where she started to notice Nick happened to coincide with a musical shift. Her teacher called it "a new depth to her sound." Coincidence?

Meghan propped the guitar on her right leg and began to strum. He watched her closely—too closely, his gaze rushing across her, unexpected and intense. She closed her eyes and began to sing the words to a song she'd written months before.

They're nothin' like me—and I
I try to fit into their world like a puzzle piece
Shoved into a space that's not mine—and I
Wonder if you'll ever notice me for who I am—or
Will you only want me if I'm just like them?

Her mind started racing and she played the wrong chord. Embarrassed, she stopped.

"Why'd you quit?" His eyes fixed on her and her stomach dropped.

"It's just dumb. . . ." Her words came out jumbled and she doubted he even heard what she said.

"You wrote that?" He leaned forward, his thigh pressing up against hers.

She stared at her fingers, still hovering above the strings. "Yeah."

"You are different," he said. "From all the other girls."

"I know." She looked away, drawn to two seagulls hopping on the sand a few feet away.

"You say it like it's a bad thing."

Her eyes found his.

"It's not." He turned sideways on the bench, facing her. "It's my favorite thing about you."

She didn't respond. Her voice seemed frozen somewhere in the middle of her throat. He leaned closer, his eyes intent on hers, and she didn't move.

She'd never kissed a boy. She'd always been too shy, too reserved, too afraid. But Nick didn't seem to notice any of that. He had confidence enough for both of them.

He'd kissed plenty of girls. She could tell by the way he drew her in. He knew how to make her feel like she was the only girl on the beach, like he'd never thought for a second of being with anyone else.

His kiss startled her at first. Soft lips pressed against hers, and for a brief moment she panicked. What did she do now? But he scooted closer, rested his hand on her cheek, and pulled her in to him. The rest came naturally. Moments later when he broke their embrace, she wished he hadn't stopped. She savored the way his skin smelled, the way his eyes locked on to hers. The quiver in her stomach hadn't even begun to dwindle when he leaned in and kissed her again.

Then he pulled back and covered his mouth with his hand. "I'm sorry."

She looked away. Mistakes he now regretted.

"I don't want to mess this up, Meghan."

"Mess what up?"

"This." He flicked his hand in her direction and then back toward himself.

She leaned the guitar up against the bench and scooted back. "Then don't."

He picked up her hand and held it. He had a gentle way about him that didn't match his reputation. And given his turbulent childhood, it didn't match his circumstances.

As they watched the sun set, Meghan leaned into him, his arm draped around her shoulder. Once the sun plunged behind the horizon, she stood to leave, and he followed. A full foot taller than her, he looked down and held her face for a long moment, studying her eyes as if they told a story.

"I'd like to do this again sometime, if it's okay with you."

She nodded.

He brushed his thumb across her cheekbone then kissed her again, not like an eleventh grader kisses his first girlfriend, but like a person who'd been searching to be understood had finally found what he was looking for.

She walked away, the decking beneath her feet like a yellow brick road leading her away from Oz. When she turned around, he still stared at her. She turned away to conceal a smile.

It had been like that since that day—Nick always watching her, protecting her. Meghan tucked the pages back inside her bag. He'd been the one person who understood her, who knew all her secrets and loved her anyway. And she'd thrown all of that away.

She never expected those stolen kisses under the setting sun to turn into her *happily ever after.*

Things didn't work out in real life the way they did in fairy tales.

The humiliation of Nadia's words rushed back with the force of a Mack truck.

Who's that lady?

Those words had crippled her for days now.

That lady is your mother. And she's not going to stay a stranger for long.

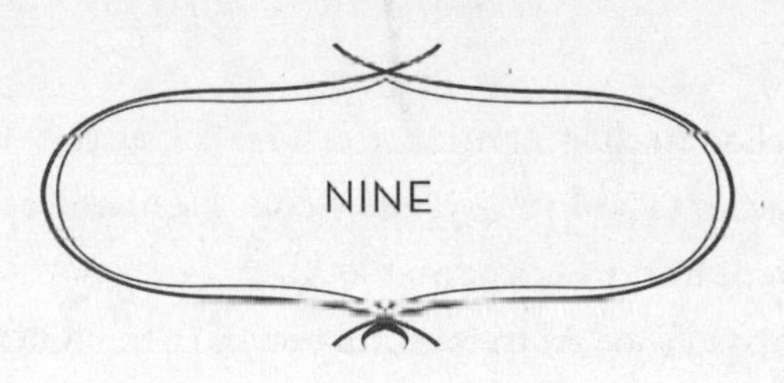

NINE

Adele

After Meghan's visit, Adele had spent the next several days showing the twins photos and telling them stories of their mama. Why hadn't she done that before? Why hadn't Nick? Now, as she drove the back way to Nick's house to drop them off, Adele wondered if he knew Meghan had come back to town.

And could he shed some light as to why?

She shook the thoughts away, reminding herself not to pry.

Besides, Meghan would find him when she was good and ready. She hoped.

Adele glanced at the kids in the back seat. They chattered on about bumblebees and a turtle they'd found in the creek near their house, and Adele couldn't help but think moving back to Sweethaven had been good for them. Nick tried to make Nashville his home after he and Meghan split, but it hadn't worked. He'd only been there for her in the first place. Nick had never warmed to the city life—part of why they didn't last, Adele figured. Maybe Meghan did know what she was doing by leaving them.

She chastised herself for the thought. The twins needed a mama no matter where they lived.

"Where's Daddy's truck? Isn't he home?" Finn scooted forward as they pulled into the driveway.

"I think he's playing baseball tonight, Finn."

She watched in the mirror as the boy's face fell.

"I don't want to go in there, Me-maw." He stared at his lap. "Can you just take us to Daddy's game?"

Adele turned around to face the two of them. She frowned.

"What's wrong with you two?"

They exchanged a quick glance and then stared at her, wide-eyed.

"Out with it. One of you. Tell me what's the matter." Adele's playful tone changed to concern.

"She's not nice, Me-maw," Nadia said. "She's mean to us when Daddy's not home."

A numb feeling skittered through Adele's chest. Violet Rhodes was a troubled woman. Everyone in town knew it—it was part of the reason Adele had been so insistent on having the twins at her house so often. Adele studied the two tiny faces in her back seat. She didn't want to alarm them with a string of questions, but she did want the truth. "What do you mean she's mean to you?" Adele checked her tone, forbidding it to be anything but light.

Maybe the kids needed discipline. They were young, after all.

"She makes us stay in our room and locks the door."

"And she never gives us dinner."

"She yells at us to be quiet all the time."

"She smokes around us even though she tells Daddy she doesn't."

"She squeezes my arm so bad it hurts."

Their confessions ping-ponged back and forth, and Adele's heart raced with each admission.

The kids stared at Adele, who turned and watched the house. From the front window, she saw the curtain move.

"You guys stay here." Adele trudged up the walk to the front door. It opened as she walked up the steps.

"Where're the kids?" Violet wore sweatpants and a baggy T shirt and reeked of smoke.

"They're in the car. I was stopping by to let you know I'd like to keep them overnight if that's okay with you."

Violet's eyes narrowed. "Why?"

Adele frowned. "I haven't seen them as much as I'd like, and we were in the middle of having fun this evening. I'd be happy to take them off your hands. Give you the night off."

"Don't think I don't know what you're up to, Adele." Violet stepped out on the porch as the door slammed behind her.

"I'm sorry?"

"I know she's in town." Violet's expression accused as she crossed her arms over her chest and stared at Adele. "She came by last week looking for Nick. No good can come outta that. She'll pull that sweet talk and try and get Nick to run off with her again. Either that or she wants the kids. It's not happening."

Adele took a deep breath and reminded herself she was a Christian woman. "I don't think you know what you're talking about, Violet."

"Why else would she be here?"

Adele scanned her mind for something—any reason—that would explain Meghan's sudden presence in town. Meghan said she and Nick had things to talk about—who knew what that meant?

What if Violet was right? What if her daughter had finally realized she missed Nick and wanted him back? In another environment, the thought would've brought a smile to Adele's face, but with Violet's firmly set jaw and shadowed eyes staring at her, she couldn't entertain her joy.

"She got the papers, that's what, and she's so mad she could spit." Violet pushed past her and made a beeline for the car. "Come on, you two. Out."

Adele followed her to the car, wishing she'd had the foresight to lock it.

"Don't think I'm stupid enough to believe you two aren't up to something." Violet pulled the door open, and Finn hugged his backpack to his chest. "Out, Finn. Now."

"Where's Daddy?" Finn's eyes filled with tears, and Adele's heart raced with fury.

"Violet." Adele slammed the door and pushed her way in front of it. "I can promise you that Meghan and I are not up to anything. I would like to have them at my house tonight for some dinner and ice cream and that is all."

Violet stared at her. "You're going to have to take overnight visits up with my son. And he's not here right now so you're out of luck."

Violet went around to the other side of the car and pulled the door open. Nadia screamed as her grandmother reached in and dragged her from the car. Finn looked up at Adele, unmistakable fear on his face. Adele gasped as she watched Violet haul Nadia up to the front porch and shove her inside the house. She looked back at Finn, who was crying now, and a helpless feeling washed over her.

What could she do? One child was already inside. She couldn't leave Nadia alone.

Before she had time to make a decision, Violet had returned.

"Where's Nick?" Adele stood in front of the car door.

"Get out of the way. You know you have no legal rights to these kids. Nick lets you see them out of the goodness of his heart."

"Now I'm wondering if he lets me see them to get them away from you." Adele planted her feet into the gravel driveway.

"If you don't get out of the way and let me get my grandson, I will call the sheriff on you, Adele."

Adele knew she fought a losing battle. Violet was right. She had no legal right to the kids. But maybe she should think about having that changed. She opened the door and leaned down so only Finn could hear her. "Listen, little man. I'm going to go find your daddy. You go in with Nadia and be a good boy."

"I don't wanna go, Me-maw."

"Hurry up, Adele." Violet closed in on them.

"I know. But I'm going to find your daddy. Okay, buddy?" She watched Finn square his jaw and she smiled at his courage.

"Okay."

Adele moved out of the way, and Violet pulled Finn from the car. "Get inside and up to your room."

Finn did as he was told, and Violet turned back to Adele. "Don't even think about trying to bring these kids to that daughter of yours. Far as they're concerned, she doesn't exist."

"That's not true. They ask about her all the time at my house." Adele cringed inside. She hated to lie, but how dare Violet?

"In our house, she might as well be dead."

Adele gasped.

Violet continued. "I don't think anyone in your family should be near the twins. We're fighting for sole custody. I imagine that's why she's back here." The smug expression on her face dashed Adele's hopes that her daughter had come home for other reasons—reconciliation, forgiveness, a relationship with her.

Adele shook her head. "You want to keep them from seeing their uncle Luke? And me?"

Violet's expression changed and a peculiar calm came over her. Slowly, she smiled. "Nothing gets by you, does it, Adele?"

Adele had made an enemy of her son-in-law once before, and she'd vowed to never do it again. It had taken him months of living in Sweethaven, months of avoiding her cheery hellos at the grocery store and quickly shuttling the kids out the door after church, before he finally came around and let her see them. Adele suspected it took that long for his loyalty to Meghan to fade.

Finally, Nick came around—thanks to Luke, she imagined. And now Violet threatened to take it all away?

"You can't do this, Violet."

"Watch me." She turned and walked up the steps.

Adele glanced up to the second-story window where two little faces watched, terror in their eyes.

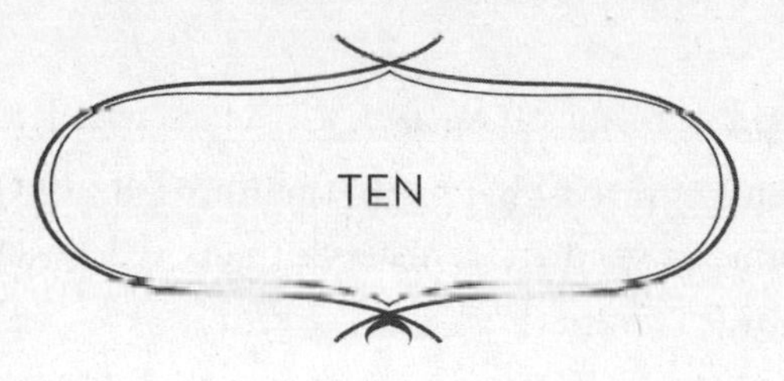

TEN

Meghan

Meghan was becoming more and more like the paparazzi she worked so hard to avoid. Finally tired of sitting in the chair feeling sorry for herself, she had a new obsession. Spying on her family. For the third day in a row, she'd waited on the shoulder of the road to watch Nick leave with the twins, then kept a safe distance from the car as he drove them to her mom's house. Again, she fought back the feelings of inadequacy that seeped in the corners of her mind.

Of course Mama should be the one watching over them. Was there anyone better at caring for children than Mama? But, oh, how inadequate it made her feel.

Violet surely told Nick that she was in town, so she was staying low until she was ready to confront him. Finally, after days of hovering in the shadows, Meghan had more or less figured out their schedule. She knew when they were with Nick, when they were with Mama and when they were in day care. She knew that Nadia's hair looked like a rat's nest until after she got to Mama's house, and Finn regularly wore two different socks—one long and one short. She knew Violet let them play in the front yard even though they lived on a highway and there was no fence.

She also knew that she hated being on the outside looking in, and with every hour that passed, the reminder of what she risked losing intensified.

And so did her anger at Nick.

Permanently shutting her out of their life felt like the worst kind of punishment—more than a smack in the face. More like a knife in the back.

When she spotted Nick's truck ambling down the driveway, something inside her snapped. Two heads of red hair bounced beside him as he drove right past her rental car without a glance in her direction.

She knew they didn't know she was there, but it still hurt. The feeling of being ignored by the people who are supposed to love you no matter what. She'd pushed those feelings down so deep she didn't think they were reachable, yet in an instant they'd sprung to the surface. Meghan's mind galloped at high speed, memories flooding with the force of a pack of wild horses.

The musty basement smell of the apartment building's entryway accosted her nostrils. The backpack over her shoulder held all her things for a long weekend. She'd packed carefully and even found the perfect Christmas gift. A snow globe paperweight with Lake Michigan inside. She'd wrapped it carefully in a T-shirt and stuffed it in the very top of the backpack.

When he hadn't shown up at the airport, Meghan assumed Daddy must've gotten called into work. Or maybe his band had caught an unexpected gig. She wandered up the stairs to the third floor, looking for 312. The hallway stretched in front of her, dark and dank. She shuddered as a cockroach scurried from the hallway under one of the apartment doors.

A dim light over the door cast a shadow on the metal numbers. 3-1-2. She'd found it. All by herself. If Mama found out, she'd be on the first plane to Nashville forcing Meghan to come back home. It had been hard enough to convince her to let her go in the first place.

A door opened behind her, and a large man with a gold chain around his neck stuck his head into the hallway. "You ain't Sid," he said, staring at Meghan.

"No, sir."

His eyes narrowed and he looked her up and down. She pulled her jacket tighter around her, his eyes too interested—too intent. He lifted his chin, still sizing her up, when the stairway door opened and a tall skinny man with a moustache walked in.

"Sid, 'bout time. I thought I was gonna have to track you down," Gold-chain said. He grunted after he spoke, then cleared his throat. "You got the stuff?"

Sid glanced at Meghan, who'd been stunned into a frozen position, unfortunately still staring at the two of them.

"Let's go inside," he said.

"Right." Gold-chain tossed one more look in her direction and then slammed the door.

At that moment she realized she'd been holding her breath. She hurried toward Daddy's door and pounded, long and loud, so he'd hear her even if he'd fallen asleep on the couch.

When no one answered, she pounded again. This time she pressed her ear against the door, but no sound came from the other side. She stood in the hallway, in the faint circle of light cast on the floor by the dim bulb above her. She stared at the 3-1-2 for what seemed like five minutes straight, unmoving.

Gold-chain's apartment door swung open, and Sid appeared in the hallway again. He shut the door behind him and stared at her. "I was never here," he said.

She nodded, backing against the wall across from Daddy's door. She slunk down onto the floor, sitting on her backpack for fear of getting her new skirt dirty. The skirt she'd picked out special just for this occasion. Seeing Daddy after all this time.

He promised to pick her up. Promised they'd have a great long weekend together. They'd go ice skating outside now that it had gotten colder, and maybe even drink hot chocolate in the park. He said so.

So why wasn't he here?

She stared at the door, waiting for it to open. Waiting for Daddy to explain.

But he never did.

Meghan shook her head, clearing her mind of the memory, and shoved the car into drive, pulling out onto the highway. She followed Nick at a safe distance until he turned into Reynold's Field. As daylight waned, the lights shone bright over the ball fields, three in all.

Ah, the Friday night Sweethaven softball tradition was alive and well.

She imagined Nick and Luke probably played for the same softball team. Most likely the two of them had stayed close. Even as she shuddered at the thought of spending her summer nights playing church league softball, a pang of jealousy rose up inside her.

She shoved it aside and found a parking spot.

From a distance she watched Nick hop down from the truck and help the twins to the ground. He balanced baseball bats, a glove, and Nadia with ease. How did he do that? He looked so comfortable in this role.

Rather than being happy her kids were in capable hands, the whole notion stirred the bitterness that had begun to bubble inside.

Nick walked over to the bleachers where he met a girl—blonde and pretty. She smiled and knelt down in front of Finn, who wrapped his arms around her in a tight hug. Then the girl stood up and held out her hands in Nadia's direction. Meghan's stomach wobbled when the little girl offered her own arms in return. The blonde girl squeezed Meghan's daughter like she knew her—loved her. And Meghan could do nothing but watch.

Nick exchanged a few words with the girl, tousled both red heads of hair, then slung the bat over his shoulder and ran toward the field. Meghan studied the girl. Blondes had never been Nick's type before. And this girl looked young—too young, really. Why was he bringing their kids around her? Clearly they knew her.

And she was probably the reason why Nick was so anxious to get full custody.

The girl sat down in a blue sling-back chair, then motioned for the twins to sit in the two child-sized folding chairs beside her. Once they sat down, the girl opened the bag Nick had given her and pulled out snacks.

How sweet. He'd packed snacks for his trampy girlfriend to feed them.

Heat rose up Meghan's face and her heart pounded so loud she swore she could hear it. How dare he? How could he cut her out just to start over with someone else? He wanted to be a quaint little family with a brand-new wife? A wife he'd be proud to waltz through the chapel doors. Was that the plan?

No one—not even Nick—was going to get the better of her. Those kids were *her* flesh and blood. His ploy to oust her from their lives had backfired—and he didn't even know it yet.

Her mind spun as she opened the door, and for a second, she seemed to be outside her own body, watching herself as she slammed the car door and headed full force toward the ball field where Nick now stood, covering second base. The lights of the field shone a spotlight on him, and she kept her eyes locked on the side of his face, daring him to make eye contact as she trudged forward. In the distance she heard rumblings from the crowd—the stray questions she'd gotten used to ignoring over the years now echoing in her mind.

Is that Meghan Rhodes?

Oh my heck, Meghan Rhodes is back in town!

We've got to get an autograph—that's her!

Meghan shoved the chattering aside. As she passed Blondie, she shot her a look that she hoped said "Don't mess with my family." The girl's eyes widened and she looked away.

Meghan pushed through the chain-link fence. It clanged, rousing the attention of the players. The pitcher held the ball, watching her as she passed him on her way to second base.

Confusion washed over Nick's face as he met her eyes. His casual stance shifted and he stiffened at the sight of her.

"Meghan?"

"How could you do this?" She pushed him with both hands square in the chest. Nick stumbled backward, caught off-guard, but quickly regained his footing.

"What are you doing here?"

"You didn't think I'd come after what you did? How could you sink so low?" She pushed him again.

"Stop it, Meg." He grabbed her arm and lowered his voice. "This isn't the place to have this conversation."

She glared at him. "What's the matter?" She raised her voice even louder. "You don't want everyone to know what a lowlife you are? You've got your cute new girlfriend and your precious family man persona and you think everyone's going to just forget who you really are?"

Nick's face fell and the pain she'd just inflicted ricocheted back and slashed through her skin, but she quickly recovered.

"You're way out of line, Meghan." Nick squared his jaw.

"You have a lot of room to talk. Does everyone know what you did? Of course they do because you sold your little secret to some stupid talk show. You sure got me there, Nick."

"Meghan, please. Let's go somewhere and talk about this."

Her laugh mocked him. "*Now* you wanna talk about this." She ripped her arm from his grasp. "You're a little late for that, don't you think?"

All the humiliation of sitting under the studio lights rushed back.

From behind, a hand rested on her shoulder, and she turned to see Luke at her side. "Come on, Meg."

She looked back at her ex-husband. He stood in front of her dazed, and for a split second she almost felt bad for him.

"This isn't over, Nick. You chose the wrong time to pick a fight with me." The standoff held for a few more long moments, and Meghan found it nearly impossible to tear her eyes from his.

Finally, she turned around to see a crowd had gathered, many of them now pointing cameras and smartphones in her direction. Meghan groaned. From how many different angles had her outburst just been recorded? Duncan would have a fit.

Luke wrapped his arm around her and walked her off the field, the stunned silence of the crowd eerily following behind. As she reached the twins, she told herself not to look at them, but she couldn't help it—just one glance.

In an instant, she wished she hadn't. Both of them stared at her, unmistakable fear in their eyes. Meghan knew she had seconds before the tears came, so she picked up the pace, rushing away from Luke's protective grasp.

When they reached the car, she hurried inside, surprised when Luke opened the passenger door and sat down.

They sat for a few moments in silence, and her mind replayed the scene she'd just made in front of the entire town.

"I've been wondering when you were going to stop by," he said.

In spite of the tears that streamed down her face, she let out a laugh. "I really know how to make an entrance, don't I?"

"I would expect nothing less." He smiled at her. Always accepting, no matter how bad she messed up. No one else understood her like Luke.

"Sorry I haven't come to see you yet." She wiped her nose with the back of her hand and stared out over the crowd. By now one of them had probably already posted the video online, and it was only a matter of time before Meghan's public breakdown would be tabloid fodder for the late night news. She shook her head and rubbed her face with her hands.

"It's all such a mess," she said. "How did we get here?"

"You really want me to answer that?"

"No." She stared at him for a minute. Her baby brother had grown up—and she'd missed that too.

"I know something that will cheer you up," he said. "Drive to the café."

"You're going to feed me something, aren't you?"

He grinned.

*****

The café had been renovated and now looked nothing like the old diner that had been in this building when Meghan was a kid. She hardly recognized the place. His time in the city must've inspired Luke to class it up.

She followed her brother in and sat down at a table in the back while he went behind the counter and ordered their drinks from one of the employees.

Her cell phone started buzzing—with the kind of fervor only an angry call from Duncan could rouse.

The caller ID told her she was right, so she clicked it off and shoved it back in her purse. The last thing she needed was one of his lectures. She already knew she'd screwed up—she sure didn't need him to remind her.

Luke plopped down across from her, his eyebrows raised as if he waited for her to defend herself. Or maybe he simply wanted to hear what she'd been up to. Luke had been to Nashville about a year ago, but since then, she'd barely even kept in touch with him—and besides Mama, he was the only family she had left.

She'd built quite the wall around herself in the past couple of years.

"I can't believe you took time away from your busy life for Sweethaven." His smirk hung lazily on his face, and she saw a little bit of the boy she still thought of when Luke came to mind.

"I didn't have much choice."

He frowned.

"Don't pretend you don't know. Nick's doing everything he can to destroy me. Great timing too—my new album just came out." She sighed at the thought of the promoting she wasn't doing.

"That's not his style, Meg, and you know it." Luke stared at her. He knew their history—all of it—and he was right. Nick had never done anything to hurt Meghan.

"Well, I guess he's got a new style." Her scoff fell flat when the door swung open and a group of men dressed in baseball uniforms identical to the one Luke was wearing strode in.

She shot her brother a look, but he'd already stood to greet his teammates.

Meghan wanted to crawl under the table, but before she could move, a cute waitress with ringlet curls appeared beside her, blocking any hope of escape. She held two soda fountain glasses, and before Meghan even tasted it, she knew Luke had ordered her a root beer float—her favorite.

In an instant, she was transported back to lazy summer days on the Boardwalk. Mama and Teddy used to insist on root beer floats every Saturday.

"Nothing says summer like a root beer float," Mama would say.

It had been years since she'd indulged in one, but she could already taste the creamy vanilla swirling into the root beer—instant comfort. The comfort of being *home.*

If only she could enjoy it alone and not in the company of the people who'd just watched her assault her ex-husband.

One of the guys strolled by the table and grinned at her. "Way to go, Slugger," he said.

The waitress slid the floats across the table and smiled. "Did you need anything else, Miss Rhodes?"

A do-over button.

"No thanks. I'm good."

Finally, Luke sat back down and smiled. "Root beer floats. Just like Dad used to make."

His dad. Teddy. Not her dad. All her dad made was trouble.

"I think I should get going." Meghan looked around the room and caught more than a few people staring at her.

"Let 'em stare. Aren't you used to it by now?"

The ringing bells above the door signaled another arrival, and Meghan finally sipped her float. Before she could swallow the drink, though, she found her eyes locked on Nick's, and her appetite skittered away.

"You should talk to him," Luke said.

"Not a good idea."

"You can't ignore him forever."

Meghan tried to avoid Nick's eyes, but they pulled her in, just like they always had, and she found herself unable to turn away as he moved across the room and found a seat at the counter. Still wearing his red jersey and a backwards baseball cap, he looked like the kid she'd known all those years ago. The one she'd fallen in love with.

Her pulse raced and she tried to remind herself that things had changed between them. They weren't in love anymore. They weren't even on speaking terms.

If only someone would tell that to her heart.

No, she wasn't here to rekindle anything. Only to fight for the only family she'd ever have.

Meghan glanced at Luke, who stared at her again with a raised eyebrow.

"What?" Meghan said.

"I don't know who is more stubborn—you or him."

"Shut up, Luke." She slid out of the booth, dragging her oversized purse behind her.

"You can't leave now. You just got here."

"I'll call you tomorrow." Finally, she lugged the purse over her shoulder and walked back in the direction she had come—through the kitchen.

"But your root beer float . . ."

"You drink it."

She stormed through the kitchen door and didn't look back, but she could feel Nick's eyes on the back of her head. She'd been programmed to know when he was nearby, and even when he avoided her, they were always aware of each other.

That hadn't changed.

Meghan tried to compose herself. In her purse, her phone had started buzzing again, but she could scarcely find enough air to breathe, let alone talk to anyone. Sweat beaded across the back of her neck and she cursed July's humidity.

Who was she kidding? The lake cooled everything down in the evening—her sweat had more to do with her own humiliation.

Behind her, she heard the kitchen door open. She turned.

Nick.

She froze, eyes on him, then looked around to see if anyone else could see them. Were there more cameras pointed toward her or were they really alone?

Which terrified her more?

Nick started toward her, his eyes locked on hers, and she couldn't move. Couldn't look away. He stopped only inches away from her—so close she could smell his familiar aftershave. It sent her mind spinning. That same smell that had filled her senses the night they first made love—the night she became his wife. He'd been so tender with her, gentle and kind. He'd always been that way—even when she made him angry. Always forgiving.

"I'll never hurt you, Meghan," he'd told her. "I promise."

But she hadn't believed him. She'd spent years waiting for him to hurt her—for him to realize he didn't love her and leave. Just like everyone else.

She'd pushed him away—she knew that now, though she'd never admit it. She'd been so wrapped up in her own insecurity, she'd convinced him she didn't love him and pushed him away.

No man would put up with that kind of treatment. No matter how much he loved her.

If not for that, would any of this be happening now?

Now, with him standing so close, the memories flooding her mind, she couldn't think straight. She needed to focus on why she'd come. Because he'd leaked the photos and served her with papers—because he wanted to take her kids away—to force her out of the family for good.

She turned away, afraid to look in his eyes for all the confusion she felt.

"Quite a scene you put on back there," Nick said, hands on his hips, waiting for her to respond.

"I'm sure you'll see it tonight on the news."

"You're not doing yourself any favors, you know." Undecipherable emotion filled Nick's eyes. She expected to find hatred there, instead she found only sorrow.

"What's that supposed to mean?"

He looked away. "Forget it. Let's just start over. Can we? Please?"

Meghan shook her head. "You want to pretend like everything's fine after what you did?"

"What *I* did? You said you didn't love me anymore, Meghan."

She went to open the car door, but he leaned against it, jamming it shut.

"Didn't you say that?"

Meghan closed her eyes, trying to forget the horrible words she'd said to him—what she'd said to convince him to leave.

"Why'd you come here then?"

She stared at him. She'd come to keep him from taking the kids away from her. She'd come because there was a gnawing emptiness in the pit of her stomach and it had been there for years. Her mind raced through other things she could say. Anything but the truth.

"Suzanne died."

"Two months ago. Why are you here now? I thought you'd just sign the papers and I'd have them free and clear."

"So you can start your family with your cute new wife?"

He sighed. "Meghan . . ."

"What you do after hours is your own business, but you had no right to ambush me on national television."

He took his hat off and ran his hand through his hair. "That wasn't supposed to happen."

She glared at him. "It sure does help your case though. And those photos? How could you do that to me?"

Nick let out a sigh. "I had nothing to do with that. Let me explain. . . ."

"You can explain it to my lawyer. When he shows up here in Podunk Sweethaven, you remember who started this whole thing."

Meghan got in the car, slammed the door shut, pulled out of the alley and didn't look back.

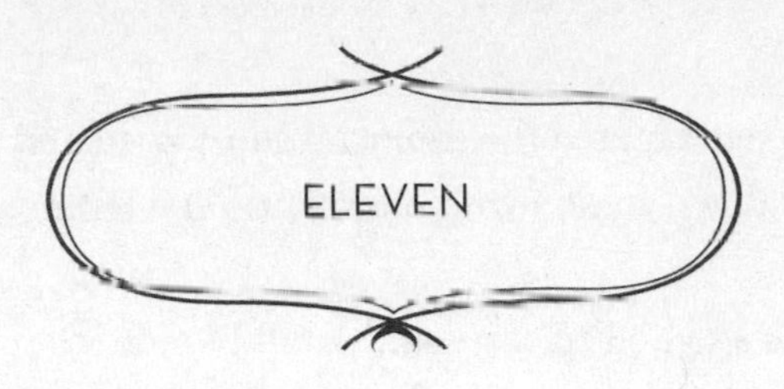

ELEVEN

Jane

"You're being paranoid," Graham said.

After the announcement about her Bible study went into the bulletin, Jane had several women stop her and ask for more information. Now that the following Monday morning had arrived, she had butterflies in her stomach and a distinct fear that no one would show up.

"We've had lots of calls to the office. You're going to have a great turnout."

Now, though, as she straightened the circle of chairs and went over what she'd prepared to say, Jane didn't feel so certain.

She glanced at the clock. Nearly ten and no one had arrived yet. She walked over to the windows, double-checked the window AC unit, and opened the blinds. As she did, she spotted several women in the parking lot. They hugged like long lost friends, and Jane smiled as she watched them walk toward the entrance to the church. Then, an unwelcome idea entered her mind. What if *she* was the outsider of this group? It had been years, after all, since she'd been in Sweethaven.

She shoved her insecurities aside and turned away from the window, preparing to welcome the women. Moments later, the hallway outside the room filled with chatter, and Jane forced her stomach to settle down. Suddenly she felt ill-prepared and terrified.

Four women entered the room, all sun-kissed and put together. Jane glanced down at her own khaki capris and tennis shoes and felt her face heat.

"Jane, it's so good to see you." A tall blonde woman with sunglasses propped on her head walked up to Jane and pulled her into a hug. "We're all so excited about this."

"I'm so glad you all decided to come. I've got name tags for everyone here on the table."

One by one, the women wrote their names in black permanent marker on the red-rimmed stickers she'd set out earlier that morning. She pointed them in the direction of the coffee and snacks and welcomed a few more women to the group. Once everyone had found a seat, Jane glanced around the circle at several pairs of eyes focused on her.

Suddenly she felt on the spot, and she wondered what on earth she was thinking hosting a Bible study in the first place.

The hum of the window unit distracted her. "Is that going to bother anyone?" She pointed at the old machine. The women all shook their heads. "It's hotter than usual this summer," one of the women said. "That thing will save us till we can all head down to the beach later."

Polite laughter waved through them, but at her silence, Jane saw their confidence in her hanging in the balance.

"Well," she said and then quickly took a sip of water. "I don't want this group to be me talking all the time. I want to hear what you all have to say."

Glances crisscrossed the room, and after a moment of awkward silence, Jane cleared her throat. "Maybe we should focus on a specific topic. Something like service or grace or hospitality or forgiveness or . . ."

A young woman across from Jane raised her hand. Her name tag said Amber.

"I'm voting for that. I'd love to get your take on forgiveness. Or do a study on it or something."

The other women nodded.

Jane grimaced. They couldn't possibly know how she'd struggled with that very topic.

"Service would be good too—we could do an outreach or some sort of community project," Jane said, hopeful.

"I think Amber's right," said the woman next to her. "I think we could all benefit from your knowledge in this area."

"My knowledge?" Jane folded her hands in her lap.

"You seem to be so put together," Amber said, glancing down at her own hands. "I'm just . . . not."

Jane waited for the other women to disagree—to tell Amber the truth. That Jane was anything but "put together," but no one did. Instead, she found them all watching her, and if she wasn't mistaken, most of them wore a look of admiration.

"I'm not sure I understand what you mean." Jane leaned forward slightly.

"Well, we all know about your son," another woman with a Southern accent said quietly. "And look at you—you're still here. Still smiling. Still serving God."

"Where else would I be?" Jane took last week's bulletin from her Bible and began fanning herself. The air wouldn't keep her cheeks from getting red, though, and she knew they were well on their way.

"I'd be mad, I think. Isn't God supposed to be the Great Protector?"

The women all nodded.

"Can you tell us how you did it? How'd you forgive?" Amber's face looked almost pleading, and Jane stuttered to find the words. They thought she had the answers, like she'd taken a magic pill and suddenly forgiven everyone for everything that had happened.

"I'm not sure what to say," Jane said. "I was mad for a long time. I didn't think it was fair."

"It wasn't fair," a dark-headed older woman said.

"I blamed God. I blamed myself. I didn't think I'd ever be happy again."

"But you are?" Amber looked hopeful.

"I am. And I feel peaceful now. It's been a long road, but I've discovered the freedom of forgiveness." She reached into her bag and pulled out her little blue scrapbook. "This helped."

The women watched as Jane opened the small book, full of her thoughts as she processed what it really meant to lose a son. Jane flipped through it but refused to read the words for fear of being found out. Some days the pain could be as fresh as the day he died.

"I wrote down every thought, every fear, every memory. It helped me work through some of the worst moments." Jane met Amber's eyes. "It can really help you process things."

The woman sitting next to Amber put a hand on her shoulder. "You should do that, sweetie." Then she glanced at Jane. "Amber lost her son too."

Jane's heart sank. *No.*

Amber swiped a stray tear from her cheek.

"I'm so sorry," Jane whispered. Amber seemed far too young to endure that pain—but then, did age ever prepare people for something so awful? Parents weren't supposed to outlive their children, no matter what.

"I just wondered how you seemed so positive and upbeat. I noticed it Sunday at church. I thought I'd feel justified somehow when I saw you. I expected you to carry the same heaviness that I do—but you don't."

Guilt plagued Jane's mind and she knew she should tell Amber—and the rest of them—the whole truth. She should tell them she'd only recently begun to forgive herself and God and Meghan. Heat crawled to her cheeks. She didn't have it all figured out, but these women thought she did.

For once, it felt good to be the one with the answers.

"Could we make scrapbooks like that?" The blonde woman Jane had misjudged from the start ran her hand through her long hair and glanced around the circle. "We've all got our baggage. Maybe it'll help us like it's helped you, Jane."

Jane smiled. "Forgiveness is a process, I'm afraid. And yes, I was thinking maybe we could all make journals in this group. You'd have to get a journal or scrapbook and then decide how fancy or simple you want to make it." Jane smiled. She was glad they liked her idea. "I'm thrilled you want to do this. I don't think you'll be disappointed."

Amber looked up at Jane. "I don't think so either. I need to get to where you are." She smiled. "One way or another."

Again, guilt grabbed at Jane's heart and she felt like a fraud, but she couldn't let on to these women that most days she had to remind herself that she'd forgiven the sins of the past. It hadn't come naturally and she wasn't inherently *good*.

For the rest of the hour, the women got to know one another, introducing themselves and sharing how and why they needed to work on forgiveness. Jane marveled at their transparency, each one of them sharing their struggles with such ease. She longed to be that honest, but as their leader, she thought it was important to stay a bit removed, to hold on to some of her secrets.

As the hour came to an end, Jane prayed and thanked God for bringing them all together. Then she asked Him to help these women this week as they struggled with the toil in their hearts. By the time she said "Amen," she felt like she needed to repent of her own dishonesty, but surely God understood—she was simply trying to be a good role model.

The women stood and began to mingle around the room, helping Jane clear the refreshment table and thanking her for being willing to spearhead their little group.

As Jane wiped the crumbs off the table, Amber walked over and stood beside her. Jane stopped and looked up.

"Thank you, Mrs. Atkins," Amber said.

"Please, call me Jane."

"Jane. How long did it take?"

"How long did what take, hon?"

"How long until you wanted to get out of bed again?" Amber's eyes welled with tears. "I have a daughter. She needs me, but I don't have any energy to take care of her. My husband and I hardly talk."

Jane remembered that. All the times she pushed Graham away—all the times she was angry with him because he wasn't grieving the way she thought he should. But Amber didn't need to hear all that. She needed to know that she'd worked it out. She was all better now.

"Grief is different for everyone, hon," Jane said, putting a hand on Amber's shoulder. "We're all built differently. But with God's help, it does get better. I promise."

Amber nodded, but a disappointed look crossed her face.

"I'll pray for you." Jane pulled her into a hug and watched as the younger woman turned to go.

"Thanks again, Jane."

She smiled, looking forward to their next meeting later that week. They'd voted to meet twice a week. They must've had a good time if they wanted to do it again so soon.

Jane collected the Styrofoam coffee cups and threw them in the garbage. As she did, she glanced up into the parking lot and felt her smile fade. Only yards away, a woman paced the parking lot, scuffing the gravel with her shoe.

Meghan.

Jane never dreamed she'd have to face her here—in the church. Confronted now with her own dishonesty, Jane glanced around the nearly empty room and prayed that no one could read her mind.

After having just paraded herself as the woman who had it all figured out, Jane knew the tight ball lodged in her stomach told a very different story.

Meghan

Meghan found herself staring at the old church where she'd grown up. It had been years since she'd stepped foot inside a church, but she'd grown up here—Mama had taught her when you're hurting, run to Jesus.

Still, she was convinced that even Jesus couldn't welcome her with open arms. Not after all she'd done.

She stood outside the tiny chapel, knowing that whoever had taken it on for the summer would likely have heard of her. Would the pastor be able to separate fact from fiction and advise her as an unbiased third party? It was what she needed right now, and she didn't know where else to get it.

Maybe leaving Nick alone really was best for everyone. Did she have any right to fight for kids she barely knew? She had, after all, been gone for two years. It didn't matter that she had reasons for leaving. It didn't matter that those reasons were valid.

All anyone could see was a woman who'd abandoned her kids.

It's all she saw when she looked in the mirror.

Meghan kicked at the gravel in the parking lot, trying to talk herself into going inside. A pastor had been trained to hear the worst about people and love them anyway. He'd be unbiased and she could use that right about now. He'd tell her she wasn't going to hell because of the mistakes she made.

Even if no one ever forgave her.

She glanced down at her phone and saw she'd missed another call from Duncan. And one from Mama. Two people who were worried about her for completely different reasons—both valid. Duncan would leave her a scathing message for missing *Good Morning America* and whatever else she'd missed. She'd deal with it later.

Was it too much to ask for a couple weeks off to save her family?

She shoved the phone in her purse and turned toward the church. When the doors opened and a group of chatty women emerged, she quickly turned away and stared toward the cemetery out back. She waited for them to get in their cars and drive away before finally working up the courage to walk toward the doors, open them and go inside.

The familiar smell of old hymnals and stained wood hit her as soon as she entered the lobby. The smell of her childhood. How many Sundays had she spent right there in that sanctuary? How many times had Reverend Carter's words rushed back to her—words that told of a gracious and merciful God? How many times had she convinced herself that grace and mercy were for *other people*?

Even God wouldn't excuse a mother who abandoned her own children in favor of fame and fortune.

And who could blame Him?

She stood in the aisle staring at the image of Jesus behind the pulpit. His eyes looked welcoming—and for a moment, she almost believed He could redeem someone as far gone as her, but the sound of someone behind her brought her back to reality.

"Can I help you?"

Meghan turned and saw a handsome middle-aged man standing at the back of the sanctuary. He wore jeans and a white button-down, his hair graying around the temples. He looked dignified. Good. *Familiar.*

She looked away. "I'm sorry to intrude."

As he walked toward her, recognition washed over his face. "Meghan?"

She stared at him for a long moment, the shock of his identity sinking low in the pit of her stomach. Words eluded her.

"It's good to see you."

Graham. Not some pastor who'd read about her in a trashy tabloid at the checkout counter of the supermarket.

Was Jane's husband a good liar or did he really mean it? His tone held no contempt for her. Could she really have been wrong about people—about church people—all this time? She'd only experienced judgment, but Graham's kindness already proved she may have been mistaken.

She struggled to find her voice. "You too," she finally said.

"I heard you were in town."

Just as Meghan had expected, video footage from the baseball game had hit the Internet moments after she stormed off the field. Not only had she humiliated herself, but she'd given away her location. She'd already caught two men with cameras in the woods behind the lake house and ignored three more angry calls from Duncan.

"I'm sorry to barge in like this," Meghan said, looking around the empty sanctuary. "I . . . didn't have anywhere else to go."

Not entirely true. She could've gone back to Nashville and closed this chapter on her life forever.

"It's fine. Would you . . . like to talk?" Graham's kind eyes watched her, full of concern and devoid of any trace of lust. That alone set him apart from most men.

"If you're uncomfortable talking to me, I understand. I don't even think God would expect you to be nice to me." Meghan hoped the hair covering her face concealed her humiliation at asking for help from a man who had every reason to turn her away.

She had nowhere else to go. How pathetic.

"Don't be silly. My office is this way."

He led her out the back door of the sanctuary and to a small office with an oversized desk. She took a seat in a leather chair across from him and noticed he left the door partially open.

"There's no one here," he said. "So you can talk freely."

Meghan forced a smile. "I'm not sure I should even be here."

He crossed his hands and leaned toward her. "Here in the church?"

"And here in Sweethaven."

"Take your time. I don't have anything else on my calendar today." His smile was warm—she didn't even question its sincerity.

Something about Graham's eyes encouraged her to confide in him. They seemed to whisper *It's safe here.*

And she couldn't think of the last time she'd felt that way.

After she told him the whole story, she braced herself for what he would say. The part of her that wanted to run away couldn't wait for him to tell her to go back to Nashville and focus on her career, but the other part of her—the part that needed those kids and her family in her life—agonized over the idea of leaving without a fight.

Graham shifted in his chair, then steepled his fingers in front of him, index fingers covering his lips. Finally, he leaned forward and said, "Do you want to know the truth?"

She chewed on the inside of her lip. "Maybe not."

"I think you should follow your gut."

"So you think I should leave?"

He stared at her. "It sounds to me like there's a lot of passion between you and Nick."

Meghan looked down. "I think you're confusing passion and hatred."

"It's a fine line." Graham smiled. "What if you tried to work it out directly with him? Maybe the two of you could come to an agreement?"

Meghan shook her head. The thought of going to him and trying to keep things cordial only made her nervous. How could she forgive him for the things he'd done?

"Right now Nick's goal is to make me look bad—to show the world what a terrible mother I am."

"So you're going to give up then?"

Meghan stiffened.

Graham leaned back in his chair and shrugged. "The way I see it, you have two choices. Go back to Nashville and get on with your life or stay here and fight for your family. Only you know what your gut says." He met her eyes then and held them for a few long seconds. "But I do know that if there's one thing in this life worth fighting for, it's your family."

Meghan wondered if they weren't talking about her anymore. How had things been for him and Jane since Alex's death? She had avoided thinking about it for a long time—how her carelessness had cost them everything—but now, sitting across from him, she wondered how a man who had been through so much could have such a visible peace.

She studied her folded hands in her lap. "My kids don't even know who I am anymore," she whispered.

"Then give them a chance to find out."

She met Graham's kind eyes again. "How can you say such nice things? To *me*?"

A smile crossed his face. "You see yourself as a lost cause, Meghan, but I see you like God sees you—as someone with great potential."

She cleared her throat, willing her voice steady. "Do you think Jane sees me that way?" The question surprised her. She hadn't intended to mention Jane at all, but as she did, her heart ached. She hadn't allowed herself to acknowledge it, but she missed her friend.

"You'd have to ask her," Graham said.

She looked away. "I doubt she ever wants to see me again." Meghan wondered if he could tell how much she wanted him to disagree with her.

He didn't. He didn't say anything, simply smiled at her and watched as she fidgeted her way to a standing position. "Thank you, Graham. I really appreciate your time."

"Anytime, Meghan. It's what I'm here for."

As she walked to her car, she replayed their conversation—the surprising way the pastor hadn't judged her, and how he hadn't told her what she wanted to hear. He'd gone deeper and told her the truth. But he'd left the ball in her court.

The next step was hers to take.

THIRTEEN

Campbell

After two weekends in Sweethaven, Campbell discovered having nothing to do didn't sit well with her. At least not for very long. She'd settled in to the little guest room in Adele's quaint cottage, but that woman knew how to keep busy. Luke had been out of town on business on both weekends, and she'd yet to reconnect with her mom's friends.

Every afternoon, Campbell ended up at the beach, lounging in a chair and watching kids chase the waves as they rushed to the shore.

So far, all this trip had done was make her miss her mom.

The one person who probably would have time for her—her grandfather—was also the one person she avoided. She had Tilly to thank for that. Her warnings about the old man had Campbell on edge, even though she'd forgiven him for abandoning her and her mom.

Thanks to e-mail, she had struck up something of a relationship with her father, though guilt plagued every exchange. He'd made it clear he and Lila weren't doing well, and they both had her to thank for that. Still, when she got word he'd arrived in Sweethaven, Campbell's excitement—or relief—kicked into high gear. Finally, someone to share the day with.

Mid-July in Sweethaven meant shorts, tank tops, flip-flops and a lack of concern for how sweaty you got. Campbell welcomed the cool air of the Main Street Café as she pulled the door open and searched the space for her father. Tom waved from a table near the back.

She'd romanticized what it meant to have a dad for as long as she could remember, and now, walking toward the father she thought she'd never find, the only thing she felt was sadness. She'd caused this chasm between her dad and his wife, one of her mom's best friends, and she had to figure out a way to fix that.

Would he even want to get to know her now?

He stood, unsure of how to greet her, and she moved into an awkward hug.

They ordered their drinks and sat silent for a few long moments. Campbell searched her mind for something to talk about, but she came up empty.

Finally, Tom spoke. "I went back over to the art gallery. Your work still looks wonderful."

Her mind spun back to the night of her first showing. The night she discovered the truth about who Lila's husband was.

Campbell started to tell him about Deb selling the gallery, but something behind her pulled his attention. She turned just in time to see Lila stroll in. She was dressed for the beach, but she still looked pristine and elegant. Tom caught her eye and she quickly looked away.

Guilt crept up Campbell's neck. She should've called Lila. Made sure it was okay for her to spend time with Tom.

Campbell had been so caught up in her own troubles, she'd almost forgotten why he really came to Sweethaven. It wasn't to get to know her, it was to try and repair his broken marriage.

Why did that sting a little?

Campbell glanced back at Lila, who ordered an iced something and hurried out the door. Not even a "hello."

"I thought I'd surprise her," Tom said. "I hoped she'd have forgiven me by now. Turns out I've only made it worse by coming here."

Campbell stuck the spoon back in her drink and stirred.

"I'm sorry. What a downer. We're not here to talk about my marital troubles."

Sadness lingered above them and Campbell struggled to push it away. "I'm really sorry."

"Sorry?"

"Sorry about you and Lila."

Tom shook his head. "It's my fault. You can't blame yourself because I was a jerk. She has every right to be mad." He took a drink of his coffee. "I've been keeping my distance—giving her space, but maybe it's time I let her go."

"What do you mean?" Campbell frowned.

"I've been holding on to this idea that she'll forgive me, but I know Lila better than anyone. It's not in her nature. It may be time to face the fact that she's not coming back."

Campbell's heart sank. He couldn't give up on Lila. Campbell couldn't be the reason they split up. As much as she wished he'd come there for her, to build the relationship they never had, she understood that right now Lila was more important.

And she had to figure out a way to help them.

"You still love her, right?"

His face grew serious. "More than ever."

"Then you can't give up." Campbell studied her father's eyes. For a moment she imagined her mom sitting at his side, her arm laced through his, their hands intertwined.

She looked away. No. Tom had never belonged to her mom. She couldn't fantasize about what they could've been. It had been wrong from the start.

"You don't know Lila. She's the most stubborn woman I know." He set his coffee on the table and folded his arms. "I'm not sure what else I can do."

"Well, 'giving her space' isn't going to get you anywhere. You need to look for a way to get back into her life."

"I don't know where to start. Lila feels far away from me now."

"Divorce is not what she wants. She still loves you."

"Did she say that?" Tom's eyes were hopeful.

"She didn't have to. I can tell. I think women like to be pursued. And maybe she's feeling a little insecure." Campbell looked away. She wouldn't get into her own relationship woes. Luke barely had time to talk on the phone, let alone any kind of real conversation. She glanced toward the kitchen and wondered if he was back in his office.

Tom pushed his coffee mug toward the center of the table, drawing her back from her mental wanderings. "I guess you're right. Lila's always been hard to navigate, but leaving her alone isn't working, so what have I got to lose?"

Campbell shrugged.

The door to the kitchen swung open and Luke appeared. He held the phone to his ear and didn't even glance in Campbell's direction. She looked away, but Tom must've caught the hurt in her eyes.

"Men like to be pursued too, you know," he said.

Campbell glanced at her father, who gave a quick nod in Luke's direction.

"We're not all as confident as we seem."

But it wasn't the time or the place to explain this had nothing to do with Luke's confidence and everything to do with his being preoccupied and busy. How could she pursue someone who didn't have time for her?

Tom smiled. "I should get going. Thanks for the pep talk."

She met his eyes and nodded. She hoped it helped. Tom left and she watched as he walked out the door, thankful he'd decided not to give up, but sad that his attention had fallen solely on winning Lila back. How selfish could she be even hoping for a sliver of his time when she'd caused the rift that had separated them in the first place?

She glanced at the counter and saw Luke making drinks. He met her eyes and smiled, but he felt so far away. She hated how little she'd seen of him, but what could she say? He owned a business. She couldn't argue that it needed his attention.

Everyone had something taking up their time. Everyone, that is, except her. How foolish she'd been to imagine lazy days at the beach with friends. People did have to work.

But how would she keep herself occupied when everyone else clearly had their own lives to tend to?

She glanced out the window and spotted Deb standing outside the gallery. She extended a hand to a man in a suit—most likely a prospective buyer—and her heart fell.

Maybe she should take her own advice and pursue the things she wanted most.

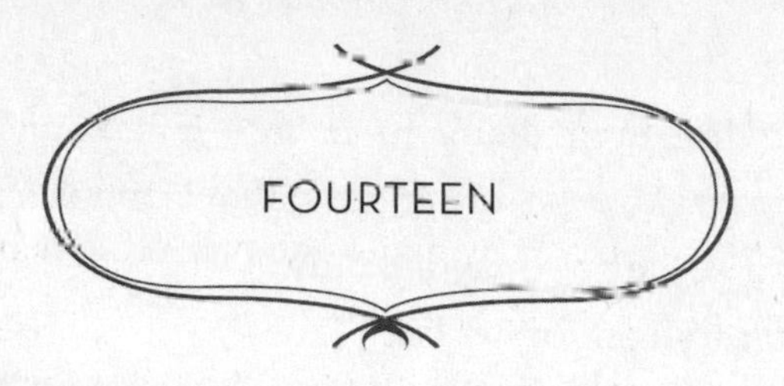

FOURTEEN

Jane

Jane stood in the Bible study room, paralyzed, pacing and wishing she had the courage to face Meghan, but mostly she wondered what her old friend was doing in the building at all.

Finally, after about forty-five minutes, Meghan emerged out the front door, and Jane gasped when she saw Graham following close behind. They spoke for a few moments and then Graham extended his hand. Meghan bypassed it and hugged him instead, then left him standing on the cement sidewalk as she went to her car and drove away.

Jane grabbed her purse and trudged down the wide hallway of the Sweethaven Chapel, her skin tingling with anger, determined to make her husband explain exactly what he was doing even speaking with Meghan—and letting her hug him? Unthinkable.

She met him in the lobby, and judging by the look on his face, she'd caught him off-guard.

"What was that all about?" Jane prayed the church was empty—she couldn't be held responsible for her temper.

Graham's eyebrows shot up and he stared at her. "What are you talking about?"

"I saw you. With *her*."

"Hon, calm down. I can explain."

"What is she even doing in town?" Jane spun around and searched for a way to expel the anger without completely losing it. A punching bag would've come in handy.

"She came to fight for her kids."

Jane laughed. "You can't be serious." How long had Meghan been here? How hadn't she heard?

"She was looking for some guidance."

Jane's fingers twitched. "Guidance. From you? Isn't it more likely she'd find her guidance at the bottom of a bottle?"

Graham's eyes widened. "What's gotten into you?"

Jane cringed. She knew she was out of line. "I'm sorry. I'm sorry. I know. I just didn't expect to see her like this. I didn't think she'd be here this summer. I thought I could move on—but here she is right in front of me." Just when Jane thought she'd made peace with everything, it smacked her in the face all over again.

That couldn't be a coincidence.

"Pretty safe to say there's still some things you need to work through." Graham walked toward her. "I think she's at the end of her rope, Jane. She could really use a friend right now."

Jane's jaw went slack and she stared at him. "Are you telling me I need to be friends with the woman who let our son die? You want me to sit there and listen to her problems and pretend I think she's fit to be a mother?"

He pressed his lips together and stared at the floor. Jane knew that look. His disapproving look that told her she'd gone too far. She hated the condescension.

Most of all, she hated that he was right.

She had gone too far. She'd allowed her feelings to dictate her actions—and it had proven that everything she'd discussed that morning with the women of the church had been nothing more than a charade. She'd pretended to be perfect.

And who did that serve?

Jane turned away and avoided Graham's eyes, anxious to leave but certain they weren't done talking.

"I would just appreciate it if you didn't talk to her, Graham. For me."

He walked in front of her and forced her to meet his eyes. "Hon. You know I can't promise you that."

"You can't or you won't?"

He stared at her. She understood the demands of being a pastor. He didn't get to pick and choose who he helped. He helped anyone who needed it—regardless of his personal feelings.

Regardless of *her* personal feelings.

She stood her ground for a long moment and then finally turned around and walked toward the door.

"Jane, wait." He called after, but she didn't stop and she didn't turn around. Instead, she marched all the way to her car, got in and drove off.

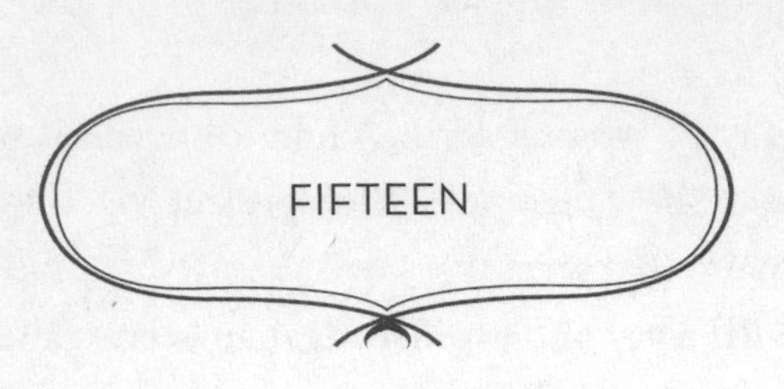

FIFTEEN

Meghan

After speaking with Graham, Meghan was surging with renewed commitment. The next day, she followed Nick to a job site, a house out beyond the town limits. It butted right up to the lake, and as Meghan parked her rental car, her memory spun back six years. The summer she'd come to Sweethaven to get clean. They'd stayed in that very cottage. They'd dreamed about buying it one day.

Meghan still remembered walking through it, telling Nick all the things she'd want if she lived there. It had been a safe haven for them—that is, until Alex.

The house had already been transformed. Meghan marveled at the way Nick could take something like a run-down house and breathe new life into it. He saw beauty where everyone else saw trash.

He'd always seen the best in her too. Even when no one else did. She watched as Nick unrolled the blueprints on the table fashioned from two sawhorses and a sheet of plywood. He instructed two men wearing hard hats and they disappeared inside the old house, leaving Nick outside alone.

It's now or never.

Meghan's face flushed with heat, and she knew she couldn't blame the hot summer sun. Nick, lost in thought as she approached, studied his blueprints, seemingly unaware of her presence.

"Did you come to say sorry?" he asked without looking up.

"Didn't think you saw me." She looked down at the blueprint and saw Luke's name at the bottom. So she was right. The two of them had stayed close—close enough to work together anyway. She thought her brother had given up being an architect.

"Been seeing that car in my rearview mirror a lot lately." He threw a sideways glance at her but she shook it off. "Is one of those for me?" He stood upright and eyed the coffee in her hand.

She held the cup out to him. "Black. Just the way you like it." He reached for it, removed the lid and took a sip.

"Is this a peace offering?"

Meghan's stomach turned at the idea that she'd given in somehow, that her being here was throwing in the towel. "Sorry about the game." She looked away. It didn't matter how much time passed since that night on the ball field. She'd never live it down.

He leaned against his truck, eyeing her, a look of amusement on his face.

"What's so funny?" She took a deep breath, trying to calm herself down. "Aren't *you* going to apologize?"

"For getting you back here? Not a chance."

She frowned. One of the carpenters poked his head out the front door.

"Got a problem in here, boss." When he spotted Meghan, his face brightened. "Oh, sorry to interrupt. Didn't know you had company."

Nick waved him off. "I'll be there in a minute."

The man disappeared back inside, leaving them standing on two opposite sides of an imaginary line.

"Nick, please. Can we talk like grown-ups?" She set her drink down on his makeshift table and crossed her arms over her chest. "You know I don't want to give them away. I had no intention of being gone this long in the first place."

"But you haven't seen them in over two years, Meg. I tried for months to get you to take them, to stay in their lives—you stopped taking my calls."

"So you had to go through the tabloids to get to me?" Her raised voice didn't bode well for a polite conversation.

"How else is anyone supposed to get your attention?" He put his cup on the table and took a step closer.

Her mind flashed back two years. The night she'd relapsed. The night she pushed him away for good.

She'd won three Country Music Awards, and the after parties were in full force. All night, with Nick by her side, she'd drunk nothing but club soda—but he got tired and went home, leaving her to fend for herself. Three hours later, he pulled her off the floor of the bathroom at one of the clubs, carried her to the car and drove her home. Home, where she was responsible for two sleeping two-year-olds.

"How could you do this, Meghan? After everything you've been through to get sober?"

In her drunken state, with heightened emotions, she couldn't make sense of what had happened. "You have no idea the kind of pressure it takes to be me," she said.

He took her by the arms and forced her to look at him. "Try being me," he said. "Try being the guy who has to keep picking up the pieces every time you do something like this, Meghan."

"Then don't do it anymore." She pulled herself from his grasp. "Just take the kids and go."

He stood straighter. "You don't mean that."

"Yes, I do. Just go. I don't want you here anymore anyway."

She knew just what to say to hurt him.

A lie that she couldn't take back.

That night, as Nick packed his bags, Meghan crept into the nursery to say good-bye to her sleeping babies.

She stood over Nadia's crib, smoothing the tousle of red curls matted to her face. "Sweet girl," she whispered. "Your mommy . . ." Her voice broke as she thought of what she needed to say to her daughter. "Your mommy is sick. And if you stay here with me . . ." She wiped the tears from her cheeks. "It's just better for you to go live with Daddy. It's safer that way. For everyone."

Her heart had broken that night, and it broke now as she replayed it in her mind. She'd told herself it was best for them—that if she couldn't stay sober for them, she didn't deserve them. But she'd been miserable ever since.

He faced her again. "You have to figure out what you want, Meghan. Once and for all. It's time to grow up and make a decision. I can't let you keep hurting us. If you say you want them and then walk away again, it's not fair to anyone. They're not babies anymore. They're four years old. And you're missing out on them."

"Boss?" The carpenter had returned. "We need you."

"I have to get back to work." He stood in front of her for another few seconds, but she couldn't think of anything to say.

Nick didn't want to play nice. He wanted to teach her a lesson. To show her what it meant to be a responsible adult.

And she was happy to show him just how grown-up she could be. She pulled her cell phone out of her purse and headed back to the car.

"Taylor, Kaufman and Pierce," a woman's voice on the other end of the line answered.

"This is Meghan Rhodes. May I speak with Mr. Pierce, please?"

"Certainly, Miss Rhodes, may I tell him what this is regarding?"

"A custody battle that I have to win."

Meghan

"Mr. Pierce, thank you for coming."

When Meghan's attorney arrived on her doorstep the following day, she was all nerves. By bringing James Pierce into it and flying him to Sweethaven at a moment's notice, she'd made up her mind. She wasn't going down without a fight.

Duncan had hired Mr. Pierce to handle Meghan's legal affairs, but she'd never actually met the man. She'd always assumed he was older, given that he was a partner in a high-profile law firm, but the man in front of her couldn't have been much older than she was.

Handsome and well dressed, everything about James Pierce said he meant business. He entered the lake house and extended a hand in her direction. "Good to finally meet you, Miss Rhodes."

"Please, call me Meghan."

"Then you must call me James." He flashed two rows of pearly whites in her direction. Professionally bleached, Meghan thought. "So, let's get down to business, shall we?"

They sat in the living room and Meghan told James everything, from the shady way Nick had ambushed her on television to their conversation earlier that week. She left out the part about practically stalking him for nearly three weeks and accosting him at a softball game in front of half the town.

"So, the best option here is to leave no stone unturned. We need to find dirt on your ex—and fast." James looked up from his legal pad. "Can you do that?"

Meghan's mind raced. Who would turn on Nick to help her? Even her own family would be on his side at this point.

"I'll do some digging on him too," James said, obviously sensing her concern. "Don't worry, I'll find something. I always do." He reached over and rested his hands on hers. When she met his eyes, she shifted in her seat, but he quickly retracted. "Now, this girlfriend. She's young, right? Do you think that could be an issue? If he's spending time with someone who wouldn't make a good mother . . ."

"I don't know who she is," Meghan said. "She didn't look unfit to me though. My kids seemed to really like her." She stared out the window and spotted the tree house. How different would this lake house be with the sounds of happy children rushing in from the yard?

"Meghan, if we're going to do this, you're going to have to be willing to make some enemies." James leaned forward. "He hasn't given you much choice."

She sighed. This wasn't how it was supposed to be.

"Listen. Why don't we take a little break for now? I've got my investigator with me. Whatever dirty little secrets Nick's hiding, we'll find them." He stood. "There's a little café right downtown. I bet they have a decent sandwich."

Meghan laughed. "My brother owns that café."

"No kidding? Does he know Nick?"

Meghan nodded, remembering the blueprints—Luke's blueprints—at Nick's work site.

"Maybe he'd help. If he lives here, he might know what your ex has been up to for the last couple years."

Meghan nodded. It was worth a shot, but as she got in James's rented Mercedes, a sinking feeling came over her. Did she really want to know how Nick had carried on without her? Did she want to hear the dirt on him? Did she want to destroy the man she'd always loved?

SEVENTEEN

Adele

Finally, after too many days of mismatched schedules, Adele drove to Luke's café to meet the girls for lunch to discuss their new and improved version of The Circle. They wanted to make a new scrapbook, like the one Campbell's mother and Meghan had made with Lila and Jane when they were young. But with summer more than half over, they hadn't even figured out how to go about it yet. It seemed like their only option might be to plan one of their big scrapbooking parties at the end of the season. But at this rate, would any of their plans come together?

She couldn't help but consider calling Meghan to come along—she belonged there, after all, but all of her calls to Meghan had gone unanswered.

She'd kept the twins several times since her run-in with Violet, always returning them to Nick's care—not his mother's—and considered telling him of her suspicions about his mom's mistreatment of his kids. Always, something stopped her. Fear of making false accusations. If she was wrong, Nick would never let her see the kids again. Besides, Finn had told her Grandma Vi had hardly been around lately.

A blessing, to be sure.

Adele parked the car in front of the café and saw Luke at the counter. Campbell and Jane sat at a table. She smiled, grabbed her purse and greeted them. They found a large table near the window and waited for Lila to arrive. In a matter of minutes, Adele could tell something was wrong. Jane refused to meet her eyes and Campbell seemed sullen.

"You girls look about as happy as a preacher at a funeral. What's wrong?"

"Did you know Meghan was in town?" Jane stared at her.

Adele's eyes darted from Jane's glare to Campbell's surprised expression.

She sighed. "I did. She came by my house the Friday after the Fourth."

Jane's eyes widened. "She's been here for almost three weeks?"

"I'm sorry, darlin', she hasn't returned my calls. I wasn't positive she was still here." Adele bit the inside of her lip. She'd trained herself to do that every time she told a half-truth. But did Jane really need to know she'd driven by the big rental house nearly every day since Meghan stormed off her porch her first week in town just to be sure her daughter *was* still here?

"She went to Graham for *counseling.*" The contempt in Jane's voice came through loud and clear.

Adele tried to muster empathy for Jane, but she had to acknowledge the relief that she felt knowing Meghan had sought help from someone so wise. "Maybe Graham can help her," she offered.

Jane shook her head. "She's got some nerve."

Adele had never seen Jane like this. She seemed angry—and that didn't suit her young friend.

"Oh, look," Campbell said, breaking the tension. "Lila's here."

Thank goodness.

Lila waved and approached the table, but before she reached them, a distinguished older man stood and blocked her path. "Lila Adler," he said.

Adele watched as Lila stopped in front of him. "It's Lila Olson now."

The flirtation in her voice was unmistakable.

"You don't remember me, do you?"

Adele glanced at Jane and Campbell, who were both waiting to find out who this man was.

"I'm sorry. You look a little familiar, but I haven't been back to Sweethaven in years," Lila said. She glanced at their table, a helpless look on her face as the man blocked her path.

"And Sweethaven has noticed your absence," he said.

"I'm sorry, do I know you?"

"Name's Patton Gallagher. We met years ago when I was just starting out. Your father invited me to your wedding." He spoke loud enough for the entire café to hear.

"Oh, that's right. I remember. It's been years." Lila smiled at him.

"You look the same." He stood and extended a hand in her direction.

"It's not polite to tell lies, Mr. Gallagher." Lila took his hand and shook it. She seemed to be enjoying his attention a little too much, Adele thought.

"Did you accept my father's invitation?" Lila tossed her hair behind her shoulder.

"Unfortunately, no. I wasn't able to make it to see another man steal you away before I ever had a chance." He winked. "Are you here for the summer?"

Jane's eyes widened as she stared in Lila's direction. "Does he know she's married?"

Lila flashed a smile at Mr. Gallagher. "I am, are you?"

"Every year. We should catch up. Can I take you for coffee tomorrow?"

With that, Adele bolted toward the barricade of a man and tapped him on the shoulder. “Excuse me, Mr. Gallagher.”

He spun around. “I’m sorry, have we met?”

“No, but you announced your name to the whole restaurant. I thought I’d come and retrieve my friend here.” She took Lila by the hand and pulled her past Patton Gallagher. “Good to meet you.”

She shoved Lila toward the table.

“Adele, what are you doing?”

“Saving you.”

“From what?” Lila tossed him a flustered smile.

“From yourself,” Adele said. “That man might as well be wrapped in caution tape, and you were flirting with him like a dopey teenager.”

“Oh, I wasn’t either,” Lila said. “Hi, girls.” She hugged Jane and then Campbell and sat down at the table. “He’s quite handsome, though, you have to admit.” She glanced at the man, who stared in her direction with a lazy smirk on his face.

“Lila,” Adele said. “You’re a married woman.”

“Not for long.”

Jane straightened. “What does that mean?”

Lila waved her question away. “Let’s not talk about my love life. We’re here to talk about The Circle.” Lila stole one more glance at Patton Gallagher before he walked out the door and down the street. Adele noticed he stole a look right back at her and she shook her head.

“Trouble, that one.”

“What’s the big deal?” Lila feigned innocence well.

“For one thing, he knows you’re married and he still asked you out.” Campbell looked away.

“Tom and I are separated.”

"But *he* doesn't know that," Jane said. "Doesn't speak well of his character, Lila."

"Can we please talk about the scrapbook?" She pulled a small album from her bag. "Are we all going to work a book together after all, or should we just get together and work on pages for our own books?"

They stared at each other, no one wanting to jump in and dictate their plans. Adele looked around the table, studying each of them. Jane, clearly still struggling with her feelings for Meghan, Campbell displaced and lonely, and Lila, losing her marriage of twenty-five years. How had they gotten here?

If only a big batch of gooey chocolate chip cookies could cure all their problems.

"Y'all are the ones who insisted on getting The Circle back together again," Lila said, oblivious to the tension hovering above them. "So, what, should we work on our own pages and then go to your house and put them in one book, Adele? At the end of the summer? Or maybe after Labor Day when it's not so god-awful hot outside?"

"Sure, hon. After Labor Day sounds good."

Lila stared at her. "That's all you have to say?"

Adele forced a smile. Her own woes had made their way to the forefront of her mind, and she now stewed about her daughter and the twins.

"What is wrong with everyone?" Lila looked at them all, one by one. "Y'all look so depressed."

No one said a word.

The bell above the front door clanged again, stealing their attention from the tense table.

Meghan sailed in, and a collective gasp escaped their lips.

"Oh," Lila said.

EIGHTEEN

Meghan

As Meghan entered the café, James Pierce at her side, she met Luke's eyes and smiled, but the look on his face quickly dashed any feelings of happiness she might've had. Meghan followed his gaze to the back of the café, where Mama, Jane and Lila sat with a thin blonde girl who bore a strong resemblance to Suzanne.

Campbell.

Mama glanced at Jane, and Meghan could see the sympathy on her face.

Still worried about Jane. Worried about what Meghan's presence would do to Jane.

What about me?

Seconds that felt like hours passed, and Luke appeared at her side. "You've got great timing." He watched her for a few long seconds. "Meg, you okay?"

She couldn't find words.

"Luke Barber. Meghan's brother." He extended a hand toward James.

"James Pierce. Meghan's lawyer."

Luke shot Meghan a look. "You brought your lawyer here?"

"Don't start in on me, Luke. I tried to be nice to Nick." She sighed. This wasn't what she wanted. She didn't want to cause problems for her brother—he'd been one of the only other people who hadn't accused her of killing Alex with her reckless behavior. Their already strong bond had strengthened because of it. The way she saw it, Luke was the only family she had.

Seconds passed and Mama bustled over. "I was beginning to think you fell off the face of the earth, young lady. If I didn't know better I'd say you were avoidin' my calls."

Meghan watched as Mama turned her attention on James Pierce. "Who's this handsome fella?"

"James Pierce," he said. "I'm Meghan's—"

"Friend. He's a friend of mine from back home. James, this is my mother."

"Pleased to meet you, Mrs. Barber."

Mama giggled as James shook her hand, then finally looked at Meghan again. "Well, we were just gettin' ready to eat some lunch. Why don't you both join us?"

Meghan glanced back at Jane, who avoided her eyes. She imagined her old friend was praying in her head, begging God to take Meghan away someplace where she didn't have to see her ever again.

"I don't think that'd be a good idea, Mama."

"At least come say hi, darlin'. And meet Campbell. Your brother's quite smitten with this one—she could be your sister someday."

Meghan looked at Luke with a raised brow. "That so?"

"I have to get back to work," Luke said as he walked away.

"The girls would love to meet your handsome friend, too, darlin'."

"I can't stay, Mama. I wish I could."

James shifted away, pretending to be interested in the menu board. Sweet, Meghan thought.

From across the room, Meghan spotted Lila. It would be unfair to leave and not say hello. But Jane . . .

Before she could decide, Mama had her by the arm and was pulling her toward the table.

Meghan let out a stream of hot air. "This is a bad idea."

A few steps and they were standing in front of a large round table. Lila walked around to the other side and hugged Meghan, fiercely, the way an old friend clings to someone they love. Meghan hadn't been hugged like that in years. "I've missed you," she said in Meghan's ear.

When she pulled away, Meghan saw tears in her old friend's eyes.

"And Meg, this is Suzanne's daughter Campbell." Mama motioned toward the young blonde girl with Suzanne's features. She could see why this girl had stolen Luke's heart. Poor guy never stood a chance.

Campbell stood and extended a hand. Meghan shook it and the girl smiled. When she did, it carried her back to simpler times, times when she and Suzanne hung their feet over the dock into the water of the lake. When none of them had kids or bills or ex-husbands or cancer. All they had before them was the promise of a bright future.

"It's so nice to finally meet you, Meghan. I read all about you in the scrapbook." Campbell sat perched on her chair.

"I haven't seen it in years." Meghan avoided Jane's eyes, but she could feel them staring at her.

"Did you bring your pages? I was kind of hoping to put the whole thing back together again," Campbell said. "It's on display at the art gallery across the street."

"Campbell had an art show there last month," Adele said.

"You're an artist?"

"Photographer. Mom was the artist."

"I remember." Meghan looked down at her polished toes. "I did bring my pages. Maybe I could drop them off to you sometime."

"I'd love that. And you'd get them back, but having the book together in the gallery would be a dream come true. I think it would make Mom so happy." Campbell beamed as she talked about Suzanne. They must've had a great relationship. Close friends. Not like her and Mama. Not like her and her own kids if some things didn't change.

Meghan noticed Lila staring over her shoulder and she only then remembered James. "Oh, I'm sorry. James Pierce, these are my oldest friends—Lila and . . ."

She couldn't rightfully call Jane a friend anymore, could she?

Jane stood. "I'm going to go."

Meghan dared to look at her. For the briefest moment, their eyes met, but Jane looked away. "No, I'll go."

"Don't be silly, girls. Both of you sit down." Mama stood between them.

"I'm sorry, Adele. I just can't." Jane clutched her purse with both hands, holding onto it like a life preserver. She looked at Meghan again. "I can't believe you had the nerve to come back here. Why couldn't you have just stayed away?"

Jane's voice had attracted looks from the other customers.

"Mrs. Atkins?" A cute young woman holding a little girl stood behind Jane, and judging by the look on her face, Jane didn't know she'd been there to hear her outburst.

"Amber. I'm . . ." Jane heaved her purse over her shoulder. "I've got to go." She flashed one last look at Meghan and marched away.

"Should I go get her?" Mama looked at the blank faces on Lila and Campbell.

"I told you, Mama. I shouldn't have even come over here. James, let's go somewhere else. We can talk to Luke later."

Her lawyer turned to go, but Mama's words stopped him.

"Don't be ridiculous. You girls are gonna have to talk sometime."

Meghan closed her eyes and inhaled a long, deep breath. "You can't do that, Mama."

Innocence splashed across her face. "Do what?"

"You can't make everything better by waving your magic wand over everyone. You might hate that Jane doesn't want to talk to me, but you can't change her mind. Just let it go."

"Me? Let it go?" Mama scoffed. "I don't think you should be the one handin' out relationship advice, little girl." As soon as she said it, Meghan could tell Mama regretted it, but it didn't matter. The damage was done.

"I didn't mean that, darlin'. I'm sorry."

"What's that you used to say, Mama? 'Out of the abundance of the heart the mouth speaks'?"

Mama's shoulders fell.

She caught Luke's eye and he motioned for her to follow him. Hopefully he had an office or something behind the swinging doors he walked through.

Meghan slung her purse over her shoulder, glanced at Lila and Campbell and forced a smile. "Good to see you again, Lila. And Campbell, I'll see about bringing those pages by."

They both nodded, apparently stunned to silence.

She turned to James, who'd already taken away one guy's cell phone to keep new videos off the Internet on his client's behalf. "I'm going to wait out here," he said. "You go ahead."

"Thank you." She forced a smile.

In the solace of Luke's little office, Meghan tried to release some tension. Her neck felt tight and the pulsing pain in her temples showed no signs of retreat. "This is such a mess."

"It'll blow over, Meg. It always does." Luke closed the door then sat behind the bulky desk.

She studied him for a long minute. "You're always the optimist, aren't you?"

He grinned. "Doesn't do any good to worry about it. You can't fix it all right now."

"That's all you've got for me? Those are your words of wisdom?"

He shrugged and kicked his boots up on the desk.

Behind him, the wall was papered with blueprints. Of what, she couldn't tell, but he obviously hadn't forgotten how to be an architect.

"Why do you stay here?" she asked.

"What do you mean?"

"You could be doing that." She motioned to the blueprints. "You were great at it."

"I didn't like wearing a tie."

"But you're still designing. I saw your blueprints at Nick's."

"He told you about that?" Luke looked surprised.

"He didn't have to. Your name is on them." She leveled her gaze, knowing she was about to put her brother in an awkward situation. "I need your help, Luke."

"Anything."

"I didn't come back here to reconcile with Mama or even talk to Jane. I came back for my kids."

He rubbed a hand over his stubbly chin and inhaled a deep breath. As he slowly let it out, something caught in her gut and she could tell he had something to say.

"Just say it, Luke. Say that if I really wanted the kids I would've seen them more and this isn't about getting my family back together. It's about putting Nick in his place."

"Is it?"

"No." She let out a breath. "No. It's not. It's about the kids. If Nick's going to release those pictures to strengthen his case, then I need to get some dirt on him."

"Is that what your shady lawyer told you?"

"He's not shady. He's one of the best."

"I'm sure he is. But the best in a custody battle usually means shady." He dropped his feet to the floor. "You're wrong about Nick. He didn't leak those photos."

"He was the only one who had them, Luke. You can't tell me it's a coincidence that they showed up the same time as his custody papers." The humiliation had returned.

"He wouldn't do that to you." Luke took his backwards ball cap off and ran his hand through his hair. "It's not his style. Besides, he still loves you."

"He's got a funny way of showing it." She glared at him. "So, are you going to help me or not?"

He frowned. "Meghan, I know you've been gone awhile, but I still live here. And so does he. He's . . . he's the closest thing to a brother I've got."

Heat crawled up the back of Meghan's neck, and the pulsing in her temples graduated to a pounding.

"You're not going to find anything on him anyway. He loves those kids. He rearranged his whole life to take care of them."

"Not like me."

"That's not what I said." Luke stared at her for a long moment. "I just meant that he's got a successful business. He's in church every week. The kids are his main priority. Just go talk to him—he wants you to be a part of their lives."

Meghan stood. "You know, Luke, I expected Mom to side with Nick. It's what she does. But you?" She scoffed. "See ya later."

He called after her, but he didn't follow. She stormed out, the rawness in her stomach gnawing at her. If her own family wouldn't support her, what chance did she have?

Her mind drifted back to the moment on Mama's porch when Nadia bounded outside and stared at her. Not being recognized by her own child had been more humiliating than the time she slipped on stage at the CMAs.

She found James sitting at a high table near the door. If no one was going to help her, then she had no choice but to do it James's way. Dirty.

Campbell

Five. Six.

Campbell counted the number of rings as she held the phone to her ear.

"Hi, you've reached Luke. Sorry I missed your call—"

Campbell blew out a sigh and hung up.

The sun baked the pavement, and its unique smell wafted to Campbell's nose. She inhaled. The smell of summer. While most people would covet her free time and her suntan, Campbell had grown tired of living off of Adele's generosity. She needed something to do.

And judging by the way things had been going, she had to wonder if Luke regretted convincing her to spend the summer in Sweethaven in the first place. Their relationship, their conversations, had been so easy in the beginning, and now, something between them just felt off.

This summer wasn't supposed to remind her how alone she really was.

Across the street, a man in a suit emerged from a shiny silver BMW. He walked toward the Sweethaven Gallery, and Deb met him at the front door.

Campbell's heart sank at the thought of some stuffy businessman owning the gallery. She and Mom had always dreamed of running a gallery, filling the world with art.

But who was she kidding? She didn't know the first thing about owning her own business.

Still, as if moved by an imaginary force, Campbell traipsed across the street and wandered into the gallery, pretending to be interested in the artwork, but trying to overhear the conversation. Deb led the man around the building, showing him the ins and outs, explaining all the benefits of ownership. He'd be crazy not to buy it, really. With its perfectly restored wood floors, high ceilings and lovely light, the Sweethaven Gallery was a steal at any price.

As they approached the front of the gallery again, Campbell tuned in.

"The apartment upstairs is a lovely addition. If you decided on a manager, he or she could live up there or you could rent it out. It has its own entrance in the back." Deb glanced at Campbell and smiled, excitement glimmering in her eyes.

Campbell felt guilty for begrudging Deb her Italian dreams, but the gallery was more than just a building. How could Deb consider selling it? Especially to this guy?

"I'm thinking of changing things quite a bit. We'd make the gallery more modern, sleek, like something you'd see downtown. I think it could be a nice draw for city dwellers who spend their summers here." He turned his attention to the artwork on the wall. "I have some connections, so I'd only hang prominent artists. Be nice to bring some culture to this sleepy little town."

Campbell's eyes narrowed as the man laughed and shook Deb's hand.

"We'll be in touch," he said.

As he walked out, Campbell approached Deb, whose smile seemed plastered to her face.

"You can't let him buy the gallery."

Deb's smile faded. "Why ever not?" She walked behind the counter and fussed with a pile of papers.

"You heard him. He'll ruin it. People from the city come here to get *out* of the city. They want the charm and beauty of Sweethaven. The gallery has that. If he gets his hands on it, all it'll be is another stale, shiny, white-walled museum wannabe."

Deb raised an eyebrow and stared at her over the top of her reading glasses. "You're awfully worked up. This is great news, my young friend. If that man buys the gallery, I don't have a care in the world. I can run off to Venice and Tuscany and Rome and paint to my heart's content." She stopped and leveled her gaze with Campbell's. "This is an answer to my prayers, honey. I can't stay here because of some sentimental attachment."

"But everything you've created will be destroyed."

"I don't have much choice, hon."

"Let me buy it." The words slipped out before she had a chance to think about them, surprising Deb as much as she surprised herself.

Deb laughed. "You're only here till the end of the summer, Campbell. Another month, maybe a month and a half?"

"I know, but I could stay."

Deb frowned. "What if you hate it? Don't romanticize what it takes to run a business. The work is hard. The hours are long. And here in Sweethaven, you make most of your money during the summer, meaning you have to budget for the rest of the year."

Campbell tried to run the numbers in her head. Would buying the gallery outright wipe out the account her father had set up for her? Or could she still live on it for a while—just until things took off?

Her heart jumped at the thought.

Campbell nodded. "I understand all that. And I'll take care of it. Just like you would. I could still offer classes and bring all the things to this town that you have for so many years. That man isn't going to do those things, Deb. You heard his plan. Is that really what you want to become of this place?"

Deb took her glasses off and looked Campbell square in the eye. "Hon. Why would a girl like you want to run a gallery like this?"

Campbell looked around, surrounded by Mom's art and the photos she'd worked so hard to perfect. "It was always our dream. Mine and Mom's. And you were the first person to believe in her talent. I can't explain it, but it just feels like the right thing to do."

Deb looked around the gallery, as if she were mulling things over in her head. Finally, she turned back to Campbell. "It's not a big money maker. You have to do the classes to make up for what you don't sell in art."

"Okay."

"And I wasn't lying about the apartment upstairs, but there's no air-conditioning, so it gets pretty warm."

Campbell stifled a smile. "You're not giving me the hard sell, are you?"

"I'm giving you the truth. There's nothing I'd love more than to see you here, but only if it's going to make you happy." Deb took her hands. "You sure you want to do this?"

Campbell thought about it for a long moment. Did she? She had her whole life ahead of her—she could do anything. Was she crazy for wanting to fill it with work? She looked around the gallery at the paintings on the walls. Paintings she'd hauled here in the back of her car the first time she came. She could practically feel her mother's arms around her in that very moment. *You can do this,* Mom would say. *You can do anything.*

She smiled. "I'm sure."

Deb's face brightened. "Good. I don't like stuffy suit-wearing businessmen anyway." She took the For Sale sign out of the window. "They'll never understand what it really means to be an artist."

She handed Campbell the sign.

"Now, let's go look at the apartment."

*****

Later that night, Campbell left Deb's, a feeling of excitement practically lifting her off the ground. For the first time, she had a purpose. She knew exactly what she wanted to do with her life. Never mind that she hadn't intended to stay in Sweethaven beyond the summer.

As she crossed the street toward the café, Campbell wondered how Luke would feel about her living in Sweethaven indefinitely. Maybe he needed to know she was serious. Maybe he'd find reasons to stay in town on the weekends now.

The café had cleared out and Luke sat at the counter near the back. As she approached, she noticed a sheet of paper in front of him, but when he spotted her, he stuffed it inside his notebook and tucked it under the counter.

"Back so soon?"

Why did she feel like an intruder?

"Do you want something to drink?" His smile looked forced.

"No thanks, I just came by because I have news."

"Oh?"

Campbell took a breath. "I'm buying the art gallery." She smiled, expecting him to be excited for her, but instead, Luke stuttered as if he didn't know what to say.

"Wow. That's big." His tone fell flat.

"It's good, right? My mom and I always wanted to do it, and now I'm going to."

He crossed his arms and nodded. "It's great, Cam."

She frowned. "What's wrong? I thought you'd be excited."

Luke sighed. "I just don't know if you know what you're getting into. It's a lot of work, owning your own business. And are you sure Sweethaven is where you want to settle down?"

What was he saying? He was in Sweethaven—shouldn't he want her to settle down there?

Unless . . .

"Luke, this doesn't have anything to do with you and me. You should know that. I'm not getting all serious on you or anything. I just thought you might be excited for me is all."

"That's not what I meant." He looked away but didn't offer any more explanation.

"I'm sorry I bothered you," she said.

As she walked out, she forced herself not to cry, but it took everything she had. Just as she was about to make one dream come true, she was about to make another one run away.

And that broke her heart.

Lila

After several days of successfully avoiding Tom, Lila began to wonder if he'd given up and gone back to Macon. A strange ball of disappointment formed in her stomach at the thought, but she shoved it aside.

How could she blame him for doing what she asked?

Still, standing inside the Sweethaven Post Office, she scanned the few patrons for any sign of her husband, telling herself she didn't want to be caught off guard, but knowing there was a part of her that hoped she'd run into him again.

She opened her box and fished out the stack of mail, flipping through it and discarding the junk right there in the post office. Lila gasped as she reached the bottom of the stack. A familiar postmark caught her eye.

Ginny Rutherford, Attorney at Law

The divorce papers had arrived. It was what she'd wanted, so why were her palms sweating? Why the sudden acceleration in her heartbeat?

Lila hurried to lock the post office box and tore open the envelope as she walked outside, the midday sun causing her eyes to water. She fished around until she found her sunglasses in her purse and scanned the papers, and a sense of finality settled over her.

She would soon be a divorcée.

"Fancy meeting you here, Miss Adler." Patton Gallagher stood at the bottom of the wide cement post office stairs, his eyes fixed on Lila as she approached. Quickly, she shoved the papers back into the envelope and into her purse.

"Mr. Gallagher, you startled me," Lila said, feeling her shiniest beauty queen smile falter.

"I apologize. I was simply admiring the scenery."

She looked away. Soon enough, it would be perfectly appropriate for men to admire her. She shoved the papers down a little deeper into her purse.

"Allow me to walk you wherever it is you're going?" Patton fell into step beside her, close enough for his arm to brush against hers as they walked up the hill.

"I'm on my way home from the post office. I come out every day about this time." Lila kept her eyes on the sidewalk in front of her.

"I'd be lying if I said I hadn't noticed that."

She glanced at Patton, who wore a hat to shield his eyes from the bright summer sun.

"I saw you yesterday and hoped it was a routine, so I put myself in your path today." He looked at her, and his confidence took center stage.

She allowed herself to smile before looking away.

"I've been waiting to run into you, but I'm not a patient man, so I took matters into my own hands. I'd like to have dinner with you." Patton's salt-and-pepper hair peeked out from under the hat. Lila hadn't been asked on a date in more years than she cared to remember. She couldn't deny she liked the attention—and Patton Gallagher held a certain charm that she didn't know how to resist.

Then she thought of the papers. She pushed her hair behind her shoulder and pressed her lips together. "I'm sorry, Mr. Gallagher—"

"Patton, please."

"Patton. I'm sorry—you know I'm married." She flashed him a look and warned herself not to enjoy this too much. She hadn't served Tom with the papers *yet.* A technical marriage was a marriage nonetheless.

"I heard through the grapevine you were getting divorced."

Lila's jaw went slack. "From who?"

"Doesn't matter, really. Did I hear wrong?"

She sighed.

"I'll take that as a no. Hardest part about getting divorced is getting back out there. I'm willing to help you take that step." He reached down and took her left hand, stared at the diamond on her ring finger.

Her hand felt small in his, and her mind drifted as she imagined what it would be like to date someone other than Tom. She never really had. She'd saved herself for a man who'd betrayed her. Could Patton Gallagher give her the life Tom never could? A life of romance and adventure? Many would consider signing the papers a mere formality. She had to admit it felt like her marriage was already over.

"Dinner would be nice," Lila said.

As soon as she agreed, she thought about Jane and Adele. Their disapproving words from the other night rushed back, and she studied Patton's eyes. Had he known then that she planned to divorce Tom? If not, he had no qualms about flirting with married women—and what did that say about his character?

She brushed the idea aside.

It's just dinner.

"I think it'll be more than nice." Patton laughed, but as they walked, Lila seemed unable to focus, her eyes scanning storefronts and passersby for any sign of Tom or one of her friends. Still, she couldn't deny there was some sort of spark between her and Patton. Handsome and successful, he exuded confidence, the kind that drew women to him.

And he seemed quite smitten with her, which was more than she could say for her husband.

As they approached the Main Street Café, Lila spotted Adele sitting on the patio.

"I should run," she said.

"So soon? We could get a drink. The café serves a not too shabby sweet tea. Perfect for Southerners like you."

She laughed and moved out of Adele's view. "I'm sorry, I think I'll have to pass."

A smile spread across his face. "I suppose I'll have to settle for dinner. Tomorrow night?"

She nodded. "That should work out just fine." She thanked him for walking with her and then crossed the street, hoping to avoid being spotted by Adele or anyone else she knew. Her friends would never approve of her talking with Patton, let alone having dinner with him.

Lila glanced over her shoulder and saw that he still stood in the same spot, watching her walk away. She waved and then rounded the corner, her mind swirling with conflicted thoughts.

Back at the lake house, Lila sat at the table, the divorce papers spread out in front of her on the dining room table. She stared at the little Post-it flag next to the line requiring her signature. Below it, another flag for Tom's. How would he react when she asked him to sign? He'd said he wouldn't give up on her—what if he made the divorce difficult?

She stared at the signature line, her pen hovering above it, poised to scribble her name and call it done. But before she took the pen to the paper, the framed wedding photo of her and Tom on the mantel in the next room caught her eye. She dropped the pen on the table and walked to the fireplace, picked up the photo and stared into her own eyes.

Somewhere along the way, she'd convinced herself that what they'd had together had never been real, but the photo told another story. She looked genuinely happy—because of the man at her side.

Adele's words rushed back to her—words she'd spoken just days after Lila learned the truth about Tom and Suzanne. "Leaving isn't the stronger choice. Stayin' is."

It went against everything she'd always believed—women, like Mama, who stayed with dishonest men were hardly admirable.

Unless they had some secret she didn't understand.

The fact remained that Tom had chosen to follow her to Sweethaven, that he said he'd fight for her—he hadn't been that romantic since they were dating. But he'd chosen to keep his distance—to do what she asked and give her space.

Like a gentleman. Like the man she fell in love with in the first place.

She'd always dismissed their love story as boring and uneventful, glossing over the details whenever they told new friends how they met. But the wedding photo reminded her of those early months of dating, those first years of marriage.

Their story had been anything but boring.

Lila slipped her shoes off in the entryway and ascended the stairs. In her old room, still frilly with rich linens and doused in pinks and lavender, she found the hope chest where all of Tom's letters were stored. Why hadn't she brought them to Macon with her? Weren't they important enough to keep with her, rather than having them stuffed in a chest in a town she hadn't visited in years?

She opened the one on the top and started to read.

August 18, 1986

Dear Lila,

You just left town with your family and I already miss you. After spending the summer with you, I'm sure of one thing. You and I are perfect for each other.

A lump of sorrow clogged her throat and she set the paper down. These letters were full of sentiments that meant nothing anymore. They weren't the same people they had been all those years ago—and now, they had a past full of secrets to contend with.

A noise in the entryway pulled her attention. She dropped the box on the plush bed and walked into the hallway as the front door opened and voices carried upstairs.

Lila's pulse quickened and every scary movie she'd ever seen rushed to her mind.

She hid behind the wall and waited, wishing she'd brought her cell phone upstairs with her. But why would someone break in in the middle of the day?

She peeked around the corner and tried to catch a glimpse of the people barging into her house, but before they moved into her line of sight, realization set in. A woman's voice, thick with a Southern upbringing, carried up the stairs.

Mama.

No.

This did nothing to slow her pulse.

What were her parents doing there? She hurried to the bedroom and paced the floor, the sound of her footsteps masked by thick carpet. Why on earth would Mama and Daddy come to Sweethaven? Lila had called them before she came to make sure they weren't planning to use the lake house.

"Oh, Lila, we're far too busy to vacation this summer. You go ahead," Mama had said. "Enjoy it. You look like you need to relax a little."

She then listed all the ways Lila's face had aged and suggested Botox to keep her "looking fresh."

Lila cringed at the memory. She never would've made the trip if she thought she'd be spending it with her parents. With her already wounded ego, Lila didn't think she could stand to be in the same room with Mama. Not even for a day. She glanced at herself in the mirror above the long antique dresser. She tucked in her shirt and smoothed her hair, then closed her eyes and took a deep breath.

"This is ridiculous," she said to herself. "You're a grown woman."

"Lila!" Mama's voice carried up the stairs and down the hall. "Are you up there?"

Lila walked to the door and willed herself to stay strong. "I'm here," she called. "Mama?"

She walked down the stairs and met Mama in the entryway, which suddenly seemed so vast it swallowed her up. Jewels framed her face, and her upswept hair told Lila Mama hadn't just given the Botox advice, she'd taken it. There was something remarkably frozen about her expression. "You look like you just woke up," Mama said, her tone as dry as crackers.

Lila bit her tongue. "What are you doing here? I thought you didn't have time for a vacation."

"Oh, we aren't vacationing. We're just here for the weekend. The Sweethaven City Council wants to present your father with a humanitarian award." She smiled. "Charitable work, you know."

Yes, her parents had always been very charitable. They doled out criticism to anyone in need.

"Is everything comfortable for you? I know you're high maintenance." Mama glanced upstairs. "I hope you don't mind staying in the smaller room while we're here." Her eyes wandered around the lake house, surely assessing Lila's housekeeping skills. Lila followed her gaze to the sitting room, then into the living room. Everything seemed to be in its place, traditional, expensive furniture the focal point of every room.

The papers strewn across the table in the breakfast nook caught her eye. *No!*

With as much nonchalance as she could muster, Lila walked toward the table and gathered the papers into a stack. "I'm already in the smaller room. Doesn't feel right to take your room." *I have no desire to be you.* Lila folded the papers and stuffed them back into the envelope, avoiding Mama's watchful eye.

"Oh, Tom doesn't mind?" Mama's eyebrows shot upward and waited for an answer.

Lila stared at her, frozen. She hadn't even considered the fact that Mama would hound her about Tom's whereabouts. And dinner with Patton? She could hardly go through with that now.

"Lila?"

"Oh no. He's not here."

"Where is he? You said he'd be joining you. Or did I misunderstand?" She motioned for Lila to follow her into the kitchen. Lila's mind raced as she tried to grab on to something—anything—that could explain Tom's absence. She couldn't tell Mama she was thinking of leaving Tom. The "I told you so" speech would be unbearable, and besides, she didn't want Mama's commentary on her life. She needed to make her own decision—apart from her mother and everyone else.

"Daddy." Relief washed over her as Lila spotted her father standing over the counter reading a newspaper.

"Afternoon, sweetheart. Have you gotten settled?"

"She was just about to tell me where Tom is," Mama said. Just once Lila wished Mama would give her an out.

"He's not here?"

"Not yet. We came up separately."

Separately was right.

"Was going to take him to play golf tomorrow morning. He still plays, doesn't he?"

Lila nodded. "It's awfully muggy for golf, Daddy."

"Are you kidding? It's blissful compared to Georgia. Besides, we'll get out early." Daddy probably wanted an excuse to get away from Mama.

"Will he be here tomorrow?" Mama stared at her, her penciled-on brows frozen over wide eyes.

"Yes. I think he will be. Our plans are still so uncertain." Lila waved her hand as if that could explain away her awkwardness. Mama frowned at her, clearly suspicious.

"Well, we won't get in your way. I expect the two of you need some time to relax." Daddy closed the paper and set it on the counter. "Ran into Patton Gallagher down at the coffee shop."

Lila's breath caught in her throat. Had Patton told them about her and Tom? Did Mama already know the truth? Was she trying to bait her?

"Said he's run into you a few times." Daddy smiled.

Lila glanced at her mother, whose expression begged an explanation.

"I saw him at the café and on the street."

"I didn't realize you two knew each other," Mama said.

"We don't." Lila decided to let her answer stand alone. Why explain anything to Mama? She'd deduce whatever she wanted anyway.

Lila took a deep breath. It would take a miracle to survive the weekend. If Patton had discovered the truth in a few days, Mama would have it in hours. A gossip magnet, she'd know every sordid rumor that had been spoken about her and Tom. Her stomach twisted.

"I'm sorry I can't stay and have dinner with you. I've got plans tonight." Lila grabbed her purse and checked for her phone.

"You're going out like that?" Mama gave her a once-over.

Lila swallowed, wishing for once she had the courage to say what she really thought. Instead she forced a smile and walked out the door.

In the silence of the car, Lila exhaled for what felt like the first time since she descended the stairs into Mama's lair. She glanced in the rearview mirror. Her eye shadow had gathered in the crease of her eye, and her mascara had smudged in the heat of the day. Mama had a point—she shouldn't leave the house looking like such a mess, but staying there didn't seem to be an option either. She grabbed a compact from her purse and tidied her makeup. Not much of an improvement, but it'd have to do.

Leave it to Cilla Adler to rip up her nerves like old carpet, exposing the underbelly of her insecurity. Lila drove down the driveway and back toward town. Next stop: the Whitmore Bed and Breakfast.

Meghan

"Don't worry, we'll find something." James Pierce was proving to be a thorough and shrewd lawyer. "And if we don't find it, we'll manufacture it. You hold the upper hand here." He reached across the kitchen table and took her hands. "You seem stressed."

"To say the least."

"Why don't you go get a massage or something? Spend the day relaxing?"

"I can't. I'm way too tense to relax."

James stood and pulled her to her feet. "Let me worry about the case. It's what I'm here for." He brushed Meghan's hair behind her shoulder and left his hand resting on the side of her neck. His nearness reminded her how it felt to be held, to forget the day's troubles and escape into the arms of a man. In her case, that man had always been Nick.

What if she needed something new? She and James were well suited, and he wouldn't complain about her fast-paced life. Obviously, he was interested, and more than likely, he'd savor every second in the spotlight.

Nick had never liked the paparazzi. He put up with it for her, but he complained every time they had a social event to attend. Her mind drifted back to those days when it looked like they might be okay after all.

"I'm not that black-tie guy, Meghan, you know that," he'd protest, and she'd agree. He wasn't a black-tie guy at all. It was part of his charm.

"Can you just wear it for me?" She'd wrap her arms around him and pull him close.

Then, that glimmer in his eye. "If you promise to take it off later." He'd lean in and kiss her, instantly falling into the rhythm of two people who'd shared their lives together. His kisses had never lost their excitement. Sure, they'd had their share of quick just-passing-through pecks on the cheek, but when he really wanted to, he could kiss her in a way that made her knees buckle—even after all these years.

"Meghan?" James's voice jarred her from her thoughts and she quickly pulled away.

"I'm sorry—I've just got a lot on my mind."

"All the more reason to get out of here for the day." He smiled and grabbed his suit coat. "I'm going to go back to the hotel. I'll come back later with a report on what we've found."

After he left, Meghan's emptiness returned. Not that James filled her emptiness, but he did keep her mind occupied. She knew he'd cook up a perfectly winnable case, but it wouldn't be easy. If they didn't do something quick, it would be too late.

And her kids would be gone for good.

Her thoughts wandered back four years to the day she'd had the twins. After a long eight and a half months, it was finally time. Nick's excitement had gotten them to the hospital in record time but had done nothing to settle Meghan's nerves.

Finn came first, then Nadia, both with tufts of red hair from the start.

"There's no question who their mom is," Nick had joked, holding his daughter, wrapped in a hospital blanket and wearing a pink cap on her tiny head. Then he looked at Meghan and beamed, pride written all over his face. "You did amazing," he said. "You are amazing."

He leaned in and kissed her, a "we did it" kiss that lingered until Finn started fussing in her arms.

There'd been so much joy between them—even then, after all they'd been through. How had she let that go?

Her fighter's instinct had waned some with James doing much of the fighting for her, but this wasn't James's battle—and the twins weren't his prize to lose.

She grabbed her purse, got in the car and sped up the road, pulling into the driveway of the old farmhouse where Nick had grown up—where he now lived. Like it or not, he didn't have full custody yet. They had joint custody, and she was tired of the runaround. They were her children and she wanted to see them *now*.

She marched to the door and started pounding. "Nick, open the door." She pounded again, then rang the doorbell.

"Have you lost your mind?" Violet's voice came from behind her. She spun around and saw the old woman standing at the bottom of the steps.

Just then, the front door popped open and the kids stood staring at her, that same scared look on their faces that she'd seen the night of the ball game.

"Get back inside, you two," Violet said, her words staccato and pointed.

The kids started to shut the door, but Meghan grabbed it. "No. I came to see them." She knelt down. "I came to see you." She forced a smile and begged her heart to slow down.

"Get away from them, Meghan. They don't even know you anymore." Violet started up the stairs. "Shut the door, Finn."

Finn looked past Meghan and his fear intensified. She glanced at Nick's mom and saw her eyes had gone black. Maybe the fear on his face wasn't directed at Meghan at all.

The little boy leaned toward Meghan and whispered in her ear, "I remember you, Mama."

"Finn!" A string of nasty words followed as Violet pulled Meghan back and pushed her way between her and the kids. The kids scurried up the stairs.

"How dare you talk like that in front of my kids," Meghan said.

Violet's laugh mocked her. "Don't get up on your high horse with me, little girl, after all you've done." Her eyes narrowed. "You're not welcome here, Meghan. I made that clear. My son doesn't want to see you and I certainly don't want to see you, so you need to stay away or I'll get a restraining order."

"I didn't come here to see you or Nick. I came for my kids."

"You gave them up a long time ago. Now get out." She slammed the door, leaving Meghan on the front stoop, hopeless and desperate. Telling a judge that Violet swore in front of the kids wasn't enough and she knew it.

She backed off the porch and looked up at the bedroom window. Two little pairs of eyes watched her. A lump rose in her throat and Meghan stopped, staring at them for a long moment. Why had she let it all come to this?

In spite of the sadness on his face, Finn lifted his hand in a wave. Meghan waved back.

"I love you, guys. I'm not leaving again!" Meghan shouted up at the house. "Not without you."

Finn pulled the window open and threw something out. Meghan walked over and saw the stuffed monkey she'd gotten him before he was born. Was he giving it to her to tell her he didn't want it anymore?

She turned it over and saw a small piece of paper fashioned in the shape of a heart pinned to the monkey's chest. On it one word. *Mama.*

Had this monkey stood in for her these past two years—giving hugs and cuddles when her son needed them?

Meghan looked back up at the window. "I love you, Finn. I love you, Nadia."

"Love you too, Ma—" Finn's words were cut off when an invisible force yanked them from the window. Violet appeared behind the glass, then pulled the curtains shut, shutting her off from her kids just like that.

Meghan ran her finger over the worn paper heart.

He said he remembered her. He loved her. In spite of everything she'd done.

She couldn't give up on them now.

Meghan

Later that afternoon, Meghan sat across from James Pierce at a picnic table under an old shade tree down by the lake, listening to the dismal state of her custody case. The lawyer had brought in an investigator to help dig up dirt on Nick, but so far they'd come up empty.

"Doesn't it count for anything that he's playing dirty? That his mother is a lunatic?"

James's eyebrows shot up. "What do you mean she's a lunatic?"

"Just what I said. The woman is crazy."

"It might help. We'll look into it. And like I said before, we've got some very creative people in our office."

Meghan cringed. She didn't want to entertain the idea of making up stories about Nick.

"What about that girlfriend of his?"

James shrugged. "Nothing so far. Everyone we've talked to tells the same story. Single dad who lives for his kids."

She sighed.

James rested his arm around her shoulder and gave a squeeze. "We're just getting started, Meghan. Don't get discouraged yet."

She sat with her back to the bench on the Boardwalk where she and Nick had had their first kiss. The fewer reminders of it, the better—it was hard enough being back in Sweethaven without thinking about every detail of their history together.

In front of her, though, something else caught her eye. A lanky guy wearing work boots, jeans and a faded red T-shirt, holding the hands of two familiar children. Hers.

James turned and followed her stare. "Isn't that him?"

Meghan looked away. "We should go."

"No, this could be good. If he knows you've hired a lawyer, he'll be more likely to compromise." He leveled her gaze. "We don't have much to go on at this point—working it out with him could be a good thing." James leaned closer. "Or maybe just make him *think* you're working it out. Get him to trust you again."

Meghan sighed. James couldn't have known the way her stomach still jumped when she saw Nick. And she could hardly bear having the kids so close, yet still unreachable.

"Mommy!" Finn spotted her and started waving, pulling from Nick's grasp and running in her direction.

When he reached her, he flung his arms around her and squeezed. Meghan closed her eyes and held him tight, inhaling the little boy scent of him. The smell of summer outside.

He pulled away and looked into her eyes. "Did you get my note?"

"I did, Finn, thank you." Meghan smiled, thinking back to the little heart pinned to the stuffed animal he'd thrown out the window. A love note—with her name on it.

He grinned, showing off a perfect row of tiny teeth. She looked up just as Nick reached the table. Nadia hid behind him, and Meghan chose not to push the little girl.

Nick glanced at James and then back at Meghan. "Sorry to interrupt. We're just getting dinner."

"Let me guess." Meghan looked at Finn. "Hot dogs?"

Finn smiled, then nodded. "How'd you know?"

Meghan looked up at Nick, memories of their nights in that very spot running through her mind. As kids, a hot dog was about all they could afford. Funny that now that she could afford to buy the whole town, the only thing she wanted was to share a hot dog dinner with her kids.

Nick shifted and looked at James again.

"Oh, how rude of me. I'm sorry, Nick, this is James Pierce."

James stood and shook Nick's hand, but her ex-husband didn't make eye contact. Instead he mumbled a "good to meet you" and then turned his attention to the kids.

"Let's go, guys, I'm starving."

"Can Mommy come too?" Finn still bubbled with excitement.

"Mommy and her . . . friend . . . probably have other plans."

Meghan shot him a look. "We do, actually."

Like digging up dirt on you.

Nick tossed a look at James. "Good to meet you, James."

"You too."

Nick watched her while he started the kids walking toward the hot dog stand. She didn't break eye contact for far too many seconds, then finally James's throat clearing grabbed her attention.

"We should go," she said.

They walked back toward the Mercedes and drove away. She looked out the window. The light changed and James accelerated, but Meghan's thoughts stayed in park. The cool breeze coming off the lake had provided the perfect backdrop for a reunion, but there she was, speeding away in the opposite direction.

"Expecting company?" James's words pulled her back to reality, and she spotted another car in the driveway next to hers.

"No." Meghan frowned.

It could be anyone—Lila, even Jane if she'd mustered the courage to come and give Meghan a piece of her mind. But as they got closer, her stomach dropped.

She'd know that nervous pace anywhere. After weeks of putting him off, avoiding his calls and coming up with excuses, Duncan had made good on his promise to come to Michigan and haul her back to Nashville.

"Duncan?" James laughed. "What in the world . . . ?"

Meghan dropped her head into her hands and groaned. "He's going to kill me."

When he spotted the car, Duncan put his phone in his pocket and marched toward their car. Before she opened the door, she could hear him shouting at her.

"Where have you been? Do you know what you've done to me? I had to go back to the doctor for more blood pressure medication. You're killing me, Meghan." He glanced at her lawyer. "Hey, James."

Meghan pushed past him and walked toward the front door, saying nothing.

"Don't you have anything to say? Do you know your new album was just released?"

"Last time I checked, it was still at the top of the chart," James said. God bless him.

"Yes, but think how much longer it would stay there if she got her butt back home and started promoting it."

"In case you hadn't noticed, Duncan, I'm a little busy up here. It's not like I just decided to take a vacation or something." Meghan threw her purse on the front table and walked into the kitchen. Both men followed her into the Pottery Barn–inspired room, with cream-colored cabinets and thick crown moldings. In other circumstances, this house would've been a dream. Whoever decorated it made it look like it simply came together without trying, laid-back and comfortable.

"We're working on her case, Duncan."

"Can't you handle that, Pierce? Isn't that what we pay you for?"

"I can. And I am, but being here and having access to the kids has been beneficial—not just for the case, but for Meghan." He glanced at her, but she didn't meet his eyes. She didn't need James pretending he cared about her getting the kids back. The truth was, he cared about his high profile case—and that was all. They both knew what this could do for his career.

"Meghan, you have appearances booked—what am I supposed to tell these people?"

She cracked open a bottle of water. "Something suddenly came up?"

Duncan drew in a deep breath, to calm himself down, Meghan was sure. She knew how to push his buttons. He turned away.

"Duncan, you know when this all blows over I will sing wherever you want me to, but right now, I have to be here."

He spun around. "How many chances do you think you get?"

Meghan felt her shoulders drop.

"The album is getting great reviews, but people are not going to put up with this from you for very much longer. You're all over the tabloids right now—with those photos and then that ridiculous outburst at the baseball game. What were you thinking?"

Meghan rubbed her temples. "I don't know."

"That's it? That's all you can say?"

"I'm sorry. I am. I didn't mean to mess everything up for you, but if you'll remember, I am the reason you're so rich, Duncan."

"And I'm the reason you still have a recording contract."

Meghan narrowed her gaze. "What are you talking about?"

"They were ready to let you go. I talked them into one more shot. 'Just one more album,' I said. 'She can pull it off.' And they finally agreed, but they made it very clear that this was our last chance. Your last chance."

Meghan sighed and sank into a padded chair. "So if I don't show up next week and do all this publicity, I don't make any more albums?"

"That's what I'm saying. Why else would I be here?" Duncan sat down across from her. "I know you're worried about your kids, but let James handle that. You come back with me and we'll work on what you're really good at—being a star."

James sat down beside her. "Maybe Duncan's right, Meghan. Being here is just going to confuse things. You go back, do the appearances and I'll handle things on this end. I promise to call every night with an update."

Meghan listened to the words, but inside, the only thing she could think about was Finn's arms wrapped around her, the little heart pinned to his toy, the way he'd invited her to dinner with them.

Duncan tossed a look at James and sighed. "You've got a second chance, Meghan. Don't mess this up."

She nodded and led him to the door. "I'll call you tomorrow."

James followed behind. "Call me if you need anything."

After they'd gone, Meghan turned and faced the empty house. It seemed to taunt her. Couches looked big and oversized, perfect for families who liked to cozy up together with popcorn and movies. The chef's kitchen was stocked with the latest and greatest, making it easy to serve up a feast for a party of twenty-five.

And yet, here she was. Alone.

In the quiet, Meghan's mind wandered back to the first night home with the twins. She and Nick had stood over their cribs for what felt like an entire night, making sure they were both still breathing. They'd fallen asleep on the floor of the nursery and woken together to feed and change them. They went on that way for weeks until finally Nick suggested they move back into their own room.

"I think they've got this sleeping thing down." He stood behind her in the nursery, looking into the cribs of their sleeping babies.

"They're perfect, aren't they?" Meghan ran a hand over each soft cheek.

"They are. You did good, Mommy."

She smiled and turned into his hug. They stood there in the moonlight inhaling the scent of baby powder and reveling in the growth of their little family.

"Everything I need is right here in this room," Nick said.

And he meant it. Even then, Meghan knew the big-city life held no appeal for him. He'd only wanted her and the kids and a little house on the lake. What more did he need?

And why did she think she needed so much more?

Meghan walked into the living room and pulled the scrapbook pages from her bag, plopping down in a red chair and a half, the kind that would be perfect for two people who didn't mind being close. She ran a hand over a photo of the four girls—so young and so innocent—and wished she could go back and do so many things over again.

Her life seemed to be a series of regrets—and now she faced a decision that could lead to one more.

Fabricating a lie to make Nick look like a bad father would ruin them for good.

And sitting there in the lonely darkness, she had to decide if she was willing to take that risk.

TWENTY-THREE

Lila

Lila parked her car outside the Whitmore Bed and Breakfast and stared at the building for at least ten straight minutes. The colonial home had been painted pale yellow, and thick white trim encased each of the nine windows lined across the building's front. Even in her current state, Lila couldn't help but admire what the new owners had done with the Whitmore. Restored it to a thing of beauty.

What was she thinking? She couldn't go to Tom. Why did she always expect him to bail her out?

But she couldn't bear to face Mama's disapproval—her snide remarks or elitist attitude. More than anything, she didn't want to believe Mama had been right about them from the start—that she'd predicted their demise before they'd even officially begun.

But hadn't she?

Lila inhaled, counted to ten and then got out of the car. Inside, the quiet B and B welcomed her. Cozy and warm, it seemed to complement Sweethaven perfectly. Dark wood floors stretched across three rooms as waning sunlight poured in from every direction.

When she saw the empty front desk, Lila explored the old house, looking for an employee. She walked through French doors into the dining room. A long farmhouse table sat underneath a vintage chandelier, and Lila wondered if Tom ate with the other guests or took dinner in his room.

Just as she was about to ring the bell, she spotted Tom in the stairway. He hadn't noticed her yet, and she could see by his eyes he wasn't sleeping well. She could always tell with him.

He made it to the bottom of the stairs before he saw her. "Lila?"

Something washed over him, and Lila prayed he didn't get the wrong idea. She wasn't there to make amends. She had a favor to ask.

"You're here," Lila said, noticing the nerves in her stomach.

"I am. I've been here all day." He stared at her. "Just got back from a trip actually." So that's why she hadn't run into him. She used to know his flight schedule by heart. Every trip had been outlined on her calendar, but not lately.

When had that changed?

"Can we go somewhere and talk?" she finally asked.

Tom's eyes narrowed for a split second before he followed her out the door and across the street, toward the gazebo where they found a bench and sat down.

Tom stared at something in the distance, refusing her eyes.

"I came to ask you a favor."

"I figured."

She crossed one leg over the other and hugged her purse. "I wouldn't ask unless it was really important. You know that."

He turned to face her. "Is everything okay?"

She let out a hot stream of air. "Mama and Daddy showed up at the lake house a little while ago."

His eyebrows shot up. "Oh."

"I know. And I know how you feel about them, but I can't tell Mama what we're going through right now. I can't hear her tell me I should've listened to her all those years ago and you were never really good enough for me in the first place and . . ." Lila said the words without thinking and then saw the way they hit Tom, like a swat across the face. “I’m sorry.” Reliving Mama’s disapproval wouldn’t do either of them any good.

“Do *you* think you should’ve listened to her all those years ago?”

She looked away.

“Lila, she wasn’t right about me.”

“I don’t want to argue about this right now.” Lila’s eyes clouded and she forced the tears away, stared at a bumblebee that hovered above the rosebushes near the gazebo.

“So, what’s the favor?”

Lila closed her eyes. Even she couldn’t believe what she was about to ask. “Come home with me. To the lake house. Stay the week and pretend that everything is fine between us.”

Tom didn’t respond.

“I know it’s nuts, I do, but I just can’t handle any questions right now.” She stared at him as the seconds ticked by, wishing she could read his mind. “Say something.”

He watched a squirrel as it scurried down the sidewalk and up an old oak tree in the distance. “You know how much I love being around your parents.”

“Just forget it.” She started to get up, but his hand on her arm stopped her.

“But I’ll do it. For you.”

She felt paralyzed by his gaze. After a long moment, she looked away. “I wouldn’t ask, but . . .”

“I understand. I know your mother. But you know she’s going to hear about us through the grapevine. She’s the queen of gossip around here.”

“But if you’re there, she’ll tell people it’s not true. She’ll say she’s seen how happy we are and it’s crazy to think we’re split up.” Lila hoped so anyway.

"So you not only want me to show up, you want me to put on an act that will convince your mom everything's fine."

"It's too deceptive, isn't it?" Lila cringed. She'd left him because of deception, and yet, here she was asking him to put on a good show for her parents. The hypocrisy didn't elude her.

"It's not deceptive for me to pretend I'm in love with you," he said.

His words caught her off guard, but he'd thrown them out like he was simply mentioning the weather.

"I'll do it. When do you want me to show up?"

"Tonight, I guess. I could come by after dinner and we could go together."

Tom leaned back and rested his arm on the back of the bench. "Just one more thing, Lila."

She waited with expectant eyes.

"I'm not letting you go without a fight."

She stared at him, and as though there was an invisible cord connecting them, she couldn't look away. She found Tom's firmness surprisingly attractive.

He picked up her left hand and touched her wedding ring.

She tried to respond, but her voice had failed her. His familiar touch had a newness to it she couldn't quite explain. All she knew was that it shot a tingle down her spine.

And suddenly bringing him home with her seemed like a very dangerous idea.

TWENTY-FOUR

Adele

Ever since her run-in with Violet, Adele had found ways to keep tabs on her grandchildren, making up reasons for Nick to bring them over to her house and keep them overnight. But living with her suspicions about Violet had started to wear on her, and she knew she needed to come clean with Nick.

But when he picked the kids up from her house, Adele could tell something was wrong.

"You wanna talk about it?" Adele held the screen door open, but Nick shook his head and turned away, leaned against the column of her old cottage and stared at the park across the street.

She joined him on the porch. Nick Rhodes. Broken since the day she met him. She feared her daughter had only torn the scabs off of old wounds where Nick was concerned. She put a hand on his shoulder and waited for him to meet her eyes.

When he did, she smiled. "You're a good man, Nick Rhodes."

He looked away. "I didn't want it to go like this."

"She's stubborn, son. You know that." Adele cleared her throat. "Nick, I know we haven't always seen eye to eye."

Her mind raced back to that day after Alex's accident.

"How could you ask her that, Adele? She's clean. She's been clean—do you know what you've done?"

Adele would never forget the desperate look in his eyes. It was as if he knew that day, he'd lost Meghan. And Adele had been the one to push her off the edge.

Nick had always been squarely on Meghan's side—it had been part of the reason it took him so long to let Adele spend time with the twins when they returned to Sweethaven. She couldn't risk upsetting him—not with Violet already gunning for her.

Nick shifted.

"But I want you to know how much I respect you, son."

"I'm not sure I follow. I always thought you were nice to me so you could see the kids. Figured you held a grudge against me. I assumed you thought I walked out on your daughter."

"She pushed you, I'm guessin'."

"She . . . yeah, I guess."

"Far as I'm concerned, you're one of the good ones."

"Not sure she sees it that way, Mrs. B."

"Meghan's always looked at the world a little sideways, I think."

He sighed. "I'm mostly worried about the kids. I get her not wanting me anymore, but I don't get how she can keep herself from them."

Adele tensed at the mention of the children. "Nick. You know I love those kids. And I love my daughter, but I'm inclined to think maybe she's not telling us everything. Maybe she has a reason we don't know about."

He looked at her. "Not one that justifies leaving your kids. I thought if I . . . never mind."

Adele stared at a couple of kids on swings at the park, and she sensed her opportunity slipping away. "How are you doing with the twins, Son? Everyone okay?"

"Sure. We're fine. You had them today—do they seem okay to you?"

Adele nodded, her insides twisting in conflict. Did she tell him about his mother? She didn't have proof, but her heart told her she was right. But Nick could choose not to believe her. He might even keep her grandchildren away from her and she couldn't bear that. Not again.

Then there was the matter of hurting him. How could she suggest that he'd put his own children in harm's way without realizing it?

Nick glanced at her. "I should go. I need to get the kids. Are they ready?"

"They'll be with you tonight?"

"'Course, where else would they be?"

Adele inhaled, but as she studied his eyes—his pain as visible as the conflicted emotions he felt for Meghan—instead of speaking her mind, she went inside, packed up the twins and watched them as they drove away.

Adele waved as he backed out of the driveway and turned the truck around, her mind drifting back to the first day Meghan brought him home. She had seen a broken spirit in him even then, but Meghan wouldn't tell his secrets—not to Adele, not to anybody. Years later, Adele learned the truth about the abuse Nick had suffered, and yet he had turned into a gentle, protective soul.

And Meghan had run him off.

She sighed as she boxed up the banana cake she'd made that morning and set it on the front seat. As she drove toward the lake house Meghan had rented, she asked God to give her wisdom. She had such a way of setting her daughter off in the wrong direction—and with their volatile past, Adele needed all the help she could get.

"Jesus, just don't let me say anything stupid," she said, as if Jesus had anything to do with her inability to control her tongue. She put the car in park and headed up the sidewalk toward the front door, relishing the breeze coming off the lake. Late summer could be almost pleasant thanks to that wonderful body of water. Summers were hot, but bearable.

She knocked on the door and waited for an answer, certain Meghan was inside since the rental car was parked in the driveway. She cupped her hands around her face and peeked in the windows.

"You look like a Nosy Nelly." At the sound of Meghan's voice, Adele spun around. Her daughter stood in the yard at the edge of the porch.

"You scared me to death."

"Because you're looking in my windows?"

Adele laughed. "Because I was expectin' you to answer the door."

"I was out by the lake." She walked barefoot across the porch and opened the front door. "What brings you by?"

"I made you a banana cake." Adele followed her into the kitchen.

"As an excuse to come talk to me about what?" Meghan opened the fridge and pulled out a bottle of water. Adele pushed away the fleeting thought that it was so much better to see her drinking from that bottle than the kind she used to prefer.

She set the cake down on the counter. "Do I need an excuse to come by? I just thought you could use some home-baked goods. Lord knows you need some meat on your bones."

Silence fell between them and Meghan took another gulp of water.

"Awfully warm to be baking, Mama. You should make some homemade ice cream."

"Oh, the twins and I did that last . . ." Adele snapped her mouth shut at the sad expression on Meghan's face.

Her mind whirled back to her car-prayer and she begged for a little divine intervention.

"I saw Nick this morning." The hole she was digging just kept getting bigger.

Meghan stopped mid-drink and set the bottle on the counter. "I don't want to talk about Nick, Mama."

"What's going on with you two? I could tell he was upset."

"You come here to find out what I did to hurt him? Is that it?"

"Don't be ridiculous." Now would be a good time to bite her tongue.

Meghan walked into the sunroom and plopped down in the wicker chair facing the lake.

Adele followed her, unable to help but marvel at this big, beautiful home. It had been professionally styled but lacked the fussiness you might expect. The sunroom boasted three walls of windows, couches comfortable enough to sleep on, and a modern style that would suit any young family.

How was Meghan coping without hers?

She remembered Violet's mention of Meghan getting "papers." Custody papers, she assumed. Why would Nick try to take the twins away from her now? Adele sat across from her daughter. "There has to be something you can do to work this thing out between the two of you."

Meghan stared beyond Adele toward the lake, her eyes glazing over. "The only thing left for me to do is to fight him. Either that or give up."

"What do you mean by 'fight him'? With your career, that's gonna end up in the papers and everything else."

"His choice, Mama."

"What about the kids, darlin'?" Adele folded her hands to keep from fidgeting.

Meghan shook her head. "What else am I supposed to do? He pushed me too far."

They were quiet for a long moment, and then Meghan seemed to reenter the room, her eyes focused on Adele. "You know Nick as well as anybody here, right, Mama?"

Adele shrugged. "I suppose so."

"You can help me. Find me something I can use against him in court. I don't even have to actually use it, I just have to be able to threaten him with something."

Adele's mind wandered to what she suspected about Violet. Something like that—like Nick putting the kids in harm's way—could certainly strengthen Meghan's case. But it would destroy Nick, and most likely her grandchildren in the process. Her stomach twisted and she shook her head.

"What is it, Mama?"

Adele felt her eyes widen.

"I can tell by the look on your face that you know something." Meghan leaned forward and glared at Adele.

She shook her head. "I don't know anything."

Meghan shook her head. "First Luke, now you. After everything, you're still taking his side. Don't you think you owe it to me to do this one thing? Is that too much to ask?"

"You don't know what you're asking."

"I'm asking for help. In all the years of therapy, I learned how to ask for help, and what good is that doing me now?"

A rush of panic ran down Adele's spine and she felt like Benedict Arnold. She could give Meghan the dirt she wanted on her ex-husband, but at what cost? The kids would certainly pay the price. But if her suspicions were right, they were already paying.

The impossibility of her situation didn't escape her, and Adele silently prayed to God for a Solomon-sized dose of wisdom.

Somehow, she had to make this thing right.

TWENTY-FIVE

Jane

Jane sat at the kitchen table, a mess of patterned paper, glue and embellishments surrounding her. She'd spent the morning creating pages for the prayer journal she hadn't intended to create in the first place. She thought she didn't need it anymore, but seeing Meghan had told her otherwise.

She hadn't said more than two words to Graham since, and he didn't seem the smallest bit fazed by her silence. He'd learned to leave her alone during these moods, but having to work through it on her own only upset her more.

The journals had been her constant companion in the first months after Alex died. The blue one in which she spilled her feelings about losing her son, and the small spiral-bound journal she'd started at the suggestion of her therapist.

"To help you remember that Meghan needs God's love too."

Praying for Meghan had been the hardest thing Jane had ever done, and it didn't always make her feel better. Sometimes she wrote the prayers feverishly and with clenched teeth. Others were written through tear-filled eyes.

This morning's prayers were a mixture of both. Mostly she asked God to give her a new perspective on Meghan—empathy would make her own journey to forgiveness a lot easier. Somehow, she'd found that if she could put herself in the other person's shoes even for a second, it seemed to make the forgiving part easier. It hadn't always worked with Meghan, though, given her status and wealth. She seemed to have everything she could ever want.

Jane studied the page she'd created. Pages without pictures had become the norm for her. A handwritten prayer on the right-hand side of the two-page spread was outlined with strips of various patterned papers. She'd spent over an hour on the prayer part of it and still felt unsettled even though she'd written "Amen."

The women from the Bible study came to mind. She'd convinced them she had all the answers. She'd walked the slippery slope and had emerged stronger and wiser—but she didn't feel either. Instead, she wrestled with this same demon once again.

She'd always promised herself she'd be transparent—not one of those pastor's wives who pretended to have it all together. The ones who answered every question with a biblical quote and seemed to have no life experience. Jane knew that helped no one, so she made a point to always be real, but right now "real" felt too painful.

She closed the cover on the book and made a choice to let the prayer work for her. No sense on dwelling on everything—she'd taken her cares to God. She had to believe He'd help her through the big mess of bitterness that seemed to threaten her at every turn.

TWENTY-SIX

Meghan

Two oversized suitcases sat beside the front door. Meghan only had a few more things to pack and she could get back to her real life—to focusing on anything other than digging up dirt on Nick or risking running into his girlfriend.

Her heart dropped at the thought of Nick with someone else. She couldn't stay in town for one more second if it meant running into the two of them with her kids. She'd stop by the café to say good-bye to Luke, then swing by Mama's out of courtesy—but then she had to go. Like Duncan said, James could take care of the case—it was his job, after all. Why did anyone need her digging up dirt when they were paying an investigator to do it for them?

She couldn't risk staying in Sweethaven one more day. If she missed another appearance, she'd have trouble booking anything—and she needed this album to sell.

The album was all she had.

Besides, the memories here were too painful.

Meghan's cell phone buzzed, moving in a snake-like pattern across the kitchen table. Meghan glanced at it from across the room but didn't get up to get it until the buzzing stopped and it beeped that there was a new voice mail.

"Meghan, it's Duncan. Let's talk later today. We need to make arrangements to get to New York. Call me back so we can work out the details. Otherwise, I'm coming over." Duncan paused and Meghan could imagine the face he'd been making—eyes closed as he pinched the bridge of his nose. "I don't mean to be blunt, but if you don't get your act together, you'll be yesterday's news. You really need to think about what you're doing." The voice mail ended abruptly.

Meghan sighed. The cancellations were stacking up and she was starting to become a punch line on the late-night comedy shows. The more she read about herself online and saw about herself on the entertainment channels, the more she felt the pull to return to what she did so well—perform. To make people happy with her music. It would be so much easier to call Duncan to tell him he'd won: she'd be at *Good Morning America* whenever he set it up, she'd sing wherever he wanted, and she'd do everything she could to restore her image.

Especially with Mama working against her again.

It had been a long road, the path to fame and glory. It hadn't always been high heels and stadiums. In the beginning, Meghan had waited tables and sung in bars just to make ends meet—just to say she was a professional singer. And the pictures proved that she'd done almost everything to make her dream come true.

Then, one day, Duncan walked into her bar, heard her sing and made her an offer. Her mind settled on the memory of running all the way home that night to tell Nick. His happiness had been so genuine—he wanted to make her dreams come true too.

But in so many ways, it was that dream that had torn them apart. She'd sacrificed everything to get where she was today.

If she missed another appearance, she'd have trouble booking anything—and she needed this album to sell.

In many ways, the album was all she had left.

The doorbell rang, and Meghan's heart jumped. Was Duncan on the porch when he left the message?

She walked to the door after the bell rang again and found Suzanne's daughter standing there, looking a little out of place.

"Campbell?" Meghan waited for her to speak.

"Your mom told me where you were staying. I hope it's okay that I'm here."

"Oh, the scrapbook pages. I'm sorry, I've got them inside, come on in." Meghan stood to the side so she could walk past, then shut the door behind her.

"No, that's not really why I'm here, but I'll take them if you've got them." She glanced at the suitcases. "Are you going somewhere?"

"Uh . . . yeah. Duty calls. I have to get back to Nashville, then I have some appearances scheduled." Meghan handed her the stack of pages. It was the first time she'd actually had time alone with Campbell. "Do people tell you that you look like your mom?"

Campbell laughed. "Yes. A lot. Especially people here, people who knew her when she was younger."

An awkward pause hung between them and Campbell shifted her weight. Meghan knew the girl had something to talk to her about—something other than scrapbook pages—but what it was she didn't know. "Would you like some lemonade?"

Campbell's face brightened. "I'd love some. I won't take too much of your time."

"It's fine. It's not like I have a lot of visitors out here." Actually, that wasn't completely accurate. "What's up?"

Campbell took the glass of lemonade and sighed. "I just wondered if you'd spoken to any of the others lately. Your mom or Jane?"

Meghan sat down and watched Campbell fumble for the right words.

"Things are weird between everyone, and I was just thinking if we could get everyone together in the same room, maybe it would help clear the air?"

Meghan turned her glass around in circles, then wiped the condensation from her hands. "I appreciate that, Campbell, but there's a lot of history we're dealing with here. You saw how badly it went the other night."

"I know." She cracked her knuckles and stared at the table, visibly upset by the rift between her mom's old friends.

And why wouldn't she be? They were all she had left of her mom's past—and none of them were speaking. "I'm really sorry, hon. And I don't think I'll get much of a chance to patch things up before I leave."

"How much longer are you here?"

Meghan looked down. "If my manager had his way, I'd already be gone."

"Can I tell you something, Meghan?" Campbell stared at her folded hands on the table.

"Of course."

"It won't be better for anyone if you leave. Not for you or your ex and especially not for the kids."

Meghan watched her, trying to piece together where this was coming from.

"It would've changed everything just to know my father had fought for me. Even for one day. But he didn't. He paid for me and walked away." Campbell ran a hand through her hair, her eyes filling with tears.

"But I *am* fighting. It's being taken care of as we speak."

"I'm not trying to tell you what to do, Meghan, but I can tell you that someday, maybe years from now after they've given up hope that you'll return, they will realize that you walked away. And they'll wonder what they did to make you leave."

"It's not about that." Meghan looked away. She knew how it felt to long for a parent's love—to come up empty and feel unworthy. In her mind, keeping her distance from the twins had always been about saving them.

"They won't know that."

Meghan met her eyes just as Campbell swiped a tear from her cheek.

"I'm sorry about your dad, Campbell," Meghan said. "It's not fair."

"No, it's not."

Meghan swept her hair into a ponytail and wrapped an elastic band around it, then smoothed it out with her hands. "Nick's got a lot of dirt on me, and from what I can tell, that man has turned himself into a bona-fide saint. What judge is going to side with me?"

"You're Meghan Rhodes. What judge wouldn't side with you?"

"One who reads the tabloids."

"Maybe you could talk to Nick."

Meghan shook her head. "I tried that already. It didn't go well."

Campbell frowned. "I overheard Luke talking to your mom about Nick's mother. Isn't her name Violet?"

Meghan stiffened. "Yeah, that's her. What about her?"

"I'm not sure. Something though. I got the impression that something was wrong." Campbell stared at her for a long moment and then stood. "I don't mean to butt in." She hugged the scrapbook pages to her chest. "Thanks for these."

Meghan nodded and followed her to the door. After Campbell left, Meghan went out back and stared out across the lake for a long time. Her suspicions were right. Luke and Mama did know something, but they'd chosen not to tell her. They'd chosen Nick. Again.

Her little chat with Campbell had been just the kick she needed to fire her up all over again.

This custody battle—one that proved in writing to her and everybody that she was flawed—it made her want to fight for what really mattered. More than anything.

Duncan would have to wait. Her career would have to wait. The gauntlet had been thrown down, and Meghan Rhodes wasn't the type of person to walk away from a challenge.

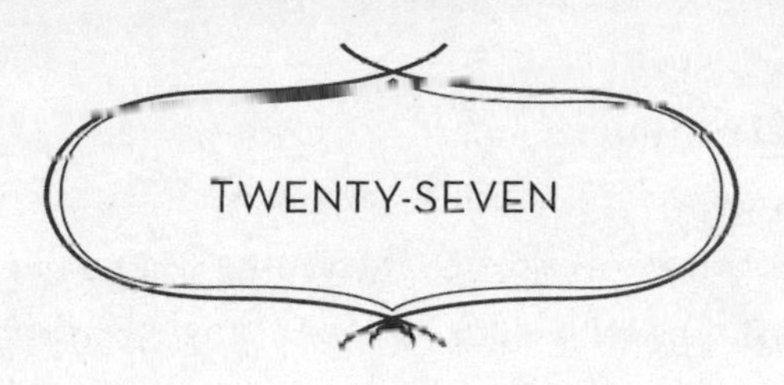

TWENTY-SEVEN

Lila

Lila had filled the evening with errands and distractions, but the rawness in her stomach hadn't gone away. Her guilt over what she was about to do ate at her, and she knew it'd be no small feat to hide the truth from Mama. Finally, Lila found the courage to go back to the Whitmore. There, she found Tom leaning against his rental car, suitcase at his feet.

He wore khakis and a crisp white polo and, as always, he looked handsome and dignified. She forced herself to think about something else.

"Can we show up in two cars?"

"Of course, why not?"

Tom shrugged. "It's your story. I just want to make sure I play my part well." He hoisted the suitcase into the back seat. "You ready to get this over with?"

Lila sighed. "We can't just pretend we're okay, Tom. Mama will see right through it. We have to sell it."

He glanced down at her lips, then back at her eyes. "I have no problem with that."

She looked away. "This is ridiculous. I should just tell her the truth. She'll claim she was right all along, but at least it'll be out there."

Tom quieted.

"What do you think?"

"I think you should decide what you want."

Lila took a few steps away, imagining Mama's contempt. Her ability to crush Lila with just a look or a single, well-placed jab. She couldn't bear the thought of Mama being right—not after she'd been so adamant that she and Tom would be together forever.

She *had* been foolish, looking back on it now.

But what was done was done. Lila couldn't stand on the street corner debating for another moment.

"Let's just get this over with." Lila walked to the black Lexus and got inside, then drove to the lake house with Tom close behind.

They pulled into the driveway, but Daddy's car wasn't the only one waiting for them. Next to it was a black Cadillac.

Great. Mama and Daddy were bad enough, but dealing with their stuffy friends might put her over the edge. She turned the car off and rested her head on the steering wheel. A few moments later, Tom knocked on the window. Time to face the music.

"You ready for this?"

She shrugged. "I guess we'll find out."

They walked up the front walk. Maybe they could disappear into the study or sit out back undisturbed. Before she pushed the door open she turned to Tom. "I'm not sure I can do this. Mama's like a vulture."

He rested a hand on her shoulder. "You won't be alone."

She studied him, aware of his sincerity.

He ran his thumb across her cheek. "I guess we'll have to make sure she thinks we're really in love."

She tried—but failed—to break eye contact. Finally, he pulled his hand away and pushed the door open.

"This is crazy," she whispered.

"But kinda fun." He smiled and followed her through the door.

Inside, Lila heard voices in the dining room. Tom set his suitcase near the stairs.

"Lila? Is that you?" Mama's voice filled the entry, and Lila glanced at Tom as if to wish him luck in this charade.

They'd been pretending in one way or another for years—why should this be any different?

"It's me, Mama."

"Oh, Lila, I heard the strangest rumor about you and . . ." Mama came into view. "Tom?"

Tom wound an arm around Lila's waist and smiled at Mama. "Evening, Cilla. Sorry I'm late getting in."

Mama's eyes darted back and forth from Lila to Tom, almost as if she were trying to read what they weren't saying. Mama had a sixth sense for these things. If there was a rumor floating around, she'd reel it in.

"Nonsense," she said. "We're glad you could join us. I thought you were coming in tomorrow."

"Isn't it a wonderful surprise?" Lila had learned how to pretend after watching her mother for years.

Tom smiled. "Smells wonderful in here. Did you cook?"

Lila raised an eyebrow. She didn't want to join her parents and their guests. She wanted to hide away somewhere and not exhaust herself with all this pretending.

"I did. You must be starving. You're probably *dying* for a good, home-cooked meal." Mama glanced at Lila.

"Oh, not at all, Cilla. Your daughter is a wonderful cook." Tom looked down at Lila and winked.

They followed Mama into the kitchen.

"Kind of late for dinner, isn't it?" Lila asked. "Maybe we could just grab a snack, Tom? Go sit out back on the porch? It's such a lovely night."

"Don't be silly," Mama said. "There's more than enough food. Your father has a business associate here, though, so we may have to endure a little real-estate jabber. You know Patton, Lila."

Lila gasped and Mama shot her a look. Tom glanced up and met her eyes.

Lila fumbled for something to say. "Tom, let's go out on the porch. It's a nice night and—"

"I don't want to be rude, hon. Your mom cooked."

Mama grabbed two white plates from the china cabinet along with silverware and napkins. "Tom, would you mind getting two glasses for your drinks?" She disappeared into the dining room, and Lila moved closer to Tom.

"What are you doing? We don't want to go in there."

"I do," he said. "You said 'sell it.' You can't challenge a guy like that and expect him to back down."

Lila shook her head. "I think one of the old biddies from town probably told her everything. She's like a black widow spinning a web. And we're the flies she's trying to trap." Lila turned away, but Tom grabbed her arms and made her look at him.

"I know in your mind we aren't together, but in mine, we've never been apart." He brushed a strand of hair away from her face, but the weight of his gaze sent her insides tumbling. She knew he'd be blindsided when she gave him those divorce papers—and after he was so willing to do her this favor. Her stomach turned at her own deceit.

She looked away. "Let's just get through this dinner and be done with it."

He smiled. "No problem."

The dining table had been set with white linens, hydrangeas and Mama's favorite silver. "Not the everyday silver," she'd have told Patton Gallagher as he arrived.

It was, of course, but Mama would say it wasn't to make the man feel important. She'd mastered the fine art of pretending.

Lila avoided Patton's stare as she entered the room, Tom close behind. But after they sat in high-backed chairs slip-covered in white linen across from him, with Mama and Daddy on either end of the long rectangular table, Lila dared a glance. His eyes held a look of amused confusion—she'd agreed to dinner with him tomorrow night, but here she was with her husband? Lila hurried her eyes away.

"Tom," Daddy said. "Didn't know you'd be joining us tonight. We thought you were getting in tomorrow." He glanced at Lila with one eyebrow raised.

"I wanted to surprise my wife," Tom said. He took her hand, which rested atop the table. "I had a couple trips I had to finish up so I could take a few weeks off. We need the time to relax and enjoy each other. Been too long since we've done that."

Lila glanced at him, but his eyes were focused on Daddy. Unlike Patton's, who were still cast in her direction. She met them briefly, shifted in her seat and fidgeted with her napkin.

"Have you met my colleague Patton Gallagher?" Daddy motioned toward Patton, who perked up at the mention of his name.

Tom squinted as if he were trying to read the man across the table.

"Don't think we've had the pleasure," Patton said. "Good to meet you, sir. You have a beautiful wife."

Lila coughed, mid-drink.

"I couldn't agree more, Mr. Gallagher," Tom said. He paused, his full attention on Patton. "She caught me when we were just kids." He looked at Lila. "Been in love with her ever since."

Patton cleared his throat. "Yes, best not to let one like her slip away." He smiled. "I know a little bit about missed opportunities."

Lila took another drink. It did nothing to hydrate her dry-as-cotton mouth.

"It's really wonderful to see you, Tom," Mama said. "It's been so long since we've all been together. I'm happy to have the whole family under one roof, though I'm not sure how long we'll all be able to put up with each other." Mama picked up her long-stemmed wineglass and sipped her chardonnay. Her smile faded as she drank.

Tom squeezed Lila's hand then passed a platter of roast beef and vegetables to her. She set it down without taking any. She wished she could point out to the room that Mama most certainly had not cooked that meal. Lila knew for a fact it had come from The Grotto.

How dare she insult Lila's cooking when she—

"I was about to tell you, Lila, I heard the strangest rumor in town."

Lila took a breath and braced herself for what was coming. Of course the Sweethaven rumor mill had already reached her mother.

"Someone told me they saw you with Meghan Rhodes earlier this week?"

The butterflies in her stomach settled down, though she had the distinct impression that wasn't the only thing Mama had been told.

"I saw her at the coffee shop," Lila said. "She's been back for a few weeks."

"We should get her to play a concert while she's here," Daddy said. "The big Labor Day celebration."

"But you won't be here for that, will you?" Lila noted the hopefulness in her own voice and reminded herself to dial it down a notch.

"No, but you will, dear. You could use something useful to do." Mama laughed and took a bite of carrots. "Is Meghan still a drug addict?"

Lila shot her mother a look.

"What? It's not a secret." Mama laughed. "Heaven knows everyone who reads the newspaper has heard all about her escapades."

"That was years ago. She's fine now."

"Ask her about the concert. She should do that for her hometown," Daddy said.

"She could certainly use the good press right about now." Mama's eyes widened.

"Can we talk about something else?" Lila shifted in her seat.

Mama and Daddy exchanged a look that drew a sigh. They'd laid an expectation on the table, and she was meant to pick it up and carry it with her.

"I'll see what I can do about the concert," she said.

"Very good."

The conversation continued and Lila's discomfort grew the longer she sat at the table listening to men vie for power under Mama's watchful eye.

Tom played the part of the attentive husband beautifully, filling her water glass from the pitcher at the table's center, serving her a slice of pie in spite of her uneaten dinner, resting a hand on hers whenever it turned up empty on the table. He spoke about the two of them as if they were the best of friends. If she hadn't known better, she'd have believed him herself.

"Patton is quite successful," Mama said as the conversation lulled.

Lila bit back a sarcastic response as she knew Mama's point. Patton is rich. Filthy rich. The kind of man who deserves to be married to an Adler. His graying hair dignified him, though she imagined he had a few years on her. He looked like the kind of man who'd traveled the world.

"Oh, Cilla, don't start bragging on me," Patton said, though Lila got the distinct impression that if Mama didn't brag on him, he'd happily brag on himself.

"Yes, Cilla, we wouldn't want to embarrass the man," Tom said.

Lila shot him a look. Tom was no fool. He must've picked up on Patton's bold affection for her. And like he said earlier, he was never one to walk away from a challenge.

"You should be proud, Patton. But you're so modest—someone has to brag on you. Lila, do you know this man owns three different restaurant chains?" Mama set her glass on the table and focused on obtaining Lila's attention.

She frowned. "I thought you were in real estate."

"Old Patton's involved in a little bit of everything," Daddy said.

"Or he'd like to be," Tom muttered under his breath.

Daddy didn't seem to hear, but Patton raised an eyebrow in Tom's direction.

Tom excused himself and left the four of them staring at each other.

Mama frowned, her eyes wide in fake innocence. "Is everything all right?"

"I'm sure. He's had a long couple of days," Lila said. "It's not easy piloting jets across the ocean—so many people's lives in the palm of your hand each day." She stared at Mama, daring her to compare real estate with what Tom did for a living.

"It must be hard for the two of you to be apart." Patton watched her from across the table, a smug expression on his otherwise handsome face.

Lila grew weary under the weight of Mama's gaze.

"Yes, Lila. It must be difficult for the two of you to be separated like you've been."

Had she lingered on that word: *separated*?

"Well, he has had more work than usual," Lila said. "But we're used to it after so many years together." She glared at Patton, then turned to Mama. "If you'll excuse me, Mama. I think I'm going to retire for the night."

Mama nodded as she folded her napkin and put it in her lap. Her lips pursed the way they did when she was annoyed. Lila pretended not to notice. For once, she didn't care.

She expected to find Tom in the kitchen, but it was empty. As were the living room, the study and the sunroom.

She opened the front door and stepped out onto the porch. The stars shone brighter in Sweethaven, unobstructed by air free of pollution. Or maybe Sweethaven was closer to heaven than the rest of the world. She marveled at the crisp night sky overhead, trying to mark it in her memory. She wrapped her arms around herself to ward off the chill in the air.

"It cooled off," a voice from behind startled her, but before she turned, Patton had placed a jacket around her shoulders. "Feels like rain."

She didn't respond.

"Surprised to see you here tonight," he said. "At least with Tom."

"He's my husband." Lila stared up at the stars, remembering the day Tom showed her Orion, the first constellation she ever spotted. They were in junior high.

"Is he though?" Patton stood beside her, too close. She could smell his cologne. Musky and unfamiliar. "Why was he at the Whitmore when he could've been here—with you?"

Lila clenched her jaw and turned to face him. "How did you know about that?"

Patton stared up at the moon. "I own the Whitmore."

Lila frowned. "Well, he's here now."

After a long pause, Patton said, "All I know is if you were my wife, I wouldn't spend a single night away from you." He took a step closer, and for the briefest moment Lila entertained the idea of spending time with someone other than Tom, but as quickly as the notion entered her mind, something else accompanied it. Guilt.

In a flash, she recalled the look on Tom's face the day he asked her father for his permission to marry his daughter. Mama had been there and she openly shared her thoughts on the idea. By the time Tom returned to Lila, he looked deflated. Her respect for him had multiplied that day—because he'd known walking in that it wouldn't end well.

But he still went—because he loved her. Just like he came here tonight—because he loved her. And it couldn't have been easy.

"Are we still on for dinner tomorrow?" Patton took her hands in his. "I made reservations at The Grotto."

"I'm not sure how I can make it work now with Mama and Daddy in town."

"Your parents love me." Patton laughed. "Your mother told me she wished I'd come along a few years earlier—I would've swept you off your feet and everything about your life would be different now." His intent gaze unnerved her.

"She did?"

He brought her hand to his lips and placed a gentle kiss on it. At the touch of his lips, her mind whirled with possibilities, and she tried to pretend it didn't feel good to be pursued.

"I noticed you got a letter from your lawyer the other day—divorce papers, I presume?"

Lila's eyes narrowed as she tried to figure out how he could possibly know that. "You were snooping through my mail?"

He laughed. "You're not very good at hiding things. You stuck it in your purse with the front label facing me. Maybe a small part of you wanted me to know you'd filed for divorce."

Lila eased her hand from his grip and took a step back. "I should go."

He took a step back and studied her. "Are you sure? I understand the charade you put on for your mother, but we're just two old friends out here. Your secret's safe with me."

She held his gaze for a long moment. "I don't have any secrets. Just a few things I'm choosing to keep to myself." She hoped he'd drop it and let her keep her dignity. With his advances piling up, Lila felt herself weakening. How much longer could she pretend he didn't intrigue her?

"Here's my card. Cell number on the back. We could go somewhere private tomorrow—no one will ever have to know."

She took the card and stared at it.

He reached up and touched her face, but she looked away before the feel of his skin on hers could register. He smiled, took his jacket from her and walked to his car, then started the engine and pulled away.

Lila watched for a moment and then turned to go inside, but movement in the shadows at the back of the porch sent her pulse racing. She stopped and squinted, her heart pounding in her chest when a figure stepped out of the shadows into the blue moonlight. Tom moved toward her, eyes intent on hers, and Lila couldn't think of a single thing to say.

He'd been too far away to hear their conversation, but he'd certainly been close enough to see that his wife had captured the affections of another man—and she'd done little to stop it.

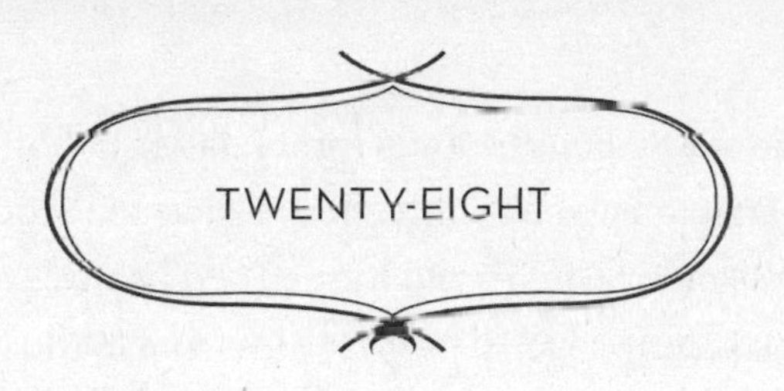

TWENTY-EIGHT

Lila

Tom brushed past her but stopped before going inside. "Lila, are you interested in that guy?"

Guilt scratched at her as she met Tom's eyes. How could she do this to him? Especially after the position she'd put him in.

"What do you mean?" She kept her voice calm to better feign innocence.

He spun around and took a step closer to her. "Don't pretend you don't know what I'm talking about."

She didn't recognize the look in his eyes and she couldn't place the tone of his voice. This was a Tom she'd never seen before. Was this what desperation looked like on him?

"I said I'd do this favor for you, but don't humiliate me with this guy. Not in front of my face."

"I didn't know you were there." Lila turned away. "I'm sorry."

He drew in a long breath and then let it out. "Are you . . . seeing him?"

She let the question hang between them for too many seconds, and Tom finally took her silence as a response.

He left her standing on the porch, staring out into the blackness of the trees across the driveway.

Did she want him to know the pain of betrayal? Did she want to get back at him for hurting her?

After too many painful moments, Lila rushed into the house and up the stairs. It wasn't until she reached the landing that she realized Tom would be in her old room. He'd be there because she'd begged him to come. Her heart raced as she walked toward the closed door. How could she face him?

She took a deep breath, wiped her palms dry on her pants and opened the door. Tom sat on the edge of the bed, head down, the stack of letters he'd written her all those years ago strewn about on the bed beside him. She startled him with the door, and his expression changed as he met her eyes.

"What are you doing?" She closed the door behind her.

"Reading." He held up the stack. "The trunk was open. I saw them sitting there. I can't believe you kept all of these."

"Tom, I'm sorry."

Tom held up a hand to stop her.

She gathered the letters and tried not to think about the nonsense they represented. No sign of those two lovesick kids in that room.

"Have you read these lately?" Tom asked.

Lila shook her head, not wanting to admit the truth. She'd glanced through enough of them to jog her memory.

Tom held a letter up in front of him. "'Dear Lila,'" he read. "'You return to Sweethaven in six days. I'm counting. I figure this will be the last letter I write before I see you in real life—before I hold your hand on the Ferris wheel and smell your strawberry shampoo.'"

They looked at each other and after a long moment, neither could keep from laughing.

"That's enough," Lila said. "You don't have to read it out loud. I know what it says."

His eyes returned to the letter. He scanned the words for a few seconds. "I wrote about that silver locket you said you wanted. You thought your dad bought it for you. Whatever happened to that locket?"

Lila looked away. "It turned out he bought it for one of his girlfriends." She sat next to him on the bed.

Tom stilled. "I'm sorry."

"I remember that locket perfectly. It was a thick silver heart on a rope chain. I pointed it out to him at the jewelry store because I thought he might get it for me for graduation. I saw a bag from the jewelers in the back seat of his car a few days later, but when my graduation day came—no locket." Lila stared at the stack of letters in her hand. "When I saw my friend Kimberly's mom wearing it, everything became so clear. Daddy wasn't going to change. Not ever."

She looked at him. He hadn't stopped loving her—she could see that now. They'd just gotten used to each other, fallen into a pattern, but what if he deserved a second chance? Did that make her weak? Did that make her just like Mama?

Too many opinions swirled around in her head to figure out how to land on her own.

"You know I'm not your father, right?" Tom took her hand in his and ran his thumb across the top of it.

She met his eyes. "Of course."

"I mean, I've never cheated on you."

Technically, he had. Before they'd been married—otherwise, Campbell Carter wouldn't exist.

"Once I committed to you, that was it. And that's not going to change. Look at this—" He motioned toward the stack of letters.

Their love story spread out in front of them. "After all we've been through, we can't just throw it away."

She pulled her hand from his and ran it through her hair. She couldn't think about this. Not twenty-four hours a day. Not when she was so tired. Not with Mama and Daddy in the next room.

She stood. "I suppose I should get ready for bed." She looked at him, but he didn't move. It had been over two months since they'd spent a night in the same room, let alone the same bed. Over two months of getting used to the idea of being alone—of entertaining the thought that one day she could love someone else.

But even as she did, even as Patton Gallagher shamelessly flirted, something inside her ached for the warm familiarity of her husband's arms.

She found a nightgown in her suitcase and slipped into the bathroom to put it on. When she returned, Tom had already changed into sweats and a T-shirt. He stopped moving at the sight of her.

They both stood frozen, the bed between them. She hadn't thought this through.

"I always loved that nightgown," he said, staring at her.

She tilted her head and put a hand on her hip. "You, sir, have your eyes full."

He looked away, but she caught the smile on his face. "I sure do."

"I can see we need some ground rules," she said.

His smile faded. "I'm kidding, Lila. I can sleep on the floor."

"You don't have to do that," she said. "We're two grown adults." Her chest tightened with disappointment, but she shoved it aside.

"Two *married* adults." He sounded hopeful.

"Two *separated* adults." She crossed her arms. "You stay on your side and I'll stay on mine."

He got into the bed and pulled back the covers on her side, then watched as she contemplated her next move. Slowly, she sat on the bed, slipped her feet under the covers and lay down. He reached across her and turned off the lamp, and she inhaled the smell of him, missing his closeness when he lay down on his pillow. On his side of the bed.

She tried to concentrate on breathing, something that often helped her fall asleep, but her mind ran away with memories as she imagined the way his hands would feel on her bare skin. She listened as his breathing steadied and then dared a glance in his direction. His eyes were closed and his lips gently parted. He'd only grown more handsome with age.

He cleared his throat, then turned on his side, facing her, his closeness unsettling. She flipped over, faced the wall and tried to forget the way he used to make her feel, like his world revolved around her. They'd lost that somewhere along the way—and as she drifted to sleep, all she could think about was the possibility of one day getting it back.

Jane

Monday morning, Jane woke with a pit in her stomach. She hadn't seen Amber at church yesterday, but she couldn't avoid her at the Bible study—and she knew the poor girl had overheard her outburst in the café. The memory filled her with embarrassment. How could she face her—or any of them—again? Surely Amber would tell the others what she'd witnessed, discrediting Jane as their leader.

She never should've tried to lead anyone anyway. God couldn't use someone who still had so much to work through.

Just as she'd done for last week's meetings, Jane set up the room with refreshments and name tags, only this time, she placed the chairs behind tables, giving each woman a work space for her own prayer journal.

She'd been spending quality time with her own journal a lot lately, but nothing she prayed seemed to change the way she felt inside.

After things were in order, Jane glanced at the clock. No sign of anyone yet and they were supposed to start in eight minutes. Maybe Amber called the other women and told them everything—it would explain why no one would want to come back.

After another couple of minutes passed, Jane decided to go to the bathroom and splash some cold water on her face. She couldn't stand the thought of everyone knowing what a fraud she was, but she'd put herself in this position. If she'd just been honest and given the other women the chance to show they could handle her baggage, none of this would've happened.

In the small ladies' room, Jane caught her reflection in the mirror. What had happened to her? She'd forgiven herself so beautifully and yet here she was, filled with bitterness just like the day Alex died.

Back at square one.

She sighed, dried her face and then opened the door. The sound of women's voices echoed down the hallway, and relief washed over her.

When she entered the room, she forced a smile.

"We're late this morning, Jane, we're sorry." One woman—Linda—glanced around at the others. "We decided to go for a walk along the lake this morning."

"All of you?" Jane asked.

"We all need the exercise." A stout woman named Sandy giggled. "We did our homework though. We got our books and did the first page."

One by one, the women pulled small journals and scrapbook albums from their bags.

"I got mine too." A voice from behind her turned Jane around, and she found Amber standing in the doorway. Jane scanned her eyes for disapproval, but she found none. Only the knowing understanding of a woman who knew how it felt like to lose a child. "Sorry I'm late."

The other women pulled Amber into their group with their chatter, leaving Jane on the outside, studying the way these women had accepted her so willingly. She'd been foolish to try and hide the fact that she still struggled, but how did she muster the courage to come clean now?

"Can we see your album, Jane?" one of the women asked.

Jane's thoughts turned to the last page she'd created—only days ago—a dark page Jane hadn't intended to share with anyone. Ever.

"Oh, I left it at home, but remember, there's really no right or wrong way to do this. I've printed out some verses for you to meditate on this week. You can use them to kick-start your journaling. I thought we'd take a look at the peace God can offer us."

She'd purposely chosen a topic unrelated to forgiveness, though she knew that peace only came when you forgave. One thing at a time. She avoided Amber's eyes as she taught the lesson she'd prepared. Afterward, the ladies started their journals and Jane watched the seconds tick by on a plain white clock with bold black numbers. With every moment that passed, she felt closer to escape.

She glanced at Amber, who already had a page full of journaling accompanied by a photo of a little boy Jane assumed was her son. She'd been so self-absorbed she hadn't even asked how she'd been since they last met.

Amber glanced up at her and smiled, her expression devoid of any criticism. Jane knew she didn't deserve these women's respect.

After several moments of silence, Jane finally stood at the front of the room and cleared her throat. "I haven't been honest with you ladies," she said.

Pairs of eyes looked up from their pages. She stared at the floor.

"I wanted to be the strong one, the one with all the answers, and some days I feel like that person." They all stared at her now, waiting for her explanation. "But most days I don't."

She glanced outside, remembering how she'd seen Meghan there for the first time since Alex died, but she'd been unable to find any empathy for her. She'd compared her pain with Meghan's—self-made, in Jane's mind—and decided nothing Meghan went through could rival losing a son. Meghan didn't deserve her empathy.

But all this comparing had only hurt Jane and driven the wedge between them even deeper.

"I've spent so much time trying to have it all together, but if I'm honest with you, I'm not there yet." She looked at Amber. "Some days I don't want to get out of bed. And most days I discover that I haven't completely forgiven Meghan for what happened."

The women sat silent and listened as Jane confessed everything, dispelling every notion that she had all the answers and putting herself squarely on the same ground as the rest of them. When she finished, she expected them all to get up and walk out—how could they receive any teaching from someone who clearly still had so much to learn?

For several seconds, no one moved.

Finally, Amber cleared her throat. "Have you tried talking to her?"

Jane shook her head. "Only what you saw at the café the other night." She knew her face had reddened at the mention of her behavior.

"Don't give that a second thought," Amber said.

"It wasn't my finest hour."

"Amber's right," Linda said. "I finally decided to talk to my mom about our relationship and I found out *why* she's such a mean old bat."

Jane laughed. "And that helped?"

Linda shrugged. "It did. It's hard to stay angry when you understand why a person is the way they are."

The other women nodded.

"And don't feel like you have to pretend to have it all together on our account," Sandy said. "Honey, we're all a mess."

"Thank you," Jane said. She marveled at their acceptance—none of them seemed interested in judging her. She'd been foolish to assume the opposite.

An hour later, Jane embraced the women as they all went their separate ways. She'd been so exhausted trying to keep up appearances, but now she felt energized and refreshed, like she had the support she needed to move beyond her issues with Meghan.

As she stood in the parking lot, she waved good-bye to the last of her new friends, thanking God for using them to teach her a little something about the power of transparency. She fished her phone from her bag and dialed Adele's number.

When she answered, Jane almost hung up, but she forced herself to ask the question.

"Adele, can I have Meghan's number?"

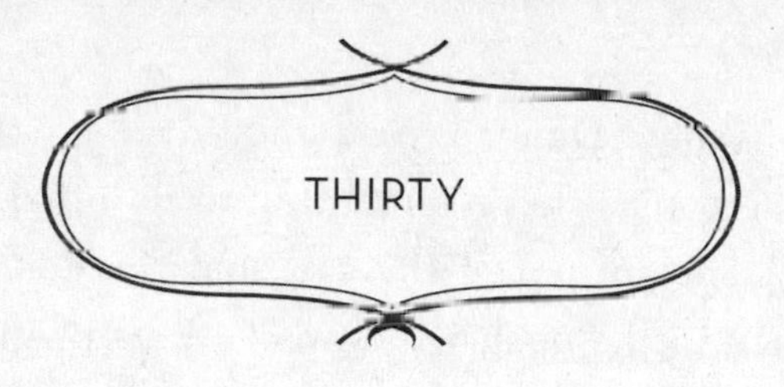

THIRTY

Meghan

"I've been patient, Meghan, but how many chances do you think you're going to get?"

From the passenger seat of his rental car, Meghan stared at Duncan blankly but didn't respond. He hadn't taken the news of her staying well.

He stilled. "Your album is floating around out there and no one even knows about it. You've missed three appearances already—is any of this worth sacrificing your whole career?"

She drew in a deep breath and looked away.

"Nick's not going to take you back, you know."

She tried—and failed—to deflect the sting of Duncan's words.

"He's out to destroy you."

"You should go back to Nashville. Just give me a few more days. A week at the most."

He shook his head, then shifted gears. "Fine," he said. "If you're going to be stubborn, we'll spin this to make you look like a doting mother—play up the hometown angle. People will eat that up." He shook his head, as if searching for more ideas. "I'll send out a press release that you have family business to attend to and you'll be back on your promotional tour next week." They pulled into her driveway. "You will be ready to leave this place by next week, won't you?"

"You're crabby, Duncan. You should go to the beach or something. You must have something to do other than follow me around." She got out of the car, shut the door and leaned her head back in the open window. "Seriously—give me a few days without your hovering. I won't make a mess of everything. I promise."

"I've heard that before."

"Bye, Duncan."

By Thursday, Meghan had started to worry. It was out of character for her manager to leave her alone. But she had more important things to focus on.

Meghan started each day the same way, peering out over the serene lake, coffee in hand. She'd never have guessed that the lake could claim so many lives if she hadn't seen it happen for herself. It had been part of her therapy to research deaths by drowning in Lake Michigan. She'd begun keeping tallies. Last summer: seventy-three. This summer: fifteen so far. Rip currents, like the one that pulled Alex under, were unforgiving.

She hadn't been in the water since that day, but that didn't stop her from feeling like she was drowning.

The phone rang. A number she didn't recognize.

"Hello?"

"Meghan, it's Jane."

Meghan's heart jumped.

"I was hoping we could meet for coffee this afternoon?" She sounded amped up. Or nervous.

"Uh . . . okay."

"Three o'clock? At Luke's?"

"Okay. I'll be there."

"Good. Bye."

And Jane hung up, sending Meghan's mind spinning with questions. Why, after all this time, would Jane ask to see her? And how was Meghan going to go to Luke's without facing Luke?

In so many ways she'd done more harm than good in coming back to Sweethaven.

But the kids. And Nick . . .

Scrapbook pages sat in a stack across the living room. She hadn't purposely kept them out of the stack she'd given Campbell, but maybe she knew better than to part with all of them at once. They'd been her comfort since Suzanne's letter came. She looked at them at least once a day—reliving some of the best moments of her life through the eyes of her much younger self.

Meghan sank into a soft leather chair and flipped through the pages, stopping on one near the top. A large red circle had been cut out and glued to a sheet of white cardstock. She could still remember passing the page around as they divided the red circle into fourths and each added a cut-out of their own head. Then, around the circle it went again, so they could take turns writing descriptive words and phrases about the other three girls. Suzanne called it a "warm fuzzy circle."

Meghan ran her hand over the photo of herself at age thirteen. Half of her long red hair was pulled off to the side, held in place by a large white scrunchie. Her smile looked strained, most likely a failed attempt to hide silver braces that lined crooked teeth.

Underneath her photo, her friends had written *Totally rad. Talented. Sarcastic. Gorgeous. Secret Keeper. Best Friend.*

Jane had written the last one. Best Friend. Jane and Suzanne had always been close, maybe to the point where Meghan envied them a little bit, but Jane had never made Meghan feel like her second choice.

And in the years after Suzanne left Sweethaven, the two of them grew closer. Long, hot summers on the beach. And when fame changed everyone else around her, Jane stayed the same. Sweethaven had been the one constant in her life.

"I'm glad you're famous now, Meghan Barber," Jane had told her at the beginning of that summer. "I've never had a famous friend."

"My last name is Rhodes now, Janie," Meghan said, not opening her eyes. "You'd think you'd remember since you were my maid of honor."

"Aw, it was such a beautiful wedding, wasn't it?" Jane smiled, but her face quickly turned serious. "You were so happy. That's why you have to give that stuff up and you know it."

Meghan removed the sunglasses. "Why do you think I'm here?"

Jane put a hand over hers. "Because you missed me."

Meghan grinned. "And those hellions you call offspring."

"Aw, come on now, they're adorable. Get yourself clean and have a few of your own."

Meghan paused, her throat clenched into a knot bigger than her fist. "You don't even judge me for my stupid mistakes. How do you do that?"

Jane shrugged. "I don't know. I never thought about it. You're just Meghan to me."

And that summed it up. She didn't think about being good. She just was.

And Meghan had broken her heart. She'd stolen the *good* from her. Now, Jane couldn't even stand to be in the same room with her. She hated herself for turning Jane into something she was never meant to be.

The sound of gravel crunching under tires pulled her attention, and she plucked back the curtains at the front window. Nick's truck bounced down the driveway and finally came to a stop next to her rental car. She walked out onto the porch and leaned against the column, watching as he made his way up the walk.

When he reached the bottom of the steps, he squinted in the sun, staring up at her.

"Hey," he said.

"What are you doing here, Nick?"

"I'm not here to fight, Meg." He looked away. "I wondered if you wanted to go grab donuts."

She frowned. "What's the catch?"

"No catch. The kids are in the truck."

She glanced over and saw two little pairs of eyes staring at her.

Nick kept talking. "I promised them donuts this morning. Figured I'd stop by and see if you wanted to come along."

Meghan crossed her arms. "What about your girlfriend?"

He met her eyes. "What girlfriend?"

"The blonde girl. From the game."

"Our babysitter. Maggie."

Heat splashed across her cheeks and Meghan pressed her lips together to avoid saying anything else stupid.

"But your new boyfriend looks sharp."

She opened her eyes and frowned. "What new boyfriend?"

"Suit guy from the Boardwalk."

Meghan laughed. "My lawyer?"

Nick's face paled. "Your lawyer." He looked away. "He's the guy who's been asking around about me, right?"

"I . . . don't know."

Nick raised an eyebrow. "Really?"

"Probably. He doesn't like to lose."

"I don't like to lose either." He held her gaze for too many seconds, and finally she looked away.

If he wanted to gift wrap the kids and set them in her lap, should she really complain? She considered James's advice to get him to trust her again, but she couldn't muster the strength to put on the charade. She could, however, use this opportunity to find out the truth about Violet—Luke and Mama might not be willing to help her, but the twins wouldn't know any different.

"So?"

Meghan glanced at her cut-off jean shorts and ratty old T-shirt. *His* T-shirt. "I should probably change."

"Please don't," he said. He held her gaze. "You look like yourself. And my shirt looks good on you."

Meghan stared at him, wishing everything was simple. Wishing she could tell him how much she missed him. She shoved her hands in her pockets, suddenly aware of his eyes on her. "Of course I'll come. Let me grab my purse." Meghan went inside, her heart racing, her mind spinning.

Back outside, she nearly lost her breath as Nick hauled both kids out of the truck and onto the ground. Her family stood right in front of her—and they wanted her to join them.

Maybe God did answer prayers. Even ones she didn't have the courage to speak aloud.

Nick wore a red-and-white baseball shirt and his same ratty old ball cap.

"We have money now, Nick. I can buy you a new hat," Meghan had told him one day out on the boat.

"Some things you just don't trade in," he said. He winked at her and kicked the boat up a notch, leading her out to the sandbar where they bathed in the sun for the rest of the day. They'd spent the night on that boat, making love and talking about the future. Everything had seemed so perfect.

How had it all gone wrong?

Meghan reached the three of them and glanced at Nadia, then Finn, then back at Nick.

"Guys, give Mommy a hug," he said.

Finn rushed over and threw his arms around her.

"Oh, I have something for you." She reached inside her purse and pulled out the monkey. She'd pinned another paper heart next to the one he'd added. This one said *Finn*.

"That's me," he said with a grin.

"I think Monkey misses you, so maybe you should take him back for a little while."

He gave the animal a squeeze.

She knelt down in front of Nadia. "Hi, sweetie. I made one for you too." Meghan held out a small paper heart. On one side she'd written *Mommy* and on the other she'd written *Nadia*. "Maybe your dad can help you pin it to one of your animals?"

Nadia nodded, still hiding behind Nick's leg.

Nick led the kids back into the truck, hoisted them into their seats and buckled their seat belts.

Meghan stared out the window, wishing for words to come easily—words that would allow her back into their lives without having to confront the past. Instead, she listened to the two of them jabbering on about lightning bugs and dragonflies.

"You know, your mom was an expert bug catcher back in the day," Nick said. He winked at her and she smiled.

"You were?" Finn leaned forward.

"But she was ruthless. She used to take the lightning bugs apart and make jewelry out of them."

"You did!?" The kids alternated between fascination and disgust, and for a brief moment, Meghan's nerves settled down.

"We made rings out of grass and lightning bugs. They were pretty fancy." Meghan smiled.

When they reached the bakery, Nick parked and turned around to face the kids. "You guys ready for some donuts?"

Squeals of delight erupted in the back seat and Meghan let it fill her up. She opened the door and pushed the seat up so Finn could get out. His outstretched hands in her direction took her off guard, but she picked him up and helped him down to the ground. Once there, he squeezed her hand, unwilling, it seemed, to let it go. Meghan stared at it, then met his eyes. He smiled at her.

"What's your favorite kind of donut?" he asked.

The lump in her throat kept her from answering.

"If I remember right, your mom is a sucker for a chocolate-filled long john." Nick smiled at her, as if he'd read her mind.

Meghan found her voice. "That's it. And it's been years since I had one."

"I like chocolate with sprinkles," Nadia said, taking her other hand.

Linked together, all four of them, they walked down the sidewalk toward Sweethaven's only bakery, Sweets. Meghan imagined that from a distance, the four of them looked like all the little families she'd always envied. Together and smiling, they appeared to have it all. And in that moment, they did. She took it in, placing the memory at the front of her mind, so she wouldn't forget how it felt to belong.

The smell of fried dough invited them into the little donut shop, and Meghan smiled at the sight of five elderly men sipping coffee and rambling on about skateboarders ruining their town. They ordered and then took their breakfast outside to enjoy the morning sun.

Meghan worked on her long john in silence, studying the dynamic between her ex-husband and her two children. He never lost his patience, even when the twins started arguing over who liked chocolate milk more.

"You're really good with them," she said after the twins wandered over toward a bed of parched flowers.

"You think?" He ate the last bite of his second donut.

She nodded. "Thanks for letting me come along."

He took a long breath in. "They need you." He watched the kids, careful not to look away for too long.

So that's why you're fighting to take them? She bit her tongue.

They sat in silence, watching the kids play.

"You've felt so far away," he said, not meeting her eyes.

The tension between them thickened, like a cloud of fog after a night of thunderstorms.

"It's been so hard." Meghan knew how small the words sounded. Did she really understand a hard life? She'd been raised by loving parents and was now one of the most successful musicians in the industry. How could she claim anything was hard?

"No one said it would be easy," Nick said. He ran a hand over his shadowed chin. "The question is, are we worth it?"

She frowned. What was he saying?

Meghan's heart dropped at the sound of an ear-piercing scream. Nadia held up her hand, tears streaming down her face. Nick rushed to her side.

"What happened, hon?" His voice turned soothing and Meghan stood off to the side, trying to stay out of the way.

Nadia screamed again. "Owie!"

"Finn, what happened to her?" Nick asked.

"I saw a bee," he said solemnly.

"A bee? Nadia, did it sting you?" Nick picked her up now and set her on the table. Nadia shook her head and held up her hand.

"There's something in there," she cried.

Nick took her hand and squinted. "It looks like a splinter." He glanced at Meghan. "A big one."

The wooden flower beds. Nadia must've scraped her hand on one.

"It hurts!" Nadia screeched.

"Okay, we'll just have to figure out a way to get it out, hon, it's okay," Nick said. He stayed calm the entire time, but Meghan's pulse raced as they pulled the attention of onlookers and passersby.

"We could run up to the store and grab some tweezers," Meghan offered. "I'll take Finn."

Nick nodded and they raced down the block to the market on the corner. They rushed to find the tweezers, then stood in line at the checkout. Meghan tapped her foot, wishing the line would move quicker.

"Mommy, is that you?"

Meghan followed Finn's eyes to the rack of tabloids. Her mouth went dry and suddenly the store felt overheated. There they were, for the whole world to see: the same photos Shandy Shore had flashed in her face, on the covers of three different magazines, along with a still from a homemade video someone had taken during her outburst at the ball field. Meghan covered Finn's eyes, threw the tweezers on the counter and handed the checker a five-dollar bill.

"Hey, you're . . ." the young girl said, her mouth agape.

"Not now." Meghan grabbed the tweezers. "Keep the change."

She gripped Finn's hand and rushed out of the store, her face hot. Who was she kidding? This was why she left in the first place. She wasn't the family type, and this only confirmed it. It didn't matter what anyone said, any more time with her would only damage her kids.

She needed to protect them from harm. And that meant keeping them away from her.

THIRTY-ONE

Jane

Inviting Meghan for coffee had been impulsive and stupid. Jane sat at the café staring at the clock. Meghan had stood her up.

Already thirty minutes late, she imagined her famous friend had more important things to do. Jane couldn't quite pinpoint how she felt. Livid would probably best describe it. And embarrassed. She was so naïve to believe that Meghan Rhodes could ever change. Jane stood, grabbed her purse and headed toward the door. Time to get on with the rest of her day.

Tomorrow, Adele had planned a barbecue, and Jane needed ingredients to make her favorite pasta salad, so she swung into the grocery store before heading home.

At the checkout counter, she scanned the tabloids, resisting the urge to throw a *People* magazine into her basket, when a headline caught her eye. *More on Meghan Rhodes Nude Photo Shocker!* The subtitle said: *And it could cost her custody of her children!*

Jane gasped. Part of a photo of her old friend was on the cover of the magazine next to the promise "more photos inside!" She picked the magazine up and flipped it around, returning it to the shelf. The magazine was already a couple of weeks old, but there it was, front and center on the newsstand. Meghan couldn't have been older than twenty in the photo. Was that how she'd gotten her big break? Was that why she'd really come back to Sweethaven?

How had she not heard about this until now?

"Shameful, isn't it?"

Jane looked up at the cashier, an older woman who stared at the magazines with a disgusted look on her face. "What is?"

"That Meghan Rhodes would do something so sinful. Some people think she had the photos leaked herself to get her more publicity."

"Why would she do that?"

The woman scoffed. "Sales, of course. Her new album just came out. I'm good friends with her ex-husband's mother. Meghan Rhodes is a mess of trouble. That issue is selling well for us, even though it's old. Have to keep restocking it."

Jane's heart sank and her feet turned to bricks. How could this woman say these things about someone she didn't even know? Meghan had made her share of mistakes, but hadn't they all? She tried to put herself in Meghan's shoes. What would it be like for the whole world to see her so vulnerable? Jane started to speak up, to defend Meghan, when the cashier spoke again.

"Are you paying with cash?"

"Oh yes. I'm sorry." Jane paid for her groceries and walked out of the store, fighting the urge to go back and set that woman straight.

Her thoughts turned to the twins. Graham said Meghan had come back to fight for her kids. The thought of Meghan losing her children made her heart ache. She didn't wish that on anyone.

Not even Meghan.

For the first time, Jane began to imagine the pain of being as lost as Meghan must be. Of living life in front of the flashing cameras and critical media. As she drove home, the anger she'd been carrying around started to fade, and suddenly, it didn't seem so important to hold on to her bitter feelings.

* * * * *

The next night, as Jane got ready for Adele's barbecue, her thoughts of Meghan were interrupted.

"Isn't Mrs. Barber Meghan's mom?" her oldest daughter Jenna asked, as she invaded Jane's bathroom and stole her mascara.

Jane sighed. "Yes. Is that a problem?"

Jenna looked at her with one open eye, her mouth agape, mid-mascara stroke. "I don't know. Is it? Will she be there tonight?"

Apparently everyone had moved on with their lives except her. "We're leaving now, Jenna. Hurry up."

With her stomach in a knot, Jane rode to Adele's in silence. What if Meghan showed up? Adele wanted to put everyone back together—Jane knew that included her and Meghan, but Jane couldn't trust her feelings of empathy to stay present if they came face to face again.

When they arrived, Jane did a quick mental inventory of the cars parked outside. Lila's Lexus. Campbell's Altima. Adele's old something or other. So far, no sign of Meghan. The stress in her gut eased a bit.

Sam ran ahead of them as soon as he saw his old friend Mugsy. The dog barely acknowledged him as Sam plopped himself down beside her.

"He really does need a dog," Graham said.

Jane shot him a look. "Over my dead body."

Jenna fell into step beside her, linking an arm through hers. "You okay, Mom?"

She glanced at her daughter, who surveyed the scene in front of them. Two long tables decorated with white linens and sprays of pink peonies welcomed them. Adele—or, more likely, Luke—had strung white lights, creating a canopy above them. Each place setting had been perfectly arranged like something you'd see in a magazine. The image nearly took her breath away.

Tom and Lila stood in the distance. When Jane caught her eye, Lila looked away. She brought Tom? Campbell wandered around the table, photographing the small details of their outdoor gathering. She'd capture the night perfectly, Jane had no doubt. Campbell held her camera up and snapped Jane's picture before she could turn away.

"I caught you." Campbell smiled. "That'll be the perfect addition to the scrapbook."

Jane searched for Adele but couldn't locate her in the yard. She must've spent the entire day preparing for their arrival.

Guilt nipped at her. She'd almost called to cancel, never giving a thought to all the work Adele had done to make this a special evening. She couldn't blame Adele for wanting to bring Meghan back into their circle. Any mother would want the same. The image of the magazine crossed her mind, and Jane thanked God for allowing her to rediscover her own humility before she made a complete fool of herself.

"Mom?" Jenna had stopped walking and now stared at her.

"What? Oh. Yes, hon, I'm fine."

Her daughter frowned. "You seem out of it."

"I'm fine. Go have fun."

Jenna strolled off just as the door opened.

"Jane, you made it." Adele bustled out and walked in her direction. "I'm so happy. And there's your handsome husband." She giggled. "If my heart ever stops beating, just stick him in front of me."

Jane smiled. She and Graham had come to a silent truce, and she couldn't deny how handsome he looked in the soft white lights. "Everything is beautiful, Adele."

It reminded her of their last big dinner here—only a couple of months before. The photos Adele had given her had been carefully placed on a scrapbook page in anticipation of her trip back—the beginning of the new Circle.

Luke helped his mom carry dish after dish from the kitchen to the table, but Adele refused to allow any of her other guests to do anything but mingle. Jane sat on a wicker love seat and took a quick inventory of where all her kids were. She'd taken to counting them anytime they were out in public. Even though the girls were sixteen and eighteen, she still located them and made sure they were okay before she could relax.

Lila met her eyes and walked in her direction, carrying two glasses of sweet tea. She sat next to Jane and handed her a drink. Without saying a word, Jane took it and sipped.

"I know what you're thinking," Lila said.

Jane looked at her. "Oh?"

"We're not back together. He's doing me a favor." Lila straightened in her seat, then met Tom's eyes from across the way. He smiled at her and she did the same.

"What kind of favor?" Jane set the drink on the small wicker table in front of her.

"He's staying with me at the lake house—just while my parents are there. I have a bad feeling their weekend trip may turn into a minivacation. I'm starting to think they'll never leave." She sighed. "I didn't have the heart to leave him alone with them for the night. No matter how mad I still am."

Jane shot her a look.

"You know my mom, Jane. I couldn't let her think she was right about us." Lila sat back on the love seat and faced her.

"Was she right about you?"

Lila stared at her left hand. The diamond sparkled underneath the twinkling white lights. She met Jane's eyes.

"I think deep down you know she wasn't. And I think you still love him as much as he loves you." Jane covered Lila's hands with her own.

Lila shook her head. "He doesn't deserve to be with me. I've only ever been with one man—him." She tossed her hair over her shoulder. "Don't you think maybe it's time I expand my horizons?"

Jane frowned. "Why would you want to? Look at him. He's handsome, strong, protective, successful. Yes, he made a mistake, but we all have."

"Not Graham." Lila stared at Jane's husband, who sat at the table chatting with Luke.

Jane followed Lila's gaze and tilted her head, staring at her husband. After her revelation at the Bible study, Jane had vowed to never shy away from transparency. Not when it could help someone. "Graham almost left me."

Lila gasped. "He did not."

"I wasn't right for a long time, Lila. Depression. Panic attacks. You want to believe that a pastor will know how to handle something like that, but the truth is, he's a man. And men like to fix things. When he couldn't fix me, he told me he didn't know what else to do and he walked out the door."

"What did you do?" Lila's wide eyes waited for her answer.

"I cried—a lot. I told myself it was what I deserved. And then I prayed. And prayed."

"And what, everything was fine?"

Jane laughed. "Not by a long shot. But the difference was, for the first time since Alex, I *wanted* to try. I'd lost my son. I couldn't lose my husband too. He came with me to counseling every week for a year."

"He never really would've left you." Lila shook her head. "You know that."

"Maybe. But I believed he would. And it saved me."

"Tom has been pretty amazing."

Jane stared at her friend—saw a gleam in her eye that told of a happiness that bubbled from somewhere deep down. A smile crossed her face.

"What's that look for?" The corners of Lila's mouth pulled upward in a slight smile.

"Nothing," Jane said. "It's just—you could've dropped him off somewhere tonight. Café. Bookstore. Yet, here he is." Jane smiled. "You must be feeling better about the two of you."

Lila sighed. "I can block it out for long periods of time, but then this nagging thought pops in my head and I pick it apart and get really angry all over again. It's like I keep mentally reliving it. Imagining them together. Imagining him raising Campbell." Lila brushed her hair away from her face. "The daughter I never had."

"Lila. You do know you control your own thoughts, right?" Jane asked.

"What do you mean? I don't pop them in my head on my own."

"But you decide how you react to them."

"So it's my fault I have a big imagination?"

"What I mean is, you can't move on if you're always looking backward." Jane folded her hands in her lap.

"That sounds like something a pastor's wife would say." Lila sounded skeptical, but Jane could tell by the look on her face she was mulling it over.

The words hovered, as if they wanted Jane's full attention. She'd given that advice to so many women—for years now, but in that moment they sounded new. For the first time, she applied them to herself.

Jane covered her mouth with her hand. "Oh wow."

"What is it?" Lila leaned toward her. "Are you okay?"

"That's what I haven't been doing."

Lila slumped back in the seat. "We're not talking about me any-more, are we?"

Jane cocked her head. "You're terrible." She laughed at Lila's dejected expression and squeezed her hand.

"All right, everyone, come and eat." Adele stood at the head of the long table, admiring the display. Dish after dish cascaded across the white tablecloth, lit by the twinkling lights wrapped in the branches of the old oak tree overhead. Jane and Lila walked arm in arm toward the crowd, and before they reached the rest of them, Jane leaned over and whispered, "Is Meghan coming?"

Lila's eyebrows knit together. "I don't know."

They stood in a circle around the table, and Jane glanced from face to face. People who'd come to mean so much to her. Some relationships rich with history, others new and fresh. She said a silent prayer of thanks for each of them.

And then she said a prayer for Meghan—wherever she was.

"I did invite a few others, but it looks like they aren't going to make it, and you know how I feel about letting my food get cold." Adele's smile looked forced. It wasn't hard for Jane to imagine the older woman's pain.

"I'd like to ask Pastor Graham to pray for our meal," Adele said.

As they bowed their heads, a noise from behind them drew their attention. Two little redheaded children ran up the driveway, their glee-filled voices shouting "Me-maw, we're here!"

Jane's breath caught in her throat, and she waited to see if Meghan would walk around the corner. Seconds later, Nick's silhouette appeared, a shadow over his face. He moved toward them, his walk and demeanor a familiar reminder of years gone by. Lila grabbed her hand.

They widened the circle and Adele met Nick's eyes. He shook his head.

Meghan wasn't coming.

Nick stayed quiet throughout dinner, but the twins chattered on and on. With red hair, freckles and big blue eyes, both Finn and Nadia captured Jane instantly. She felt inexplicably drawn to them.

After dinner, the crowd dispersed, and Jane helped Adele clear the table. On her third trip back, she caught a glimpse of her children—specifically Jenna—entertaining Meghan's twins. Jenna had woven together bracelets and necklaces out of grass and dandelions, and both Finn and Nadia seemed completely smitten with her daughter. The very notion of it sent Jane's mind whirling.

"She's got a gift," Adele said as she passed by. "She's got those kids eating out of the palm of her hand." Adele walked inside, leaving Jane struggling to make sense of why it bothered her that Jenna seemed to forgive and forget so easily. So easily that she could sit on the ground and let Meghan's children crawl all over her.

The idea shamed her. She herself had been smitten with the beautiful four-year-olds. Why shouldn't her girls feel the same?

In desperate need of air, Jane walked through the house and out to the front porch. The screen door snapped shut behind her, and she leaned on the old column at the house's front.

She closed her eyes and inhaled the warm summer air. August was just around the corner and soon it would be fall. She only had a month left in Sweethaven, and she had to find a way to enjoy it.

The sound of someone clearing their throat startled her. Her stomach lurched and she searched the darkness to determine who else had retreated to the solitude of the front porch.

When she saw Nick sitting on the ledge of the old house, both legs outstretched before him, her heart sank.

"Oh, I'm sorry," she said. "I was just passing through."

"You don't have to go," Nick said. "I can go. I don't want to upset you."

Nick had come to her the day after Alex's death. Pleaded with her to believe that Meghan had been clean, but Jane refused. She could see such desperation behind his eyes—like a man who stood to lose everything.

"You don't upset me." She turned to face him.

Nick shifted where he sat. "Spent the morning with Meghan and the kids, but . . ." His voice trailed off.

She took a few steps closer to him and sat down on one of the porch chairs.

He let his head rest on the side of the house as he exhaled.

"It must be hard for you."

Nick took off his baseball cap and fidgeted with the bill. "You have no idea." He glanced at her. "Or maybe you do."

Jane looked away.

"I went back this afternoon and bought every single copy of those stupid magazines—even the ones in the back, but the damage was done."

The silence ticked off seconds at an achingly slow pace. He had more to say, but he'd gone silent.

Jane cleared her throat. "Nick, can I ask you—what happened? I'm shocked to see you two like this. You've always been so perfect together." Jane rested her elbows on her knees and waited to find out if she'd crossed a line in asking.

"She changed, after that summer." He shot her a look. "We all did, I think."

Jane met his eyes and held them for a long moment. She'd been in such a zone of misery, she'd barely been aware of all the other people who'd suffered because of what happened to Alex that day. She'd grieved alone when she could've had company the entire time.

It felt wasteful.

"She came away from that believing she'd never be good enough for anyone. Her addiction hit the tabloids. Then there was rehab and everything else." He shook his head. "And when she got pregnant—well, it wasn't on purpose. I think having kids of her own . . ."

Jane waited for him to continue. "What?"

"It's like every day she'd wait for something bad to happen to one of them. She thought that would be her ultimate punishment, I think. Instead of falling in love with them—she pushed us away. All of us."

"I'm so sorry, Nick," Jane whispered.

"Me too." He sighed and stood up, then leaned against the post. "You were a good friend to her, Jane. She always respected you—more than you know."

The words danced around Jane's head before they settled on her ears, and she willed herself not to process them. She didn't want to hear good things about Meghan, didn't invite the sympathy she felt.

The prayers she'd journaled every day that week floated through her mind.

Lord, help me understand. Give me the strength to forgive her—really forgive her. Bring me the peace that passes all understanding.

Was showing her what Meghan had been through the past six years God's way of answering? Because for the first time since she spotted Meghan outside the chapel that day, the knot in her stomach had disappeared. In its place was a strong desire to help her old friend.

Whatever it took.

Meghan

Meghan stared at the run-down bar, nothing more than a square box building with a front porch and a sign out front, but it met a need. People went in and out, and the more time that passed, the louder it got. Everyone in there had probably seen those god-awful photos on the cover of those stupid tabloids. She didn't belong here and she knew it.

She opened the car door and trudged into the bar, her entrance raising more than a few eyebrows. The Friday night crowd of mostly men played pool at the back of the room or sat on bar stools nursing mixed drinks or bottled beer. A baseball game blared on the television in the corner.

Meghan sat at the end of the bar, knowing that it'd only be a matter of minutes before someone recognized her.

"Heard you were back in town." The bartender eyed Meghan as he wiped the inside of a glass.

"That right?"

"You don't remember me, do you?"

She stared at him, trying to imagine him without the goatee that hid his facial features. Thinning dark hair hovered atop a thick head that sat squarely on shoulders without a neck in sight.

She shook her head. "Sorry, I don't."

"Andy Boggs. We went to school together."

"Oh, Andy. Hey." She smiled, though the name had done nothing to jog her memory. Judging by his stocky build, he had probably played football. Meghan never paid those guys any attention. They'd returned her that favor.

"What can I get for Sweethaven's most famous citizen?" He grinned at her, and Meghan smiled back, her face burning like she'd just opened a hot oven and stuck her head inside.

Decision time.

She'd been at this crossroads before. The fourth anniversary of Alex's death. It had sent her spiraling again—that one night in the bar had cost her everything. Proved to her she couldn't stay sober enough to raise her kids. She had left the next day.

But this was different. Now, she had nothing to lose.

Just one night.

When she stuttered, unable to make up her mind, Andy the bartender decided for her. "How about we start you off with something easy. Fuzzy navel. Chicks love those fruity drinks, right?" He turned a glass over in front of her and filled it with ice, orange juice and peach Schnapps. He stuck an orange wedge on the edge of the glass and pushed it toward her.

She took it as an insult. "I'm more of a vodka girl." She winked. "But I can start with this."

He raised an eyebrow, then stared at her—practically salivating, she thought. She smiled. Flirted. Drank.

And every time Nick's face wandered into her mind, she shoved it aside like an unwanted insect buzzing around a picnic site.

After the incident at the grocery store, she'd hurried Finn and the tweezers back to Nick and raced home on foot. He called after her, begging for an explanation, but the humiliation pressed in on her so heavy she couldn't breathe for the weight of it.

The tears streamed down her face, but she found her way back to the house and spent the next hour sobbing at the damage her stupidity had done her little boy. What could secure her spot on the outside of their lives better than a night in the bar?

An hour went by, and Meghan had upgraded from peach Schnapps to vodka with the second drink. She'd lost count after the third glass when her head went light and she began to relax.

Andy stayed beside her the entire time, catering to her every whim. She let him. It had been a long time since a man had paid her so much attention. Unless she counted Duncan and James—which she didn't.

"How is it that we never talked in high school, Andy the bartender?" she said, her words smearing together.

He shrugged. "You were too good for me, I think." He leaned on the bar, intent on her, their faces close. She stared at him, still smiling, her eyes wide.

"You don't even deny it." He laughed. "Still too good for me?"

She shrugged coyly and took another sip of her drink.

A heavyset waitress tapped her on the shoulder. "Just one song?" she asked. "Your fans are asking."

Meghan turned and found all eyes cast her way. She glanced at Andy, who grinned.

"Just one song?" he said. "For the hometown crowd?"

She waved them off, but they persisted. The noise heightened when she stood up, and they cheered her all the way to the stage.

"You wanna hear a song?" She tapped on the microphone. It echoed through the speakers. She turned to the guitarist standing behind her. "You know any of my stuff?"

"All of it." He smiled.

"How about 'My One and Only'?"

He nodded and they started playing her hit song. It had won Song of the Year two years earlier and it was still her favorite. She'd written it for Nick, after they split up. Had he ever heard it?

She stumbled over the words of the bridge, but the crowd helped her out. When the song finished, they called for an encore, but she shook her head. "Maybe later," she said into the mike. She tapped the guitarist on the shoulder. "Thanks, man." He held her hand and helped her down the stairs. She took her seat back at the bar, right in front of Andy, who grinned that stupid smile at her.

"Pretty good," he said. "But we always knew that."

"*You* never knew that," she said. "You were one of those jock guys who made fun of me."

"What?" He laughed. "I never made fun of you. I'm a nice guy." He put his hand over hers. "You were always too caught up in Rhodes to see that, though, weren't ya?" His eyes narrowed as though he were planning to roast her carcass and eat her for dinner.

At the mention of Nick's name, regret twisted through Meghan's belly, but she quickly forced it away. Nick had no claim to her anymore. There was no ring on her left hand. In the two years they'd been apart, though, there hadn't been anyone else—there'd never been anyone else. She knew she'd ruined her one chance at the real thing.

Meghan smiled at Andy, who kissed her hand. "Time to give someone else a chance, don't you think?"

He leaned across the bar and kissed her, hard, his thick hand on the back of her head. He pulled her in close. After a few seconds, she tried to pull away, but his hand kept her from moving until he decided he was finished.

"I can show you what you've been missing all these years," he said.

The thin skin around her mouth burned from the force of his whiskered face pressing into hers. She put a hand over her lips and discreetly wiped his saliva from her mouth.

"I should probably get going home, actually."

"Nah, we're just getting started."

Andy walked around the bar and sat on the stool next to her. He turned her around to face him, their legs laced together, then tucked her hair behind her ear and stared at her.

"You're so beautiful," he said.

She looked away. "Thanks. I really do need to get going, though." Her head spun. The vodka weighed her reflexes down. Slow-motion pictures crawled across her mind.

He leaned in and tried to kiss her again, but she turned her face away.

"What's wrong?"

"I can't do this right now." She glanced around the bar, but everyone seemed to have lost interest in her. Had they all gotten used to her so quickly?

"Sure you can," he said, his tone clipped. He leaned in again, this time placing a beefy hand on her knee.

She pushed him away. "You're going too fast."

He laughed, but his grip tightened. "Please, Meghan, we're not kids anymore."

"Let me up."

"You've been throwing yourself at me all night, and now you want out? Doesn't work that way." His oversized body blocked her way.

She wriggled her wrist from his hand and tried to pull her leg away, but his grip was too strong. "I want to go home." Her voice cracked a little as she spoke, the sound of her own heartbeat pounding in her head.

"In a little while." Both of his hands held her in place, and she knew she didn't have the strength to fight him off or the clarity to outsmart him. He'd been feeding her drinks all night long, and she'd let him. Now, unable to fight, she prepared for the worst. He pulled her closer and leaned in, his face right next to hers.

"You're gonna be begging for more." The stench of alcohol wafted to her nostrils. He kissed her again, wet, slobbery kisses that missed their target and coated her chin with his spit. Her stomach churned and she pulled away, but her protesting only angered him.

"Get away from me, Andy," she said through clenched teeth.

The noise from the bar faded into the background. Clinking glasses. Rowdy patrons. Music from the jukebox as the band was on break.

She let herself go numb, like she had so many times before, when the pain gripped her with unmatched force. Then, like one strip of Velcro being torn from another, Andy Boggs's body ripped away from her.

"Get away from her, Boggs."

Nick.

Her ex threw the considerably larger man into the wall behind him and then turned around to face him.

Andy stumbled into a table and then staggered to his feet. "Rhodes, give it up. She's done with you."

Meghan stood. Nick turned and looked at her, his face a mixture of hurt and disappointment. "You okay?"

She nodded.

Then, out of nowhere, Andy hauled off and sucker punched Nick square in the jaw. He went down, the bigger man hulking over him like he'd only just begun.

Two other guys in the bar intervened, holding Andy back and keeping a close eye on Nick, whose lip bled bright crimson. He spit on the floor and looked at Andy.

"I'm not here to fight you," he said. "Just let us go."

With all the attention on him, Andy held up his hands in surrender. "Get out then." He looked at Meghan, disgust filling his eyes. "And don't come back in here." He lowered his voice as she walked past. "I don't care how famous you are, you're nothing but a piece of trash."

She walked past him and met Nick at the front door.

Outside, a hot stream of tears shot down her cheeks. Her morning humiliation had returned and multiplied times ten. How many times did Nick have to save her?

"What is wrong with you?" He took her by the arm, like a parent, and ushered her to the truck.

"My car."

"Can stay here tonight. Or I'll send someone back for it. You obviously can't drive." He opened the door of the truck and helped her inside. Through the window, she watched as he headed around to the driver's side. He stopped in front of the truck and stood there for a long minute, looking at the ground.

Talking to himself? Calming himself down? Reminding himself this wasn't his job anymore?

She'd probably never know.

The only thing she knew for sure was that once again, she had messed everything up—and she continued to rack up casualties in her wake.

THIRTY-THREE

Meghan

Talking to himself must've calmed Nick down. Meghan watched him get in the truck and shut the door.

"Meghan." He looked at her. "What were you thinking? That guy has always been trouble. He beat up his last two girlfriends. You shouldn't even be here."

Nick's eyes were full of intensity, but she had no explanation. He'd never understand.

"I'm sorry," she said.

"You're drunk."

"It's been a really bad couple of days." Her mind whirled with the memory of Finn's innocent eyes looking up at her, asking her if the half-naked woman on the cover of that magazine was her.

His mommy.

Nick looked at her. "It's been a bad couple of years."

He started the engine and they pulled away from the bar, leaving Andy the bartender and half of Sweethaven to talk about them well into the night. As usual, Nick stayed quiet. Even in her incoherent state, she knew he wanted to yell at her. How could he not?

He'd been with her as she fought for her sobriety. He'd sacrificed everything to help her get well.

And she'd just thrown it all away. Again.

"I messed up." Her words slurred. "And the whole world knows it." Meghan closed her eyes and rested her head against the truck seat.

Nick tapped the steering wheel with his thumb but didn't respond.

They pulled into the driveway of the rented lake house. She must've dozed off. She had no memory of the drive from Main Street to Lilac Lane. He stopped the truck in front of the garage and cut the engine.

She glanced at him, but he stared straight ahead, engrossed in the garage door, which shone yellow under the haze of a single lamp.

"Just say it." Her garbled words cut through the silence like a hot knife through butter.

He looked at her. "Say what?"

"Tell me what an idiot I am. Tell me I just screwed everything up. Like always. Tell me I'm a total loser."

Nick went back to staring at the garage door. After a few seconds, he opened the door and got out, then crossed around to her side and opened her door. He held out a hand. She took it and let him help her down.

Didn't he want to scream at her?

"How'd you find me?" she asked as he walked her inside.

"Small town, Meg."

Someone must've called him. Someone she wished she could thank. Images of Andy Boggs dragging her into some back room somewhere flashed through her mind. She shuddered to think what had almost happened.

Meghan stumbled up the stairs, but his strong hand on the small of her back steadied her. The warmth of his touch sent heat all the way to her cheeks. The porch spun and a wave of nausea swept over her. "I think I'm gonna be . . ." She grabbed the oversized potted plant next to the front door and threw up in it. Her knees buckled underneath her and she held on to the pot, resting her face on the cold porcelain.

"Come on, champ, let's go." Nick helped her to her feet, opened the door and led her inside.

Darkness filled the house, their steps illuminated by the light of the moon through the skylights. Nick found a lamp and switched it on. She looked at him, but he wouldn't meet her eyes. She couldn't blame him. He'd seen the very underbelly of her shame. And here they were again.

"Why don't I make you some coffee?" He sat her in a tall chair beside the kitchen table.

She didn't respond. Instead, she watched as he opened the cupboards, found the coffee, measured two level scoops and started it brewing. He looked around the kitchen, still refusing to cast a glance in her direction.

"Nick."

"Don't." His eyes darted around the room and finally landed on her. "Let's just drop it."

She stared at him, her mind reeling, conjuring images of the day she told him she didn't love him anymore. The day her addiction reared its ugly head. After a night just like this one. But she'd stayed sober since that night. In the back of her mind, she'd always imagined the day she felt good enough to come back to them, to be their mom.

She'd been so close, but here she was again. Nothing but a mess.

Nick's silence hovered, building a wall of tension between them.

"For what it's worth, I'm sorry."

He held her gaze for a long moment, then inhaled as if he wanted to say something. The coffeepot hissed and pulled his attention. He poured a cup, added cream and sugar and set it on the table in front of her.

She took a drink and let the coffee warm her. She wished it could offer instant sobriety, but she knew better. He sat in the chair next to her but stared out the window into the blackness of the backyard.

She studied him, wishing he'd tell her what thoughts were running through his mind, but she'd lost the right to know what he was thinking. Her mind wandered back to the months after Alex's death. Rehab. She knew she couldn't do it alone with that hanging over her head. Nick had come to visit her every weekend. Sent flowers to the room. "I'll be here when you get out," he'd write on tiny rectangular cards with pictures of hearts on the side. She'd saved every little note he sent while she was there, affixed them all into her little journal. They'd been her lifeline.

She'd done well for a while—well enough to go home and get on with her life, but the responsibility of losing Alex never went away.

"Maybe you should go lie down." Nick's voice broke the silence and tore her from the memory of her daunting mistakes. She opened her eyes and looked at him.

Unreadable thoughts.

She nodded and stood but faltered as her head spun. He reached up, steadied her, then stood at her side. He wrapped a strong arm around her waist, then bent down and slipped his left hand under her legs, picking her up like she didn't weigh a thing. He carried her into the bedroom and set her on the bed.

Did all their nights of passion invade his thoughts like they did hers? How many times had he led her to the bedroom, only to show her throughout the night how much he loved her? How happy he was he'd married her?

Passion had never been their problem.

The strength of their attraction hadn't lessened. If anything, in their separation, it seemed to have intensified.

As she inhaled his scent, she realized how much she'd missed his arms, his tender embrace, his kisses. He knew every curve of her body, and she'd memorized every square inch of his.

He reached down and took her shoes off, first one, then the other. Next he pulled the covers back, and she slid underneath them but kept her eyes deadlocked on him. He sat next to her and brushed a stray hair away from her face. Her breath faltered and she felt like a kid again, staying out too late in the loft of Old Man McGuffrey's barn. Nick had always had a way of giving her the stomach flutters.

Some things didn't disappear with age.

Slowly, he leaned closer to her and she met his gaze for the briefest moment. He closed his eyes and gently pressed his soft lips on her forehead, still holding her face in his hands.

"'Night, Meg." He pulled away, then stood and walked out, turning off the light as he closed the door. Not even another glance in her direction.

"'Night," she whispered.

THIRTY-FOUR

Campbell

"It was good of Nick to bring the kids over," Campbell said.

The cab of Luke's truck was filled with silence. Not the comforting, quiet kind—the kind that told Campbell something was wrong. She shouldn't be surprised. She'd walked out of their last real conversation angry, and they'd barely spoken since.

"Yeah, my mom appreciated it." Luke's eyes stayed on the road.

Campbell's heart dropped. Something between them had changed. Maybe she should've listened to Tilly's warnings.

She flipped her camera over and scrolled through the photos one by one, deleting any that were out of focus. The image of her and Luke sitting under the twinkling white lights in Adele's backyard popped up on the screen. Adele had snapped it for them, and in spite of it being a little off-center, Campbell loved it. Luke didn't have that void, distant expression he'd been wearing so often—and it was the first weekend he'd actually been in town since she arrived.

She fought the urge to ask about the work that took him away every weekend, focusing instead on the Main Street traffic lights. Luke pulled up behind the gallery and put the truck in park. She'd moved her things into the apartment above the gallery, and while she missed Adele's cooking, it was nice to have her own space.

"Thanks for the ride." Campbell turned to him.

"Of course."

She inhaled, her heart wobbly in her chest. "Do you have to get right home?" The question hung between them, leaving her vulnerable and exposed.

He sighed. "Yeah, early morning tomorrow."

She looked away. She was losing him, and she was helpless to stop it.

Luke turned to her. "I'm sorry. I know I've been a drag lately."

One quick nod was all she could muster. "I'll see you tomorrow." She popped open the door of the truck and hurried inside.

Upstairs, in the quiet of the little apartment, Campbell sank onto the couch.

She'd gotten her hopes wrapped up in this one perfect summer—this one perfect guy—and look where it had gotten her. Her mind wandered back to her previous relationships, all of which had ended. Why did she think this one would be any different? A tear slipped from her eye and rolled down her cheek.

Maybe Luke had met someone else. Or maybe she'd annoyed him by moving here so soon. Or maybe he'd decided he didn't want to be with her anymore.

She tossed and turned all night, willing herself to stop dwelling on it, telling herself to worry about what she could control, like making a real go of this art gallery.

The next morning, Campbell awoke with puffy eyes and a clogged nose. It was like the pain of the last few months had all hit her in one fell swoop, but with the sunrise of a new day, she resolved to throw herself into work. And that meant being ready for the weekend tourists. She got started with the business of the day, catching a glimpse of Luke out on the sidewalk as she flipped her sign to Open.

He set up a standing sign on the sidewalk outside the café and then disappeared back inside. Sadness wound its way around her heart.

The door opened and Campbell took a breath, hoping for a new student for the photography class she'd just announced, but instead, she saw her grandfather enter.

Guilt nipped at her heels. She'd run into her grandfather at the beach one evening and told herself she'd make a point to visit him, but Tilly's words had stopped her. While she'd forgiven the old man for the way he'd turned his back on her mom, it still felt like a betrayal to spend time with him.

But with everyone else so busy, maybe someone was trying to tell her something—like getting to know her grandfather wasn't such a bad idea after all.

He smiled as he approached. "I heard a rumor and had to come see for myself," he said. "You really bought this place?"

She smiled. "I can hardly believe it myself."

"It's a nice fit." He shifted his weight, looking thin and frail before her. He seemed unsure what to do next, and her silence wasn't helping.

"I should—"

She cut him off. "Can I do anything for you?"

He stared at her, as if contemplating what to tell her. "Deb lets me sit in here sometimes."

"Oh?"

"Once you did all this"—he motioned around the gallery at the photos and paintings on the wall—"well, it was the one place in town I could go where I felt close to her again."

Campbell stilled. He wore his pain like a badge, and she had a feeling he had yet to forgive himself for kicking her mother out when she turned up pregnant all those years ago. "I feel the same way in here. She put so much of herself into every painting."

He nodded. "I don't want to get in the way. I should be going."

"You can sit if you want. I don't mind." She glanced at the long bench facing a painting of the Boardwalk. The brightly colored Ferris wheel took center stage, with the lake shimmering in the background.

His expression changed and she could see the gratitude behind his eyes. "If you're sure?"

"Of course."

He inched his way over to the bench and sat down, staring at the oversized painting illuminated by the track lighting overhead. Next to it hung Campbell's photograph of the Ferris wheel from a different angle. She'd worked hard to get the colors just right before sending it off to the developer.

The minutes ticked by and her grandfather didn't say another word. He simply sat in the center of the gallery, staring at the images on the wall. Every time she thought of something to say, she decided against it. He seemed to crave the silence. Around lunchtime, Campbell packed up the scrapbook page she'd been working on and walked over to the bench where the old man still sat.

"I was going to grab a sandwich," she said. "Would you like to join me?"

He looked at her, a hopeful expression on his face. "Of course. Are you sure?"

She smiled, thinking of all the plans she'd made before arriving in Sweethaven. Long walks with Luke on the beach as the sun set. Hours scrapbooking and talking and telling stories with her mother's old friends. Coffee and dessert with the father she'd been e-mailing and couldn't wait to really *know.* None of those plans had included her grandfather, and yet, here he was. And while everything else had fallen apart, maybe this was the man who needed her the most.

Or maybe she needed him.

They walked outside and she locked the door behind them.

"The Main Street Café has a wonderful soup," her grandfather said. "And I know you're sweet on that Barber boy."

She sighed.

His eyebrows popped up. "Trouble in paradise?"

After a long pause, she finally shook her head. "No, it's probably nothing. I guess I just thought he'd have more time for me is all."

They walked across the street and into the café. She looked around but didn't see Luke. Had he retreated to his office again? Campbell wondered how it hurt his business for him not to be there. People expected to see him. She thought some even came back for that reason. He had a way of making people feel good.

Delcy smiled as they reached the register.

"Hey, Campbell. Are you here for Luke?"

Campbell stuttered, then finally said, "No, we're here to eat lunch."

Delcy didn't seem to hear her. "He's been on the phone all morning. All secretive back there in his office. You can go on back if you want to."

Campbell felt her grandfather's eyes on her, and at her expression, Delcy's smile faded.

"I think it's a work thing," she backpedaled.

"We'll just order."

They did and then found a booth near the back of the café. The sound of Campbell's heartbeat pounding in her head contended with the noise in the busy restaurant.

"He's a good boy," her grandfather said.

"Let's not talk about Luke."

Delcy brought their food with her trademark smile. "Let me know if you need anything else."

They ate in silence for a few moments, then Luke appeared from behind the kitchen doors. Their eyes met and Campbell quickly looked away, trying to focus on her grandfather and her turkey on rye.

He sauntered over and stood beside their table. "Didn't know you were coming in today." He extended a hand toward her grandfather. "Good to see you, Reverend Carter."

"You too, Luke. Business is booming."

Luke sighed. "It looks like it, but you'd be surprised."

She took a sip of her Diet Coke.

"Hey, are you free later?"

"I'll have to look."

"Work's been a killer lately. I thought maybe we could hang out tonight?"

Now you want to hang out? "Can I let you know?"

He stuttered an incoherent response, surprise on his face.

She turned her attention to her grandpa. "I'm sorry to run off, but I've got to get back to the gallery." She stood. "Good to see you, Luke."

He opened his mouth like he wanted to say something, but she sailed on by before he could get it out.

As the door closed behind her, she resisted the urge to turn around and see if he watched her go, resisted the urge to run back in and tell him "Yes, of course we can get together. I think about you nonstop and would love nothing more." Focused on the sidewalk in front of her, Campbell held her head high and walked back to the Sweethaven Gallery, hardly able to see for the tears that clouded her eyes.

THIRTY-FIVE

Lila

Lila awoke to the sound of birds chirping outside the window and the smell of bacon wafting upstairs. She rolled over, found Tom's side of the bed empty, and spotted a little white card and a single white rose.

Tom's notes had been coming more frequently. She'd found them in the car, stuck in her purse, on the nightstand. He never mentioned them—and neither did she. She simply read them, then shoved them inside the box in the old hope chest.

But that hadn't kept them from permeating her heart.

She inhaled the scent of the rose and smiled. He'd given her a single white rose the day he'd proposed to her.

On the front of the envelope, he'd written her name in bold black cursive, and she warmed at the thought of him going to the trouble of professing his love for her this way. Tom had never been particularly romantic—he was a man's man. She'd accepted that her life wouldn't be a dazzling fairy tale, but he'd shown a different side of himself this past week—a side she rather liked. When her parents decided to extend their stay, he went along with it. If she didn't know better, she'd say he was enjoying their little charade.

Still, just because she liked the attention didn't mean everything between them had been fixed. She opened the envelope to reveal a plain blue card. It had a decidedly masculine look to it, and Lila smiled at the thought of Tom picking out a box of blank cards at the stationery store.

Lila,

I woke up early this morning and watched you sleeping. I remember I used to do that when we first got married, still amazed that someone so beautiful had chosen to spend the rest of her life with me. I felt that way again today and then said a prayer that things between us weren't hopeless.

All I could think of was that I don't want a life without you in it. You're beautiful and strong and I know you don't need me at all, but I need you. And I want to be your husband again. Will you go to dinner with me this week? Just the two of us—no playacting, no one else watching? Say yes.

Love,
Tom

Lila closed the card and peered out the window as a boat sailed past. He'd tried so hard—but to what end? She couldn't take him back. She'd be the weak, oblivious wife—and in that label, she had no interest.

She slid a silk robe over her nightgown and followed the smell of bacon down to the kitchen, where she found Tom behind the stove and Mama sipping a mimosa and reading the newspaper.

Mama glanced up and horror struck her face. "I cannot believe you left your bedroom like that."

Heat rushed to Lila's cheeks as she glanced at Tom. He looked at Mama, then walked over to Lila and wrapped his arms around her. Lila let him hold her—under Mama's watchful eye.

"I think you're stunning."

Mama let out a laugh. "You've trained him well, daughter. I'll give you that."

Tom kissed the top of Lila's head, his nearness familiar and comfortable. She could wrap herself in his arms without a second thought.

He pulled away and winked at her.

"Are you going to eat?" Mama folded the newspaper and set it on the table. "You look positively gaunt."

"Weren't you the one who told me only a few months ago that I could stand to lose a few pounds?" Lila poured herself a cup of coffee and sat at the other end of the table.

"You clearly don't know a thing about balance. If I didn't know better, I'd think you were starving yourself again. You do that when you get stressed."

Lila took a sip of coffee and let it warm her all the way to her core. Stress did prevent her from eating—and being around Mama, trying to keep up pretenses, certainly qualified.

Tom set a plate of bacon and eggs in front of her. "I do agree with your mother on one thing. You don't eat enough."

"Not you too."

He half-grinned and then returned to the oven, where he started cleaning up the mess he'd made cooking them breakfast.

"I volunteered you for the Labor Day Festival Committee."

Lila shot her mother a glaring look. "Why would you do that?"

"You need something to keep you busy. The Adlers have long served this community—it's a tradition you're going to have to carry on." Mama peered at her with a raised brow. "We already discussed this the other night at dinner. You agreed. Tom, didn't she agree?"

Tom held up his hands as if to say "keep me out of it."

"Mama, what can I possibly do at this point? Those women have been planning for months."

"I know. And that's exactly what Meryl DuBois said when I insisted you should head the entertainment committee."

Tom cleared his throat as if to challenge her to speak up. To stand up for herself for once.

"I explained to Meryl that you, my lovely daughter, have a personal connection with Meghan Rhodes. There's a meeting today at eleven. You'll have to clean yourself up—I expect you to dazzle them with the old Adler family charm."

Lila's mind raced as she tried to think of all the reasons why she couldn't possibly attend the meeting, plan the entertainment or contact Meghan about singing a benefit concert for the people of Sweethaven, but when she opened her mouth to protest, no words came out.

Two hours later, Lila came downstairs, dressed, made up and ready to dazzle.

Tom met her at the bottom of the stairs. "You look beautiful."

"Thank you."

He stared at her, then looked down, studying his hands in front of him. "Did you . . . uh, did you get my note this morning?"

Like a nervous schoolboy, he pressed his lips together, waiting for her response. She smiled at his insecurity. "I did."

He met her eyes. "And?"

"You have very nice penmanship."

He laughed. "You know what I'm asking."

"Of course, Tom. Let's plan it this week. If I can make it through these festival planning meetings."

His face lit up, then he leaned in closer. "Don't turn around now, but I think your mother is watching us. Do you think we should make our relationship look more . . . realistic?"

Lila's eyes danced their way down to his lips, perfectly aware of his desire for her. "And how do you propose we do that?"

Now she was flirting. It wasn't fair, but he didn't seem to mind.

As he wove his hand behind her head, his thumb brushed her cheek gently. His eyes left hers in favor of her mouth and he leaned down, closing the space between them. His kiss, as familiar as her favorite sweater, felt new and exciting. Lila closed her eyes and inhaled the scent of him—clean and masculine and decidedly *Tom*.

Seconds later, he pulled away and glanced over Lila's shoulder. "I think she bought it."

Lila turned, expecting to meet her mother's watchful eye, but found the kitchen empty. She glanced back at Tom, whose grin had turned sheepish.

"She was never there, was she?"

He smiled.

She smacked his shoulder. "I won't fall for that again."

He grabbed her hand and turned her toward himself. "Admit it, there's still something between us."

She looked down.

He nodded and left her to contemplate the statement in the silence of her car. And judging by her racing pulse, she didn't need to contemplate for very long.

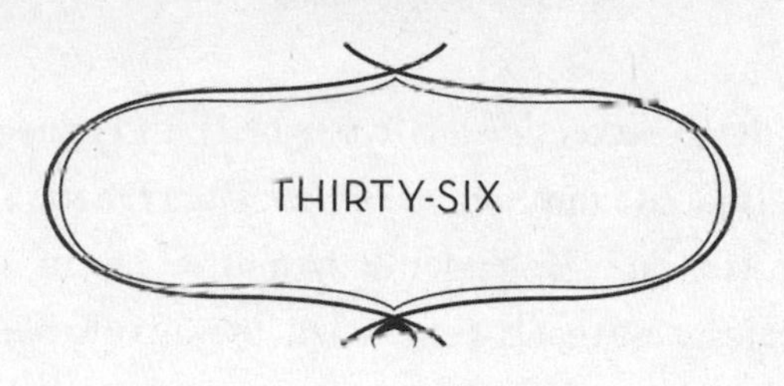

THIRTY-SIX

Meghan

After a night of fitful sleep, Meghan awoke with a heavy fog in her head. It took a moment to piece together the events of the previous night, but the pounding in her temples helped her along. The bartender's groping hands. Nick's entrance into the bar. The ride home. The way he kissed her forehead before he walked out.

The fact that her stomach still jumped at the memory of his nearness.

She hadn't come back here for this. The thought that she and Nick had anything left in their broken relationship verged on insanity.

Maybe she was just lonely.

The sound of the kids in the other room jolted her back to reality.

She sat up and looked around the bedroom. The windows faced the backyard. The early morning light pouring in, combined with the smell of fresh coffee, roused her from her tired state.

But how could she face those kids?

Meghan looked at the clock. Ten AM. Hopefully she'd slept off the remnants of the night before. She got up, still fully clothed. In the bathroom, she splashed cold water on her face, but it did nothing to disguise the dark circles under her eyes or the makeup she'd failed to remove before bed. She ran a brush through her hair and stared at her own reflection.

Regret, like a snake, twisted in her belly and squeezed. Alcohol would never hold the same appeal to her after rehab. The smell of it repulsed her, yet something about it had lured her in.

The hopelessness that had weaseled its way into her belly and set up shop, perhaps?

She forced herself not to dwell on it. She could beat herself up later.

In spite of the previous night, Nick had brought the kids over. An exercise in showing her what she was about to lose, perhaps?

The more time she spent with the kids, the harder it would be to let them go when he won them from her in court. And he would, especially after last night. She'd just gift wrapped them and handed them to Nick on a drunken silver platter. Some sick form of self-sabotage?

As she walked toward the sounds of life coming from the living room, she tuned in to the conversation.

"When's Mama getting up?" Nadia asked.

She expected a blanket "Mama worked hard last night" or something, but instead heard Nick clear his throat.

"Well, if she's sleeping late, she must need it, right?" He paused. "Finn, you okay, buddy?"

Finn's weak "uh-huh" kept Meghan from entering the room.

"What's wrong?" Nick must've moved closer to where their son sat. Probably near a corner or a wall. Withdrawn. Like his daddy.

"Those were bad pictures of Mommy."

Meghan covered her mouth with her hand, concealing a gasp. Her stomach felt hollow as she processed the words that came from her son's mouth. The shame of the day before whirled back and smacked at her like a tantrum-throwing toddler. Her son had been profoundly affected by her mistake. And she had no words to make that pain go away.

"You're right. And you deserve an explanation." Nick's voice stayed steady. Gentle.

"Why'd Mommy do that?"

"She's pretty upset about it, Finn," he said.

"Then why'd she let them put them in that magazine?"

"She didn't, buddy. Sometimes people put pictures like that in magazines because they know it'll sell more copies. They're trying to make your mommy look bad."

"But that's mean. Why would they do that?"

"I'm not sure," Nick said. "Some people like to remind us of our mistakes. I think it makes them feel better about their own mistakes."

Silence.

"You ever made a mistake?"

"I have," Nadia said, almost proudly.

"Me too," Finn said.

"Me three." Nick paused. "And Mommy too. But she's really sorry for those mistakes, so we need to forgive her."

"Why?"

"Because she needs to know we love her. Even if she makes mistakes."

"You love her too, Daddy?" Nadia had probably crawled up on his lap.

Meghan hesitated for too long, anticipating Nick's answer, then decided she'd rather not know. She walked around the corner, pretending she hadn't been listening at the door. "Morning, guys."

She smiled as the twins ran to her. Nadia hugged her around the knees, and Meghan stooped to give her a proper squeeze. Then she turned her full attention to her son. She stared at him, trying to read the thoughts behind his sad eyes. "How are ya, Finner?"

Campbell's words rushed back and Meghan imagined them—ten years from now—thinking she'd walked out on them because she didn't love them, because *they* weren't good enough.

"Good." Finn's eyes filled with tears, but he didn't cry. She hated herself for what she'd put them through.

Before she'd even known her son, she'd betrayed him by allowing the photos to be taken in the first place. She pulled him close and hugged him tight.

"I love you, little man," she said.

"Love you too, Mommy."

She looked up and caught Nick's gaze. His expression changed, but she couldn't read it.

She hated that she couldn't.

Finn pulled away. "Can I go down to the basement? Daddy said there are toys." His eyes widened with excitement.

"Sure you can." Meghan smiled.

"But whatever you get out, you have to put away," Nick called after them as they scurried down the stairs.

Meghan helped herself to a cup of coffee, then turned her attention to her ex-husband, who had moved into the eating area and now stared out the window. She stood a few feet away, following his gaze to the lake. A long dock stretched out several feet, and the lighthouse was easily visible from where she stood. With its red roof and black-and-white tower, the lighthouse had become a symbol of the small town, and it seemed fitting that it called sailors safely home.

Meghan wondered if Nick was her lighthouse.

She glanced at him. "I heard what you said."

He looked at her. "About . . ."

"The pictures. To Finn."

He looked away.

"Thank you." She watched a boat come into view and then disappear behind the trees. "Did you stay here last night?" She did a once-over of the house. Everything was in its place. Even her purse had been hung on a hook by the back door. He'd probably even cleaned out the vase she'd gotten sick in.

He nodded. "Then I got the kids this morning from your mom's and brought them here."

"Nick, I . . ."

"Your mom's coming over here in a little bit. I'll call you later to check on the kids."

She nodded, but her throat tightened, cutting off her voice. She followed him toward the front door.

Out on the porch, she put an arm on his to stop him. She'd force herself to speak if she had to. She inhaled, her heart racing.

Calm down.

"You're a really good dad, Nick. I hope you know that."

She wondered if he'd succeeded in quashing the pain. Pain she'd caused. Words she'd spoken in anger and had never meant. Words that had wedged their way between them like a vise. Words she could never take back.

He turned away from her and didn't stop till he reached his truck.

She stood on the porch, watching as he left, willing him to meet her gaze just once before he pulled away.

He didn't look back.

THIRTY-SEVEN

Lila

Inside City Hall, the air conditioner hummed a constant tune. Lila located the room where the committee met, took a deep breath and walked inside. She couldn't help but feel that Mama had forced the poor committee members to allow her to take a leadership role. She didn't expect a warm welcome.

The air turned humid as she met the pairs of eyes seated around the table.

"Miss Adler." A familiar voice filled the cavernous room. Patton Gallagher. The man seemed to be everywhere.

Then it dawned on her that Mama had pressured her there.

"It's Mrs. Olson, actually," Lila said.

"Of course. Come on in and join us. We're excited to have you on board. The entertainment has been something of a thorn in our side. We hear you may have a solution."

Lila looked at the empty chair beside him and forced herself to smile in spite of her racing pulse. "I'm not exactly sure about that."

Patton waited until she took her seat before he sat back down.

She spent the meeting keenly aware of his attention toward her, the way he purposed to bring her up to speed. He considered her—and she realized that she enjoyed the attention. At one point, when he wasn't looking, Lila studied his profile, mesmerized by his handsome looks and dignified stature. The man intended to win her affections, and if she wasn't careful, he might just succeed.

Afterward, the others on the committee hurried out, mingling and talking, everyone excited at the prospect of a Meghan Rhodes concert headlining the events of Sweethaven's Labor Day Festivities. They'd finally celebrate the end of the season in style.

Lila explained that Meghan was very busy, but the committee explained that they needed her. Tourism was important to Sweethaven, and the more people they could get in town, the better for the local businesses that had been hit especially hard over the winter.

She had been challenged to make this happen. They were counting on her.

Lila stood, hoping to make a quick getaway, but Patton reached out and put a hand on her arm. "Can you stay behind a moment?"

She nodded.

When the room emptied, Patton turned his attention to Lila and smiled. "It's nice to see you here, though I had hoped the next time we met, it might be in a less . . . public setting." He took a step closer to her and she felt her shoulders tense at his nearness. He must've noticed because his smile turned to a smirk and he took another step. "Do I make you nervous?"

Patton had none of the schoolboy charm she'd seen in Tom earlier that day. He oozed confidence. A woman would be foolish to fall for his advances—he'd clearly practiced them enough to become a pro.

Yet her palms had gone clammy and she knew her face was flushed at the very idea of him. She'd longed for this kind of attention from Tom, and it had taken the revelation of his betrayal to get it. It hardly seemed legitimate.

"Of course not."

"Have you considered my invitation?"

Lila met his eyes and put on a beauty pageant smile. "I think it's best to wait until Mama and Daddy have left, don't you?"

"Your mother was the one who first brought you to my attention all those years ago. Said we'd make a 'handsome couple.'"

Lila frowned. "When did she say that?"

Patton shuffled some papers around on the table, piling everything on top of a leather portfolio. "A long time ago."

"Before I was married?"

He picked up his things and took a few steps away from her, toward the door. She followed. "I suppose it must've been."

Lila's eyes narrowed.

He sighed. "It was a long time ago, Lila. Before you and Tom made it official. She thought if I stepped in, maybe you'd leave him—realize you could do better."

"She's got a lot of nerve." Mama had always had it in for her and Tom—from day one. The very idea that she'd tried to pawn her off on Patton Gallagher all those years ago sent her blood pressure through the roof.

Maybe Mama had intervened again. Maybe that's why Patton had been so persistent.

He stopped and faced her, his eyes intent. "She was right. When I saw you that first day in the coffee shop, I knew I should've listened to her."

Lila stared at him. "What stopped you?"

"You had that lovesick look about you."

Her mouth went dry. "And now?"

He shrugged. "Now that look's gone."

Lila couldn't concentrate on anything but Patton's intent eyes locked on to her own. He took a step closer to her and brushed a stray hair away from her face. "If you aren't ready, I'll wait until you are."

His hand lingered on her face, the warmth of it radiating down her arms, all the way to her fingertips. His eyes perused her face, hanging on her lips for too long.

As the seconds ticked by, she felt her defenses weaken. He shifted closer to her, and she swallowed, bracing herself for the newness—the danger—that his kiss promised.

She inched toward him, but as she did, the sound of the door opening behind her startled her and she knocked the portfolio from his hands, sending papers flying all over the old wooden floor. A young woman who'd been in their meeting stood in the doorway, a surprised look on her face.

"Did you find a blue purse in here?"

Patton glanced at Lila, whose face, she was sure, was fiery red at that moment. "I don't think so."

The woman frowned. "Maybe I didn't bring it with me. Thanks anyway."

She walked out and Lila let out the breath she'd been holding in from the second she realized this man who wasn't her husband intended to kiss her. And she had intended to let him.

"That was exciting," Patton said, his face lit in amusement.

"That was terrible. Now she's going to tell everyone what she just saw." She handed Patton the stack of papers she'd fetched from the floor.

"And what did she see exactly?"

Lila looked away, embarrassment settling on her shoulders.

"You're blushing."

She met his eyes. "I need to get back home."

"To your fake husband?" Patton caught her by the hand and kept her from going.

She opened her mouth to respond, but he prevented her rebuttal with a kiss, unexpected and well-placed. His lips covered hers, stunning her silent.

He pulled away and met her eyes, then smiled. "Sorry about that—but you can't blame me for being smitten with you." He brushed her hair away from her face, studying her with an unnerving intensity. "You're so beautiful."

Lila cleared her throat and pulled herself from his arms. "I'm a married woman."

He reached up and touched her face. "I'm not used to people telling me 'no.' You should know that."

Lila's face heated and she knew she walked a dangerous tightrope. She'd done nothing to stop his advances and now he'd set his sights on her. As much as that scared her, it excited her too—which maybe scared her even more.

"I should go."

The sound of her own heels clicking on the wooden floor accompanied her out the door and on down the cement stairs of the City Hall building. Lila walked to her car, wondering what had just happened, how she'd allowed it and what to make of the fact that she liked it so very much.

She'd just been kissed by a man who wasn't her husband—and the only thing she wondered was when it would happen again.

Adele

Adele drove across town, her radio humming low in the background. She waved to the passersby, neighbors she knew by name—most of whom had sampled her cooking at one point or another.

She watched as a man hung a sign advertising the Labor Day Festival on the side of a street post. Already?

Where had the summer gone?

Meghan could do well here, she thought. She'd gotten too much of the world in her and needed a place like Sweethaven to rest and recover. Unfortunately, the odds of Meghan hanging around here were about as great as Adele getting her own cooking show on the Food Network.

She parked the car in front of an old cottage on the west side of town. With a phone call to Luke, she'd learned it was where Nick spent his days working.

She pulled behind the familiar pickup truck and stared at the house. Nick had renovated more homes in Sweethaven than she could count. This one sat right on the lake, small and quaint, but with "good bones," as people said. The old bungalow needed a healthy dose of TLC, and Adele knew Nick would certainly oblige.

Her heart picked up its pace as she turned the car off, said a prayer for wisdom, and begged God to give her the words she needed to talk to the boy. She couldn't risk upsetting Nick—she didn't want to jeopardize her time with the twins, but something had been wrong with him Saturday morning when he picked the kids up, and she suspected her daughter had something to do with it.

Only neither one of them was talking. Go figure.

She walked inside, the smell of sawdust in the air. A quick glance around the house turned up no sign of Nick and sent her deeper inside.

A man wearing a hard hat passed by. He had a tool belt around his waist and carried a drill. "It's really not safe in here, ma'am."

"I'm looking for Nick Rhodes." Adele stepped over a pile of two-by-fours.

The man pointed down a hallway. "Back there. But be careful."

Her pulse quickened as she walked down the hallway. After spending hours in prayer over the situation, Adele came to the conclusion that it was time to do what her gut told her to do—protect those kids at any cost. Even if the cost was her own time with them. Still, that didn't make what she had to do any easier.

A doorway in the back led to an open room, the master bedroom, full of sunlight but otherwise empty, save one man. Nick. He stared out the window, his arms crossed over his chest.

She cleared her throat.

When he turned and saw her, his face fell.

"I'm sorry to bother you at work," she said.

He gave her a slight wave as if to tell her it was okay.

There had been a day when she'd known Nick almost as well as she knew her own children. Evenings spent at her dinner table, then out back with Teddy. They'd taken him in—and loved every second of it. But she couldn't claim to know him anymore. Still, Adele recognized a troubled face when she saw it. She took a couple of steps closer until she stood next to him. Together, they stared out the window in silence as a few long moments passed.

"What's buggin' you?" She dared a glance up at his stony eyes.

He blinked twice.

"Remember when you used to talk to me? I can remember more than once you came over looking for my daughter, and while you waited we'd have the best chats."

Nick brought a hand to his chin and covered his mouth, still not looking at her.

"You must remember. I'd bribe you with cookies to tell me why you had that look on your face. Same look you have now." She remembered all too well the pain he suffered at his father's hand.

Nick raised an eyebrow. "Did you bring me cookies?"

She reached into her bag and pulled out a container. "Freshly baked milk chocolate chip. Your favorite."

He took them from her as a smile wandered across his face and then quickly disappeared. "It's hard having her back here is all."

Adele nodded.

Nick sighed. "I picked her up from the bar Friday night." He finally met her eyes.

Lord, no. Meghan had been clean for so long. Surely she hadn't thrown it all away . . . again?

Maybe Sweethaven *wasn't* the best place for her daughter.

"I know it's the last thing you want to hear, Adele, but she's using again. Or at least drinking again."

Adele stared out the window and clenched her teeth. How did this happen? She hadn't raised her kids to become alcoholics. Or drug addicts. Or absent mothers.

But Meghan had always had a troubled way about her. She'd always kept everyone at arm's length—especially Teddy. He'd tried to be the father Meghan needed, but she'd always pined for her real father, a man who'd broken her heart more than once.

Adele shook the sad stories aside and focused on the present.

Nick held the open container of cookies out to her.

She took one and ate it. He ate three.

"I'm worried about your kids, Nick." Adele glanced at him.

He frowned. "Why?"

She exhaled. "When I've taken them home, they've begged me not to make them stay. With your mother."

Nick's expression changed to one of surprise. "They did?"

Adele turned away and pushed the image of the two of them in her backseat, begging her not to go, out of her mind. She'd juggled things so much for weeks now, but she'd been wrong not to say anything to Nick. "They said she's mean when you're not there. She locks them in their room. Won't let them eat. Other things too."

"Other things?"

"I don't think she hits them, but she's forceful. And maybe doesn't realize how strong she is."

Nick closed his eyes. "She told me you came by weeks ago. That you want the kids more often and you'd do whatever it took to get them." He looked at Adele. "She said I shouldn't believe you. That you and Meghan were planning to take them."

Adele frowned. "It's no secret I want to see the kids more. But I'm not trying to steal them away. Nick, you know better than anyone what your mother is capable of."

He looked away.

"I know you want to believe she's different now, but I don't want those kids to suffer like you did."

"With all due respect, Adele, you don't know anything about my suffering."

She turned and faced him. "We both know that's not true."

Nick stared out the window.

"I'm not telling you this to hurt you. I'm telling you this because I think you're a great daddy. And those kids deserve to be happy."

"Did you tell Meghan?"

Adele knew it would hurt Meghan to find out she knew this about Violet and hadn't told her, but she wasn't convinced her daughter was going to fight fair. She couldn't fuel the custody fire, and Nick was good for those kids. He simply didn't have all the facts. The question was, what would he do now that he did? "I didn't, but Nick, if you go through with this custody thing—keeping Meghan away from the kids—I will tell her."

Nick's glare hardened. "I should get back to work."

He walked out of the room and left her standing alone.

She quietly slipped out of the cottage. In the safety of her car, she rested her head on the seat.

"God, what is going on?" she whispered. "Everyone I love is hurting right now. Show me how to help them."

But in response, all she heard was deafening silence.

THIRTY-NINE

Meghan

Meghan sat on the back patio and watched her children in the tree house. The brick patio was a perfect square, just slightly elevated above the rest of the yard. On it was a set of metal outdoor furniture with thick, red canvas cushions and striped pillows. Meghan might not love the silence inside the big lake house, but she could appreciate the peacefulness she found in the backyard.

After getting the silent treatment for over a week, Nick surprised her when he called and asked if she wanted to see the kids. He had to work, and rather than leave them home, maybe they'd have fun at the rental house.

Meghan didn't argue. She needed the distraction. Someone had caught her drunken escapade on video and posted it online. Duncan showed up ranting about how he couldn't believe she'd do this to him and how was he ever going to fix it?

She was becoming a liability and she knew it. How many more chances would she get?

Red heads bobbed around in the tree house window as squeals of laughter resounded through the backyard. Meghan's copy of *People* fell off her lap and snapped on the ground. She reached over and picked it up but kept an eye on the tree house.

Finn walked out of the little house onto the deck and leaned over the side.

Meghan gasped. "Finn, be careful."

"I'm fine, Mommy! Look!" He put his hands over the ledge and leaned forward.

Meghan stood. "Finn. Stop. You're scaring me. I need you to stay in the house or come back down." Why did there have to be a tree house? Why not a little play shed on the ground where she knew they'd be safe?

He glanced up at her, big blue eyes wide.

"I'm sorry, hon," she said. "Just be careful up there, okay?"

He smiled. "Don't worry about me. I'm a warrior." He held up a play sword and went back inside the tree house. Relief seeped from her every pore.

"There you are!" Lila's Southern-tinged voice carried down the hill, and Meghan glanced away from the kids just long enough to wave at her. "I've been knocking."

"I didn't hear you." Meghan grinned.

"It's so nice to know you're still the same old sarcastic Meghan." Lila hugged her, then sat in the wicker chair next to her and smiled. "You have the kids."

"I do. And I'm a wreck. I keep thinking one of them is going to fall out of the tree."

Lila shook her head. "You're too hard on yourself, Meg."

Meghan didn't bother to disagree. Lila might not know the truth, but Meghan sure did. "What brings you over here?"

Lila cleared her throat. "A proposition."

"Uh-oh."

"No, it's a win-win, I think. You might even love the idea." Lila smiled.

"Let's hear it."

"You know the big Labor Day Festival is just a few weeks away, and as it turns out, I am in charge of this year's entertainment."

"No way, Lila." Meghan's thoughts rolled back to that awful Friday night. No way could she take another stage in Sweethaven. What would those people say?

"You haven't even let me finish. I propose a benefit concert, all proceeds would go to Sweethaven, and you could invite all your paparazzi buddies to come publicize it and you'll come off as the goodwill queen of the century."

"Sweethaven's not in any danger, is it?"

"I guess not, but Patton says that tourism is down and we've been hit hard by this whole economic crisis."

"Patton?"

Lila tried—and failed—to stifle a smile.

Meghan stared at her. "Lila Charise Adler Olson, do not tell me you're leaving that exquisite man God gave you."

Lila's eyebrows rose.

"Yes, you and Tom. I've always wished for what you guys have."

Lila scoffed. "I've always wanted to be like you and Nick."

They stared at each other for a few seconds and then both of them laughed. "Maybe we're both delusional," Meghan said.

"Not delusional about this concert. It's a great way to get your name out there in a positive light and sell some records. I know you've got a new album out. I keep waiting for my autographed copy to come in the mail, but so far, I'm out of luck." Lila shot her a look.

"All right."

"All right you'll do it?"

"All right I'll get you an autographed copy." Meghan stared at Lila as her face fell. Maybe it would be enough to get Duncan off her back. A charitable concert for her hometown? He'd love the idea. *If* she could muster the courage. She thought back to his words about her sabotaging herself and did she really want out of the country music industry for good?

Her heart dropped at the idea. It was all she had left. "*And* yes, I'll do the concert."

Lila squealed and pulled a poster out of her bag, thrusting it in Meghan's direction. "I'm so excited, Meg. You will not regret it, I promise. I'll get you all the details later this week."

The poster announced the benefit concert, and on the right-hand side, a photo of Meghan faded into the background. The words "Sweethaven's Biggest Star" were at the top.

"You were pretty sure I'd say yes."

Lila smiled. "I'm very persuasive." She stood and Meghan almost hated to see her go.

"Leaving so soon?"

"Dinner with Tom." Lila held up a hand. "Don't ask."

"I wouldn't dream of it. I'll see you later."

After Lila left, Meghan turned her attention back to the kids, only to be distracted by the sound of footsteps again minutes later.

"Back so soon?"

But when she turned, she found Violet standing on the back patio, arms crossed over her chest, sour expression on her face. Beside her, a Sweethaven police officer stood, hands on his belt. Did he actually have a gun?

"Violet, what are you doing here?"

"I knew your mother was up to something." Violet skulked around the perimeter of the patio, circling Meghan like a vulture eyeing its prey. "I told you she'd stolen them, Sheriff."

"What are you talking about?" Meghan stood.

"I'm not going to stand for this"—she waved her hand in the direction of the twins—"going on behind my back. Your mother was on a very short leash, and I knew she was going behind my back to make sure you got time with the twins. But as you can see here, a judge agrees with me that you are unfit to spend any alone time with these two."

Meghan glanced up at the twins. She could see their little faces peering up over the window ledge of the tree house.

"Maybe we could go inside, Violet."

"In your fancy mansion? No thanks." Violet narrowed her eyes. "The kids are coming with me."

Heat rushed up Meghan's neck and settled on her face. It took all she had not to smack the woman across the face. "They're *my* kids, Violet."

"This emergency protective order says that you have to turn them over. After your little performance at the bar Friday night, Judge Timmer felt compelled to give us temporary custody—until this can all be worked out once and for all."

"Sheriff, Nick brought the kids over here this morning. Do you think he would've done that if he was worried about their safety?"

The sheriff looked at Violet, who frowned. "He did not. We're filing for sole custody. He would never jeopardize our case like that—you've done nothing but cause trouble since you got here, and thanks to modern technology we have plenty of evidence to prove it."

"I'm afraid she's right, Mrs. Rhodes." The sheriff almost looked sad. "The kids are going to have to come with us."

"No. You can't do this. Just let me call Nick. He'll tell you he brought them to me." Shoot. She left her phone inside.

Violet took a few steps closer and got right in Meghan's face. "Don't you dare fight me on this, Meghan. You haven't begun to see what I can do to make your life a living hell."

Meghan recoiled, her heart racing.

"Kids, come on down, you're coming home with me." Violet's screech sent the kids lower in the tree house, their heads disappearing behind the window.

"You can't do this."

Meghan walked toward the tree house, but the sheriff held up his hand. "For now, this is what has to happen. You can file a complaint or take it up with the courts."

"Let me at least call my lawyer," Meghan said, wishing James would magically appear by her side.

"Give it up, Meghan. Everyone knows what a mess you are—there's no way you can take care of two little kids."

"What's wrong with you, Violet? As I remember it, you've never much cared for children in your house." Meghan wiped her sweaty palms on her shorts and stiffened, willing herself not to back down in spite of the black behind Violet's eyes.

"We all know what happens when children are left in your care." Violet's stare drilled into Meghan.

Meghan took a step back as Violet yelled again for the kids to come down.

"Do we have to, Mama?" Nadia's eyes showed pure terror, and Meghan's mind flashed image after image of Nick's childhood pain. She'd always assumed his father's abuse outweighed Violet's, but now she wasn't so sure.

"Come on, now, kids," the sheriff said, motioning for them to come down.

Meghan backed away, panicked as she watched Violet pull the kids from the tree house ladder to the ground. Images of Alex being pulled from the water invaded her mind.

Just like that day at the lake, Meghan stood by, helpless to save a child from certain danger. Only this time, the children were hers.

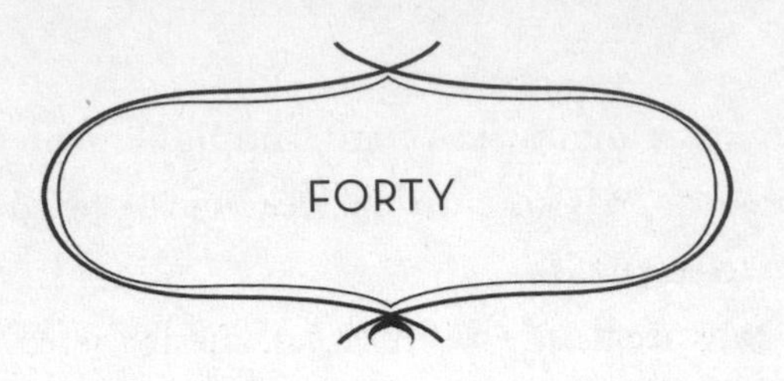

Adele

Adele's heart sank down into her belly as she meandered up the driveway toward Meghan's house. She'd taken her time getting there, wanting her daughter to have some alone time with the kids, but now that she'd arrived, panic washed over her.

A mother knows when something is wrong.

Two other cars sat in the driveway next to Meghan's rental. What on earth?

Adele pounded on the front door, peeking in the curtained window. A man on a cell phone pulled the door open. The same man that had come into the café with Meghan. Were they an item?

"Can I help you?"

"You can tell me what you're doing in my daughter's house." Adele pushed past him. "Meghan?"

Adele followed the sound of voices to the kitchen, where she saw Meghan sitting at the table and her manager, Duncan, pacing the floor and talking on his cell phone.

"Meghan? What's going on?" She rushed to the table and sat next to her daughter, whose face looked puffy and tear-stained.

"You shouldn't be here, Mama. Just go."

"Where are the kids?"

"We're handling it, Mrs. Barber." The slick-dressed man who'd let her in stood between them now. "We'll call you if there's anything new to report."

"You most certainly will not call me if there's something new to report. You'll tell me what in creation is going on over here." She crossed her arms.

The man glanced at Meghan, then back at her. He launched into some tirade about how Violet had come over with the sheriff and taken the kids. Just like that.

"Can she do that?"

"She had an emergency protective order. Judge Timmons."

"Timmons. That little weasel."

"Mama, do you think I do this on purpose?" Meghan asked after a few long moments of silence. Her voice filled with sadness.

"What do you mean?"

"I ruin every chance I have of being happy. All I've done is make one mistake after another, but when that woman yanked Finn from that tree house, I knew." Meghan turned to her. "Did you know, Mama? About Violet?"

Adele looked away. "I'm sorry, Meghan."

Meghan shook her head, fury in her eyes. "You're always saying you're sorry, Mama, but your actions tell a different story. My kids are in danger and no one told me about it. Does Nick know?"

Adele raised a hand—a meager attempt to calm her daughter down. "He doesn't, hon. Or he didn't. I told him what I suspected this very morning—"

"You told Nick but you didn't tell me?" Meghan's voice broke and she turned away. "I need you to leave, Mama."

Adele felt her jaw go slack, but she had no words—nothing to defend her actions, choosing to handle things with Violet on her own, without involving Meghan at all.

She'd wanted to avoid an all-out war between Meghan and Nick, but the only thing she'd succeeded in doing was driving the wedge between her and her daughter even deeper.

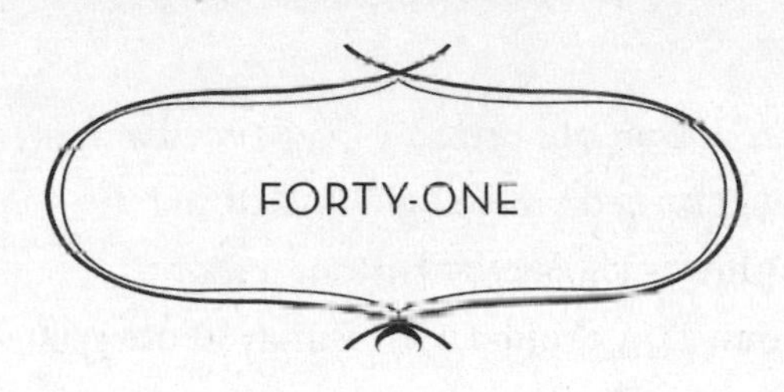

Lila

Lila stared at herself in the mirror, aware of the fluttering in her stomach. As she applied a little more makeup than usual, she thought of Tom. He wanted things to be like they were. Before.

Before he learned that he was Campbell's father. Before having a baby had become her sole purpose for living. The moment when he'd inadvertently denied her what she needed.

She'd blamed him for that, hadn't she? After all this time, she only now realized how unfair that had been.

The date had been part of their arrangement—a way to thank Tom for doing her the favor of staying at the lake house. She owed him that much at least. Especially since it looked like her parents had decided to stay through the Labor Day Festival. How would she survive three more weeks under the weight of her own deception?

A shakiness worked its way through her belly as Lila slipped into her black cocktail dress, the sleeveless one with the high belt that showed off her figure and legs. She zipped it up, found her shoes, and studied herself in the free-standing mirror in the corner of her childhood bedroom. She leaned in for a closer look. Crow's feet. Laugh lines. They were faint, but she could see them developing.

Reminders of the years she'd wasted.

After a fresh coat of lipstick, Lila glanced at her reflection one more time, then turned off the light and closed the door, willing the insecurity to stay locked away—just for a night.

Downstairs, Tom chatted with Daddy about golf or some other nonsense. Lila descended the stairway without the fanfare that used to greet her. No longer a beauty queen competing for a crown, she didn't know what she was supposed to be. She felt plain and out of place in her own skin.

But when Tom turned and met her eyes, he set her at ease without saying a word. The look on his face told her he more than approved of her appearance. Her cheeks heated at his attention, though it embarrassed her to even think such a thing.

Lila caught Mama's raised brow as she stood in the doorway staring at Tom. Her look had judgment written all over it.

"You look beautiful." Tom walked toward her, car keys in hand. He'd dressed in his gray suit, blue button-down, and silver tie with blue flecks. His blue eyes glimmered in spite of the dim light in the lake house. His looks had only improved with age—it seemed unfair.

Lila turned the bracelet around on her wrist and looked away.

"Should we get going?" Tom smiled at her, offering her his hand.

Outside, Lila welcomed the coolness of the August evening. Thanks to the lake, even the hottest days could turn into perfect evenings, and soon the leaves would turn and it would be autumn.

She inhaled, willing away the constant need for her mother's approval. Tom stepped ahead of her and opened the car door. Before she got in, she met his eyes—kind and hopeful.

They drove down Main Street, past the gallery and the café and out toward the edge of town. Rosatti's was in the country, up on a hill with a fantastic view of Lake Michigan. It would make for a romantic, if predictable, reconciliation.

The thought sent her mind spinning. What would she say? Could she take him back? She'd stowed the divorce papers away in a drawer at the lake house, but how could she give them to him now after all he'd done for her?

When Tom turned into the driveway of Frado's—a little family-owned pizza joint about ten minutes away from Rosatti's, Lila realized predictable wasn't on the menu.

She faced him. "What are you doing?"

"Eating dinner. Isn't that the plan?" He smiled and got out of the car, leaving her staring at the hole-in-the-wall restaurant. Despite the smell of tomato and garlic that wafted in the car as soon as he opened the door, Frado's hardly appealed to her—especially since she thought Tom was trying to impress her. The red sign on the plain brown building had to be two decades old. It simply read: Frado's. In dire need of a fresh coat of paint—or a complete overhaul—Frado's Pizza had no charm, no class and no promise.

When Tom opened the door and offered his hand, Lila shoved her disappointment into her purse with her cell phone. She let him help her out but stumbled a bit to walk upright on gravel in her best pair of black Jimmy Choos.

"Are we actually eating dinner here?" Lila asked as he pulled the door open.

"Of course."

They walked inside. The floor slanted, as if someone had made a mistake when laying the building's foundation. She held on to Tom's arm.

One glance around Frado's and Lila had more reason for concern. "There's no one else here."

A man walked out of the kitchen, wearing a plain white apron around his waist and a wide smile pasted on his face.

"Good evening, *mia bella*," he said.

Lila forced a smile.

"What's with the phony accent?" Tom asked.

The man narrowed his eyes at Tom, and Lila thought her husband had offended him.

"Come here, you old lug." The man chortled a gruff, Italian-style laugh, then pulled Tom into a man-style bear hug.

"Angelo, this is my beautiful wife Lila," Tom said.

Angelo took her hand and kissed the top of her fingers. "Tommy-boy always said he struck gold with you—I guess he wasn't kidding."

"You've got a table for us?" Tom asked.

Lila bit back a smart remark and they followed Angelo to a table near the back. The fireplace at the center of the room looked more like an accident than an asset. Its brown painted brick was an eyesore in an already dismal room.

Once Angelo had gone, she stared at her husband, who perused the menu as if everything were perfectly normal.

"Tell me this is a joke," she said.

His eyes darted upward and met hers somewhere above the deep-fried cheese balls and the Chicago-style pizza. "I never joke about Frado's."

"Even when I was a kid I didn't eat here."

Tom's eyes returned to the menu. "That's not true."

Lila glanced around the room. On every table, seventies-inspired orange hurricanes held faux candles that didn't so much twinkle as glow. "I think I'd remember."

"Do you want to get a pizza?"

"I don't eat pizza."

Their perfect date—his one chance to prove to her he loved her—and it wasn't off to a great start. The thought stung in a way she hadn't prepared for. If he couldn't properly win her back, then she had no decision to make. Her disappointment surprised her.

She refused to look at the menu. Angelo returned with their drinks, and Tom asked for a few more minutes.

"Take as long as you need. You are my only customers tonight." Angelo walked back toward the kitchen whistling.

"How can he possibly know that?"

"Because I paid him to close the place." Tom didn't meet her eyes.

Lila scoffed. "*This* place?"

Tom set the menu down. "I hoped you'd remember."

She frowned, scanning his eyes for clue.

"Why don't you like it here? It's cozy. It's charming."

Lila folded her hands on the table and let out a sigh. "I thought we were going to Rosatti's."

Tom lifted his chin and watched her. "Ohhhh. I see. You had tonight all planned out."

Lila brushed her hair away from her face. "I guess. I thought—oh, never mind."

Silence hung between them like a kite in need of a gust of wind.

"I admit, it's not the most obvious choice," Tom said. "But I did choose it for a reason."

"To help out your buddy Angelo?"

Tom set his menu on the table. "I was sitting at this very table the first time I ever saw you."

Lila blinked—three times in quick succession—as if that would help her process the words he'd just said. "What do you mean? We met in the park. We were eleven."

He shook his head. "I was ten. I'd just gone swimming in the lake. It was Friday night, and every Friday night was pizza at Frado's. Family tradition."

"Why didn't you ever tell me?" Lila tilted her head and watched as her husband talked. Somehow, he added life to the otherwise dreary room.

"One night, in June, we sat right here at this very table when in walks a pretty blonde girl with Jane Anderson and her family. She wore a pink dress and a pink headband, and I believe every single hair was perfectly in place. I stared at that girl the entire time she stood in the carryout line with Jane and her father—and then she left—walked right out the door.

"Afterward, all I could think about was how I could meet that beautiful blonde girl with the pink headband."

Lila sipped her water, hoping that would remedy the dryness in her mouth. "Are you making this up because you know I won't remember?"

Tom grinned. "I promise you I'm not."

"How can you possibly remember that?" Lila studied his face.

"You didn't so much as glance in my direction. The day we actually met in the park I was a nervous wreck."

Lila's mind reeled. She'd been so wrong. About everything, but especially about Tom.

Angelo returned, still showing off his wide grin. "Ready to order?"

Lila glanced across the table at Tom. "We'll have a Chicago-style stuffed crust pizza."

Angelo laughed. "I love a lady who isn't afraid to eat."

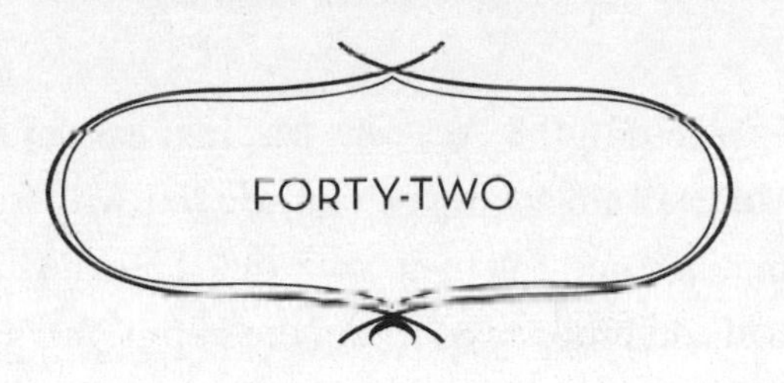

Meghan

When Nick pulled up several hours later, James advised Meghan not to let him in.

"This is going to get ugly, Meghan. Whether he likes it or not, his mother acted on his behalf, so we need to treat him the same way we'd treat her."

"I can't do that, James."

"You're going to have to. Either you tell him to get out of here, or I will."

She held up a hand to calm him down and headed out the front door, where she met Nick just as he was charging up the porch. Why was he here anyway? Hadn't they made their point getting the police involved?

"Where are the kids?" Nick's question took her off guard, sounding almost accusatory.

"Didn't she bring them to you?" Panic wound its way to the pit of her stomach.

"Who?"

"Your mom."

Nick's eyes widened. "My mom has the kids?"

Meghan nodded and recounted the whole story. "My lawyer said I can't talk to you, Nick. He's preparing for battle in there."

Mama appeared in the doorway. Meghan had let her stay after James said Mama could end up being their star witness.

"Meghan, I had nothing to do with this. I had no idea. . . ." Nick took his hat off and propped a foot on the steps. "You should've told me sooner, Adele."

Panic splashed across Mama's face. "I . . . I wasn't positive!"

Nick started to walk away. "I've got to find them." Meghan hurried after him, blocking his path back to the escape vehicle.

He stared at her and the stories came rushing back to her—stories of Nick's own childhood, stories he'd shared with her in the dark when he felt safe. They'd come to her in fits and spurts, mostly when she didn't expect them, but it proved that even as a grown man, Nick's upbringing still haunted him.

She saw the kid she'd known all those years ago—trying to be the strong, tough guy, thinking he could hide his fear from someone who knew him as well as she did. "I thought she changed after my dad died."

"I'm sure they're fine, darlin'. She probably took them for ice cream or somethin'." Mama's voice pulled Meghan back to reality, and she saw Nick shut down.

"You need to go, Mama," Meghan said, facing her.

"It's not her fault," Nick said.

"It is. It's the same thing that happened after the accident. Mama believed everyone but me. If she'd told me, I wouldn't have let your mom take them."

"But you would've come after me, right?" Nick's face fell. "And I wouldn't have blamed you."

"Let's talk about it later. Right now we need to find the kids."

Back in the house, they called everyone they knew. For Meghan, that meant one phone call to Luke and another to Lila, who didn't answer. She left her a quick message and hung up, waiting while Nick explained to friend after friend that he needed to locate his mother. He'd said the words "family emergency" to every one of them, not wanting to cause panic, but panicked was exactly how Meghan felt.

The more calls he made, the more worried she became.

He hung up and stared at her. "I've called everyone. No one's seen her."

"What now?"

He shook his head and walked toward the window, staring out over the lake. Beside him, Meghan slipped her hand in his. She felt his eyes on her, but she didn't turn in his direction.

"I never wanted full custody."

She faced him, searching his eyes.

"It was the only way I could get you back here." He looked down. "I know you, Meg. You decided a long time ago you weren't good enough for those kids, but I know better. I knew if I got you back here, you'd realize how much you love them. You'd realize how much they need you. How much we need you."

She blinked back fresh tears.

Nick's phone rang, jolting them both back to the matter at hand. His eyes widened as he mumbled incoherent sounds of agreement and then said, "Yes, got it. Thanks for letting me know." He grabbed his keys from the counter and met her eyes. "You coming?"

"Where?"

"To get our kids."

Meghan's mind raced as she followed Nick to the truck. She whispered a silent prayer, begging God to keep them safe. *I'll do anything, Lord. I'll stay clean—for good this time. I'll finally be the mother You want me to be. Just keep them safe.*

She hopped in the truck and pulled the door closed behind her, but Nick sat there unmoving.

"What are you waiting for?"

"Can we pray?"

Meghan's face filled with heat. Nick took her hands in his, bowed his head and closed his eyes. She watched as he inhaled, his exhale shaky.

"God, these kids are our whole life—"

Meghan closed her eyes, wishing she could agree with that statement, but knowing for her, it wasn't true. She hadn't given them enough of herself—and she'd filled her whole life with so many other things.

"Right now, we put them in Your hands. I pray You keep them safe. I pray You help us get to them without any problems. And God, I pray for my mom. . . ." He paused, and Meghan opened her eyes to see if he'd finished. But he still sat, head bowed, eyes closed, his shoulders shaking.

She didn't have the words and she wasn't qualified to pray, so Meghan leaned in and pulled him into a tight hug. "God knows, Nick."

Nick held her for a long moment and then pulled back, wiping his eyes. He started the truck and drove down the driveway.

Inside, Meghan replayed his words over and over again, begging God to step in where she was weak.

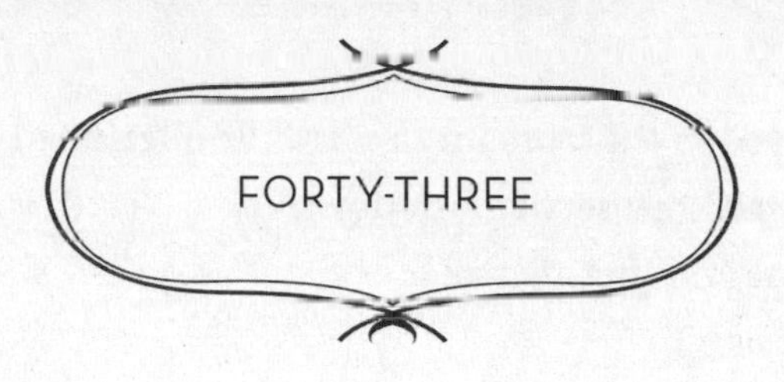

Lila

"I haven't missed much about Sweethaven, but I've missed Frado's," Tom said as he served Lila a slice, the cheese hanging in long threads, waiting to be cut with the corner of the metal spatula.

"I haven't had pizza in years," Lila said.

In spite of Lila's first impression of Angelo, he'd turned out to be the perfect host. Attentive when they needed him, but unobtrusive when they didn't. He'd brought their pizza and a bottle of red wine, along with two wineglasses, and then disappeared.

Lila cut her pizza into bite-sized pieces. "You really don't miss Sweethaven?"

He shrugged. "Sometimes, I guess. There're things I realize I love, now that I'm back."

As they ate, their conversation surprised Lila. Their dinners at home were nearly silent and fully unbearable, but something had changed between them. Almost as if their near-divorce had opened both their eyes. Lila knew that while Tom had betrayed her, he hadn't been the only one who'd let their marriage become commonplace. She'd chosen to run further away from him with every baby they lost—and while she hated to admit it, she blamed him for her inability to become a mother.

Finding out about Campbell proved the problem wasn't his. She'd been unfair, and her love had been conditional.

"I hope you saved room for dessert." Tom grinned at her.

"Oh my, no." Lila set her fork down and covered her empty plate with her napkin. After two slices of stuffed pizza, she'd had more than her fill.

"Angelo made us one of his famous cheesecakes. With strawberries."

Lila's eyes widened. "Can I get mine to go?"

Tom laughed. "Yes. I'm buying the whole thing. We can take some to your parents."

"Mama's not going to eat cheesecake."

Angelo returned with a pizza box and the check, and handed Tom a set of keys. "Be careful with her. She's my baby."

Tom smiled. "I owe you one."

Lila's eyes darted back and forth between them.

Tom stacked their cheesecake atop the pizza box and led them out the door.

She followed him to the car, but he didn't open her door for her. Instead, he opened the back door, set the food inside, then locked the car and offered her his hand. "What are we doing?"

"You'll see."

They walked behind Frado's toward a steep wooden staircase that led down to the lake.

At the bottom of the stairs, in the water, sat a big white boat. On the side of it was the word *Rosie*.

"Are we going on that boat?" Lila stopped.

Tom held up the keys and jangled them. He smiled.

The sun had begun to sink lower in the sky—the long summer days working to their advantage.

"I haven't been on a boat in years," Lila said.

Tom walked out on the dock, stepped inside the boat, then turned and offered Lila a hand.

As he started the engine and pulled away from the dock, her stomach jumped, her mind whirling back in time—to days of simplicity, when she and the girls took Daddy's boat out on the lake and spent hours anchored at the sand bar where they could get the best sun. Inevitably, Tom and his friends always showed up—and she never doubted for a second that he directed his attention to her. He'd been a part of her life almost from the beginning.

Throwing that away seemed foolish.

Tom drove them past the Boardwalk, and Lila smiled when the lights of the Ferris wheel caught her eye.

Beyond the main beach, Tom stopped the boat near one of the other less inhabited beaches. He cut the engine and she savored the silence.

"It's beautiful out here," Lila said. She admired the sun as it dipped down below the horizon. It cast pink and orange in bursts of color like flourishes from the paintbrush of a master artist.

He sat beside her, the sun hitting his face in a warm yellow glow. She studied him for a long moment as he stared out over the horizon. Tom's rugged features were only part of what had drawn her in. His loyalty and steadfastness reminded her of everything her father wasn't—and everything she wanted.

"Do you have any mints?" Tom asked, breaking the silence.

She held up the black clutch and smiled.

She opened the purse and fished through the few things she'd brought with her—mints included—but something else caught her eye. A small white box with a light blue bow. She pulled it out of the purse and glanced at Tom, who still stared at the sunset as if nothing was out of the ordinary.

"What's this?" she asked.

Without looking at her, he smiled.

"Tom?" She pushed on his shoulder.

He turned toward her. "Open it."

She turned the box over in her hand, then took the bow off. Warmth wrapped itself around her like a cashmere sweater, and she welcomed the way it made her feel. Loved.

She lifted the lid to the box and as she glimpsed what was inside, she gasped.

"How did you . . . ?" Lila ogled the silver rope chain and heart-shaped locket. Identical to the one she'd wanted all those years ago. The same locket she'd expected from Daddy—only to find it around the neck of one of his mistresses. The pain her father had caused was washed away by Tom's thoughtfulness.

Tears sprang to her eyes. He moved closer and took the locket. "Here, let me." He unlatched the clasp and she turned around, lifting her hair so he could fasten the necklace around her neck. His hand lingered on the bare skin of her back, and his touch sent tingles down her spine.

She turned to face him. "How did you find this?" She rubbed the locket between her thumb and forefinger.

"I had a little help," Tom said. He reached into his inside jacket pocket and pulled out a photograph. One she'd sent him of the locket when she'd first found it all those years ago.

"Where'd you get that?"

He pulled something else from his pocket—a small stack of letters with pink envelopes. Letters she'd written him after she went back to Macon for the school year.

"I can't believe you still have these." She flipped through the letters—holding their love story in her hands.

He stared at the letters. "I know you feel betrayed, but I wanted you to know that it's always been you."

She stacked the letters and held them tightly.

"Me and you."

Slowly, she lifted her chin and met his eyes. He watched her intently, making it clear the next move was hers.

She reached up and touched his cheek. "You do love me."

"More than anything."

Intent on his eyes, Lila held his gaze as she leaned in to him, closing the gap between them as she pressed her lips against his. He wrapped his arms around her waist and pulled her against him, then deepened his kiss, inhaling her as if she brought the oxygen back to his lungs. After several long moments, she pulled away and stared into Tom's eyes. Unmistakable desire lingered above them—deeper than she'd felt in years.

She touched her lips and looked away.

"I'm sorry," Tom said.

Lila stared across the lake to the spot where the sun had shone only moments ago. Voices prattled on inside her head and she shoved them away, determined to focus on that moment—remembering all the good about their past, and praying the bad wouldn't overshadow it. She had the choice, didn't she?

She looked at Tom, overwhelmed with a sensation that hadn't been present between them in years.

Unconditional love meant loving through the mistakes.

She'd held him to an impossibly high standard, and now she wondered if she could take it back—could she forgive him and move beyond the past?

She didn't know, but as she gazed into his eyes, more than anything, she knew she wanted to try.

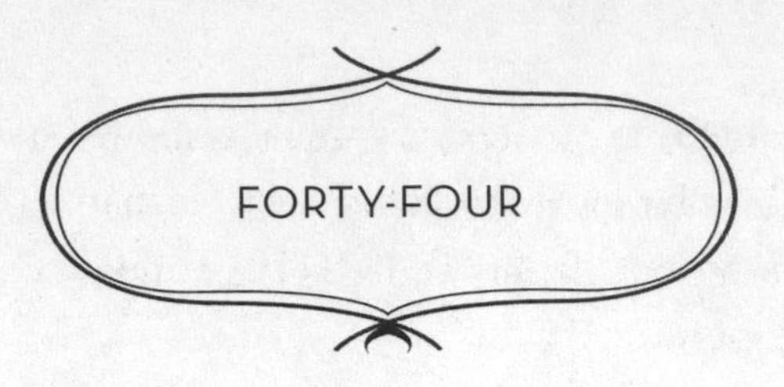

Jane

Rather than go out for the evening, Jane decided to stay in and scrapbook, but her mind kept drifting to thoughts of Meghan. She'd heard the rumors about a drunken performance at the bar, but over a week later, she'd yet to reach out to her friend.

Jane reached into her oversized bag and pulled out the little journal full of the ramblings of her heart. She couldn't even call them prayers, they were so incoherent and filled with wanderings and selfishness.

She reminded herself that she could choose to forgive Meghan—otherwise, she'd be stuck in this stagnant place for the rest of her life. A heart full of empathy helped—but she wondered, how could someone who had so much be so empty?

Jane opened the now bulky book and jotted down a few thoughts, unsure why it seemed impossible to get Meghan off her mind.

Pray.

The word came without fanfare, just a simple instruction from a place she'd learned not to ignore.

She picked up a black marker and started to write, letting the words come from a place beyond herself. *Make Yourself real to her tonight,* she wrote.

"Because she needs You, Lord," she whispered. When she finished, Jane looked at the page, adding colorful designs around the edges as if she needed to decorate it in order to seal it in tight.

But something still felt wrong, so she bowed her head and asked God to show her how she could help Meghan. "I know she needs You, God. More than she realizes, but at this point, I'm not sure I can help. Show me if I can."

Jane opened her eyes and saw her cell phone sitting beside her on the desk. She picked it up, scrolled through her contacts and dialed Meghan's number. The least she could do was check in with her. Her nerves kicked up.

Meghan answered on the first ring. "Jane."

"Hey, what's wrong? You sound upset." Was she drinking again?

But after Meghan explained that she and Nick were searching for their kids, the word *sober* took on a new meaning.

"What can I do? Let me come with you or meet you there. Something." She rushed to the living room, waving her hands at Graham in charade-like fashion. He looked at her, puzzled, but stood. She set his shoes in front of him and motioned for him to follow her.

"Where are we going?" he hissed.

"Meghan, where are you?"

"Heading out of town, near the cement plant."

"We're going to try and catch up to you. I'll call you in a little bit."

Jane slammed her phone shut and threw the keys in Graham's lap. She gave him the bullet points of where they were heading and commanded him to hurry up.

"You don't really think Nick's mom would hurt them, do you?" Graham made the turn onto the highway toward the cement plant.

Jane shook her head. She wanted to believe everything would be okay—that Meghan's children were safe, even if Violet was mentally unstable, but she just didn't know anymore. What if Violet snapped?

What if, in her delusional mind, she decided hurting the children was the only way to protect them from a life with an imperfect mother?

She forced the thoughts away, whispering prayer after prayer, begging God to protect Meghan's twins.

Because the alternative threatened to rip open her old wounds and plummet her straight back to the land of sadness. No, she couldn't allow her mind to wander off in that direction. The twins were fine.

They had to be.

*****

Campbell

The evening waned and Campbell closed the gallery, turning over the sign in the window and peering across the street at the café. She'd convinced herself she wasn't looking for Luke, but she knew better. She wanted to run across the street and demand an explanation, but she couldn't do that. Talk about desperate.

After a month in town, their time together had grown sparse with their businesses and Luke's travel. It was time to face the truth. Tilly had been right. The whole idea of Sweethaven had been nothing more than a fairy tale.

She started cleaning up the desk, having spent the day making posters to announce her upcoming classes. So far, things had gone smoothly, and thanks to the tourists who always seemed to be in a shopping mood, the gallery had been a busy place.

Good thing. The busyness kept her from thinking too much about Luke.

That and the daily visit from her grandfather—a man she hadn't expected to enjoy as much as she did.

Before she finished, a noise at the back of the building startled her, and she remembered she'd left the door to the alley open.

Her heart pounded as she crept toward the back office.

The door swung open and her heart hitched into her throat.

"Who's there?" She'd most likely violated the rules of every scary movie that had ever been made, but when she finally put the pieces together and realized the intruder was Luke, embarrassment washed over her.

"Did I scare you?" She refused to let herself be won over by that lazy grin.

"Yeah, next time you should call first." She turned and walked back toward the front desk.

He followed her, probably wishing he hadn't come into the gallery at all. She reminded herself that she had no proof he'd done anything wrong—only a series of aloof encounters and a lot of weekends away. It could be anything.

"How've you been?"

She expected him to walk to the other side of the counter, but he joined her in the too-small-for-two-people space behind it.

Campbell bit back a sarcastic response as she met his eyes. "I'm fine. How are you?"

He smiled again, almost patronizing.

"Luke, if you're here to break up with me, just say it, okay?"

He frowned. "Why would I do that?"

Campbell crossed her arms over her chest and stared out the window. Was he really this clueless? He took a step closer and pulled her hands out from their folded position. She glanced up at him, certain her eyes had gone glassy.

"What's wrong?"

Had she imagined his distance? Had she worried herself into a frenzy for no reason? "You've been so preoccupied."

He turned away and she knew she hadn't imagined it. Something was definitely wrong, and he'd come here to pretend things were okay—to put her mind at ease. But it wasn't working.

"I haven't been completely honest with you, Campbell."

Her heart rolled over in her chest. She'd been here before. Bracing for breakup, she almost asked him not to tell her. Did she want to know he was seeing someone else? Or he had an illegitimate child in another state? Or he was really married?

But the curiosity wouldn't let her turn away. "Go on."

"It's not fair to you and I know it's not, but . . ."

She said nothing, reminding herself no matter what happened, she'd be okay.

"My old firm called—a little over a month ago. They have an open position and they want me. That's why I went to the city back in June."

Campbell tried to undo the emotional damage she'd done to herself as she processed this admission—which by all accounts didn't feel like an admission at all. "Why would you keep that from me?"

He sighed. "Because I'm the one who convinced you to come here. To Sweethaven. And I've been driving to Chicago every weekend. Don't you think that's a little unfair?"

She crossed her arms. "It's not worth hiding. You're an architect—and from what I hear, a really good one. Why wouldn't you want to do what you were trained to do?" She leaned against the counter and studied him. He looked conflicted.

"I made the choice to come back here and run the restaurant and live this life." He sighed. "And when you bought the gallery, all I felt was guilt because here you were changing your plans . . . for me, and I don't even know what I'm going to do."

She wrapped her arms around him and hugged him close. "Well, you don't have to figure it all out on your own."

"I'm a guy. That's what we do."

Campbell rolled her eyes. "I'm just glad you don't have a baby out there. Or a wife. Or a Wanted poster with your face on it."

He laughed, then pulled back and looked at her. "I'd never do that to you. You need to know that now."

She nodded. "I know."

"I'm sorry you were worried. I'm just trying to sort through everything. I don't want you to resent this sleepy life someday."

She stood on her tiptoes and brought her lips to his, realizing how much she'd missed his kiss. Luke brought his hands to her face and held her in his tender touch.

His cell phone rang, jolting them apart.

He pulled the phone from his back pocket and answered. Campbell watched as his expression changed. "What do you mean they're gone?"

She waited for him to clue her in, but he seemed to be in another world. He walked over to the window and looked across the street. She followed his gaze and found Adele standing outside the café, phone to her ear, and Campbell could tell something was very wrong.

FORTY-FIVE

Lila

Tom docked Angelo's boat and tied it up.

"We should get a boat," Lila said.

He pulled the knot, waited a moment to see that it would hold, then stood. "I was just thinking that." He smiled.

She slipped her shoes off and stood two inches shorter than before. At his side, she felt protected, and she welcomed the feeling. She'd been feigning strength for too long now; even before they separated, Lila had insisted on controlling every aspect of their lives. Had she stolen a piece of his manhood in doing so?

He met her eyes and she found no judgment there, only kindness. As horrible as she now realized she'd been, Tom seemed oblivious. She ran a finger over the locket that hung around her neck. He loved her.

And she'd almost thrown it away. Suddenly Patton Gallagher held no appeal—the only thing she wanted stood right in front of her.

He took her hand and led her up the steep staircase, standing below her with a flashlight he'd grabbed from the boat.

In the dark, they found their way. Little by little, one foot in front of the other.

The thought needledLila like a pinprick to the heart. The darkness in their lives had served as a beacon of light—and now, one day at a time, they would find their way. Together.

They drove in silence back to the lake house, an air of contentedness wafting back and forth between them. When they wound up the driveway and parked the car, Lila exhaled for what felt like the first time since ascending the stairs down by the lake. Crickets chirped outside, accompanying her thoughts with their playful melody.

Tom told her to stay put, ran around to her side of the car and opened the door for her. She took his hand and happiness invaded when he didn't let it go.

Inside, darkness swept across the lake house—no sign of life to be seen. The pale moonlight filtered in through the wood blinds, casting a staggered pattern on the wall. Lila flipped the entryway light on and walked into the kitchen. On the counter, she found a note. Mama's script.

Lila & Tom,

Your father has been called away on business and we had to catch the first flight out of Chicago back to Atlanta. Unfortunately for me, that flight is at 10 PM. Take care of each other and stay as long as you'd like. The house is all yours. We won't be back.

Sincerely,
Your mother

Lila pushed the note across the counter toward her husband and pressed her lips together. "Do you know anyone else who would sign a letter to their daughter like that?" Lila laughed.

Tom read to the end and then smiled. "It oozes warmth."

He waited for a few long seconds.

"I miss you, Tom," she blurted.

He exhaled, dropping his head forward and then moving toward her, pulling her into a tight hug. "I miss you too," he whispered. "So much."

"I miss the old us. The 'us' I remember when I read your letters."

Tom took her face in his hands and studied her eyes. "Let's start over."

She clung to his words, gazing into the deep blue seas of his eyes. Breath seeped from her lips without her permission, but she struggled to refill her lungs. Finally, she found the courage to let her heart decide. "I'd like that."

He leaned down to kiss her, but his lips found first her forehead, then one cheek, then the other—then finally they swept across hers, enticing and intoxicating. She pulled him closer, but no matter how close they were, it didn't feel near enough. He kissed her like a desperate man, then pulled back and looked at her. Desire flashed in his eyes and Lila knew they'd reached the point of no return.

She wrapped her arms around his neck and he picked her up, their arms entwined, their faces drawn together like the curtains in a closed-up house.

He examined her eyes for permission, and as she held his gaze, she silently gave it. Her skin tingled with anticipation. She loved him—but she'd always loved him.

What had changed? Why did this feel like their first night together?

As he carried her up the stairs, she inhaled his scent, familiar and cozy. She'd smelled the distilled fragrance of his aftershave every night for over twenty years, but inhaling it now, it had a newness to it she couldn't place.

At the top of the stairs, her feet reached the floor, but she leaned into him, her arms wrapped around his waist, her head on his chest. "I need you, Tom." She stared down the darkened hallway, aware of what lurked behind the last door on the right. The bed they'd shared—only for appearance's sake—a bed that welcomed them to share their love, and the idea of it sent her insides tumbling.

Their marriage—and everything about it—had turned into a routine. Lila could've set her watch by it. Weekly menus rarely changed, and neither did their lovemaking. It had gone from passionate to lackluster to virtually nonexistent. She had gone through the motions—sometimes. Other times, she'd simply refused him.

But standing in the hallway, his hand on the bare skin of her neck, Lila sensed a change. A current of electricity connected the two of them, and her body responded with every kiss, every touch.

Had her decision to forgive him—to move beyond the past—changed something between them? Had forgiveness, like a bandage on an open wound, healed the mistakes of the past and brought them closer in a way she'd always desired but didn't dare hope for?

He offered his hand and led her into the darkness of the hallway, where the two of them shone like a light, illuminating the great depth of their love.

New, unconditional and fresh with possibilities.

Meghan

"They're okay," Nick said.

Tension filled the cab of Nick's old truck like a thick fog. Meghan stared out the window as they sped down the bumpy highway. Silently, she prayed to a God she'd long since abandoned. She asked for favors, bartered with future earnings—she even promised she'd go back to church.

Just let them be okay.

"I'm sure they are," Meghan said, sounding more hopeful than she felt. Her phone rang and when she saw the screen, she groaned.

"Hi, Duncan."

"Meghan, where are you?"

She filled Duncan in, watching Nick as he watched the road, and told Duncan where they were going. "Whatever you do, please please please don't leak any of this to the press."

"Of course I won't, Meghan."

Meghan hung up, not convinced he'd do as she asked.

She leaned against the window, staring outside as trees whizzed by, then cornfields—not a streetlamp in sight. Her thoughts settled on Violet and her heart clenched.

"I wish she didn't hate me so much." After a beat, Meghan clarified. "Your mother."

Nick cleared his throat. "I think you remind her of my dad."

She shot him a look.

The road clicked under the tires at even intervals as they clipped along at least twenty miles above the speed limit. The aching silence gnawed at her. Nick's dad used to get drunk every night and beat Violet till she bled—then, usually, he came back for more. When she looked at Meghan, she saw her husband—a mean drunk. In her mind, she took the kids to protect them.

But all those years had turned her into a mean, bitter woman herself. How could she not see that?

"I've changed." Meghan's voice failed her, cracking under the weight of her words. Words she didn't even believe.

Nick studied the road.

Her throat constricted over a lump of sorrow, and she struggled for air.

Her mind reeled with thoughts of the morning after she convinced Nick to leave her. He'd returned to their house for more of his things, but instead found Meghan behind the locked door of their bedroom, wrapped in the humiliation and shame of her relapse.

When she didn't open the door, he broke the lock and rushed in, unmistakable fear in his voice. "Meghan?" He pulled back the covers, searching for her—relieved when he found her still breathing. "I thought . . ." He picked her up and held her.

"What are you doing here, Nick?" Her words sounded muddled in her own mind. "Just go."

"I can't leave you," he said.

She pulled away from him and sat up, knowing that while she wanted to collapse in his arms, wanted him to make it better, the only thing left for her to do was to push him away. For good. It was best for everyone.

But Nick thought he loved her, in spite of everything. He'd only go if she forced him to.

She stood and widened the distance between them. "This is what I need to do, Nick. I need to be by myself for a while, to figure some things out."

He stood up and walked toward her, but her raised hands kept him from touching her. "You can't mean this."

"This isn't the life I want."

"Then we'll change it. Tell me what you want and I'll make it happen." His insistence, his willingness to do anything for her stunned her—even after all this time.

She turned away, fighting tears. "You should take the kids and go back to Sweethaven. I know you hate Nashville anyway—so don't stay. Don't spend another second in a life you hate."

He turned her around. "I would only hate my life if you weren't in it."

Meghan covered her face with her hands and resisted the urge to fall into his arms and let him fix everything for her again. "I want you to go."

"Meghan, don't run away—not from me."

She knew what she had to do. She squared her jaw and held his gaze. "I don't love you anymore, Nick. I want you to go."

Horror flashed across his face, and after too many moments of silence, he finally left.

She sank to the floor and sobbed until her body gave way to sleep. The next morning Duncan whisked in and pulled her out of that room, propped her up and told her everything would be fine. "Time to do what you do best," he said. "Be a star."

Now, sitting across from Nick recounting all she'd lost, sadness overwhelmed her.

Nick watched the road but stole occasional glances at her. "Meg, were you drunk that day at the lake?"

She shot him a look. "What?" Had he only been pretending to believe her?

"I can't figure out why you keep tormenting yourself over something out of your control." He looked at her. "It was an accident. You didn't kill Alex."

The words hung between them. He couldn't possibly understand.

"Did you hear me? You didn't kill Alex."

"Stop it, Nick." Her eyes welled with fresh tears.

Nick reached across the seat and grabbed her hand. "You have to forgive yourself, Meghan. Alex died—and it was terrible. Horrible. But it wasn't anyone's fault."

Meghan buried her face in her hands and let the tears come. "Why do you keep doing this? You've spent your entire life saving me—over and over again."

He glanced at her, intent. "That's what love is, Meghan."

She studied his eyes. Kind. Generous. She'd always trusted him.

"Can I ask you something?" Nick leaned back against the seat of the truck, still holding her hand.

"I guess." *Not something painful, please.*

"If I asked you to come back, what would you say?"

The question hovered in the air like a thick fog, and Meghan waited for the cloud to pass.

"I want us to be a family again."

How could they talk about this right now—they were only assuming they'd find the kids and everything would be okay. What if they were living on borrowed time?

"Let's just get through this okay first, Nick."

Nick sucked in a breath and let it out slowly.

"We can't make decisions when we feel like this." Meghan's stomach jumped as she replayed his words. *If I asked you to come back, what would you say?*

His phone vibrated, pulling their attention back to reality. The reality that Violet had finally lost it—and she had their kids. As she listened to Nick's side of the conversation, she couldn't force herself to stop imagining the worst.

This time her babies really were in danger.

And just like with Alex, she was powerless to help them.

Jane

"Where are we going?" Jane finally asked, more to fill the silence than anything.

Graham stayed a polite distance behind Nick's truck. Where was God? Did He hear her begging for mercy for those kids?

"Nick said his family has an old cabin off of Beacon Hill Highway. It's about an hour away—we should be getting close." Graham glanced at her. "You doing okay?"

She shook her head but didn't dare speak—she knew her voice would fail her. After her initial call with Meghan, she'd let Graham take the lead—getting directions from Nick as they sped out of town. Finally, after a few long moments, she said, "Shouldn't we call the police? Technically, she's kidnapped them. How do we handle this on our own?"

"Nick probably doesn't want to send his own mom to jail," Graham said, a frown on his face.

"I understand, but she's not right in the head. She never has been."

Graham kept his eyes on the highway. "I think it's Nick's call, hon."

"Those poor kids." Jane's mind spun as she imagined them, tied up in the back of the car or sleeping in the closet of a dingy old cabin. Who knew what Violet was capable of?

"I'm sure they're fine."

"How can you say that, Graham?" Jane's misplaced anger surprised her.

He held his hands up in surrender, his eyes wide.

"I'm sorry—it's just that I feel so helpless."

Helpless—like she'd felt on the beach that day.

Jane's heart raced and a familiar feeling poured over her. The ache of losing a child.

If something happened to the twins, Meghan would feel that same horror—and no matter what they'd been through, Jane had to try and spare her friend those feelings—sorrow, hatred and anger entangled together. The prison they'd created had nearly destroyed Jane. She had to protect Meghan from that at all costs.

After over an hour of driving, Nick pulled over to the side of the road and cut the engine. Graham followed suit and Jane's heart kicked up a notch.

Nick got out and ran back to their car. "I really appreciate your coming along."

"Don't give it a second thought," Graham said. "What do you want us to do?"

Nick explained he didn't want to startle his mom—she wasn't stable, and he didn't want to risk the kids any more than he already had. As he spoke, Jane could see the pain behind his eyes. She glanced at the truck and met Meghan's eyes. She should go talk to her—what her friend must be feeling in that moment.

Instead, she listened intently as Nick told them what he'd planned. "And I'd love for you to be there for my mom, if you don't mind."

Graham nodded. "I'll do whatever I can."

Nick ran back to the truck and Meghan hopped down. Jane glanced at Graham. "What are you going to say to that woman?"

Her husband shrugged. "I'm gonna have to figure that out later. God will have to give me the words."

"Better you than me. I'd love to wring her neck."

Graham put a hand on hers. "I know this isn't easy for you. Let's concentrate on getting those kids out safe."

They got out of the car and the four of them met up beside Nick's truck.

"I'm going to go around that side." Nick pointed to the left of the cabin. "Can you guys go right? Let me know if you see anything."

They nodded and did as they were told. As they strode toward the cabin, Jane fell into step beside Meghan and linked an arm through hers. "It's going to be okay."

Meghan's surprised eyes danced in the moonlight. "Thanks, Janie." She swiped away a tear and Jane smiled, then broke away from her friend, heading around the right side of the cabin as stealthily as she could.

Light from inside the little house poured through the flimsy curtain and out the window, onto the ground just between them. Like a shot, Jane backed against the cabin wall, her eyes wide, anticipating Violet's angry scowl behind the glass.

From outside, she heard rustling around and then a crash, like a bottle breaking.

"I told you not to touch that," Violet shrieked.

"I'm sorry, Grandma."

Jane gasped. She looked at Graham, who held a finger over his lips as if to remind her to stay quiet.

"Get in here—both of you. You'll spend the night locked in the bathroom if you can't listen. I told you once—I'm done with you."

"I don't want to stay in here, Grandma, it's dark."

"If you don't shut up, you're going in the closet. You wanna go in the closet?"

Jane imagined two wide-eyed four-year-olds shaking their heads in quick succession.

"Then get quiet."

The light on the grass disappeared and the bathroom door slammed.

Jane shot Graham a look. "We can get them out the window," she whispered.

"How are we going to do that without her hearing?"

Jane stilled—and listened. "The TV is blaring in there, Graham. This is our shot. You boost me up."

The window, just out of reach, could be locked—or screwed shut—but Jane had to try.

Graham knelt down and offered Jane a knee. "Be careful."

She stood on his leg and hoisted herself up. On tiptoes, she leaned into the glass and pushed, trying to pry it up. "It's stuck," she whispered.

"Try again," Graham said.

She took a breath and this time pushed harder. When the window started to budge, Jane had to stifle the joy that threatened to blow their cover. "It's working."

Once she had it open, she searched for the kids, both of whom were sitting in the bathtub, staring at her.

"Finn, Nadia," Jane whispered. "It's Mrs. Atkins. Remember me from the barbecue?"

Finn stood. "Are you here to save us?"

Sorrow washed over Jane as she nodded at the two children. "But we have to be really quiet."

Nadia stood beside her brother. "She'll be really mad if we leave. We gotta stay here and wait for Daddy."

"Your daddy's here, hon," Jane said. She paused, listening for the blaring television before she continued. "He's going to meet you outside." She wondered if she should wait for Nick to come around to their side of the cabin, but she imagined with Violet in his crosshairs, Nick would likely stay put.

The twins looked at each other, confused.

"She's going to be mean to us. I don't want to stay with her." Finn held his hands up toward Jane, who realized she might not have the strength to pull him out.

"Everything okay?" Graham whispered.

"Yes, as long as I can pull him up." Jane thought of Alex. Who had he reached out to that day? If she'd been there, could she have pulled him from the mighty current that sucked him under? Her eyes clouded and she inhaled, determined to save these children from their own wretched waves.

From somewhere inside, a burst of strength shot through her and she heaved Finn up and pulled him through the window. With Graham's help, she set him on the ground. He looked up at her, eyes full of tears, and said, "Can you save Nadia too?"

Jane's breath caught, like a vise had been wrapped around her heart, and she nodded. One glance at Graham and she was back at the window. She peeked inside, but the light filtering into the empty bathroom told her the door had been opened. Nadia must've gotten nervous.

"She's gone." Jane stepped down from Graham's propped knee.

"She's gone?" Finn asked. "My grandma found her?" His eyes widened and even in the darkness, Jane saw the pallor of his skin as the blood drained from his face.

"It's okay, buddy, we'll find her."

They rushed around the cabin before Violet spotted them out back, and Jane prayed the entire time. She held Finn's hand and pulled him along. When their car came into sight, Jane picked up her pace. "I'll take him to the car."

As they moved, a noise from the other side stopped them, and she stilled until she saw Nick and Meghan emerge from the shadows.

"Daddy!" Finn's voice carried through the blackness of the empty night.

Nick rushed toward Finn. "Where's Nadia?"

Finn pointed to the dank house.

"I think she got scared," Jane said. "I had to pull him through the bathroom window."

"She saved me, Daddy," Finn said.

Meghan shot Jane a look, her eyes glistening in the pale moonlight.

"Meghan, take Finn. I'm going to go get Nadia." Nick flipped his phone open, dialed and waited, phone propped to his ear. "Yeah, I need to report a kidnapping."

Jane gasped, then caught Meghan's eye.

Her heart raced—she prayed she hadn't made it worse for Nadia by taking Finn out the window.

Slowly, Jane walked toward Meghan. Finn stood between them, holding his mom's hand. He glanced up at Jane and then slipped his pudgy four-year-old hand inside hers. His touch shocked her, like paddles jolting her heart back to life. She stared at it for a long moment and then brought her face even with Meghan's.

Meghan refused Jane's eyes, but she could see a line of pain across her forehead. With her free hand, she reached over and touched Meghan's arm.

"Everything will be okay," Jane said again.

Meghan's head dropped into her hands and she cried, tears of fear and sorrow and regret, Jane recognized.

Finn wrapped his arms around his mom's legs and clung to her. "Daddy will save her, Mommy. God will help Daddy save her."

*****

Adele

"It's my fault," Adele said. "I know it."

She sat motionless at a little table in the café, only one faint lamp lit to deter the night owls from attempting the door. Luke paced in front of her, and Campbell sat, perched on a bar stool at her side.

"Luke, you might as well go ahead and say it. If I'd said something sooner, none of this would've happened. If I'd just trusted Meghan instead of trying to work it all out myself. Do you know what this has been doing to me? It's torn me up inside."

Luke stared at her then, his phone still in hand from his last unsuccessful call to Nick. "Mama, stop. This isn't about you."

Adele gasped. "I'm not saying it is, son, but I feel terrible." She glanced at Campbell, who looked shell-shocked. Poor girl hadn't signed up for this family drama.

"I told her." Campbell's voice cut through the silence.

Luke and Adele both looked at her, but she stared at her folded hands in her lap.

"What do you mean?"

"I went to see Meghan—I told her I overheard you two talking about Violet. I didn't know what you were talking about, but I told Meghan." Campbell glanced up at Adele. "I'm sorry. It wasn't my place."

"Don't be silly." Adele looked away. "At least one of us had common sense enough to clue her in. She's never going to forgive me."

Luke shook his head. "We can't just sit here."

"What else are we going to do? We've made a mess of things and the best place for us right now is out of the middle of it."

She couldn't save her grandbabies any more than she could save her ruined relationship with her daughter. So Adele did the only thing she knew how to do.

She bowed her head and turned all of her troubles over to the only One with the answers.

Meghan

Jane's touch jarred Meghan from a near trancelike state. Her comforting words broke something inside her, and Meghan couldn't hold back the tears. Words she couldn't say to Jane six years ago—*everything will be okay*—settled on Meghan's ears and wove their way into her heart.

She didn't deserve Jane's kindness.

A black Mercedes pulled into the parking lot and Duncan jumped out, followed by James Pierce.

"What are they doing here?" Nick asked.

Meghan shook her head. "No idea."

The two men jogged over. "We wanted to be here in case you need anything, Meghan." James glanced at Nick. "We weren't sure if you had anyone on your side out here."

Nick clenched his fists at his sides. "You both need to go."

Meghan touched Nick's arm. "We're fine, James. I'm fine. You didn't have to drive all the way out here."

"Meghan, come on, we don't have time for this." Nick stuck his phone in his back pocket. "I'm going to go inside," he said. "I think you should come with me."

"Me? No."

He lowered his voice so the others couldn't hear him. "Meghan, she needs to see that you aren't my father. She needs to understand you're not going to hurt our kids." Nick's eyes persisted, but Meghan's spirit screamed in protest. Standing face-to-face with the woman who'd put her through this agony, who'd emotionally abused her children for the past two years—she didn't trust herself.

"Meghan, I'll keep Finn out here with me. You go," Jane said.

Meghan finally met her eyes. Words tumbled through her mind—so many things she wanted to say to Jane. She'd said them all to herself so many times before. But standing beside her—the recipient of unwarranted compassion, words failed her. Instead, she nodded, kissed Finn on the forehead and followed Nick toward the cabin.

Nick pounded on the door. "Mom, I know you're in there. Let me in."

The door popped open, but the chain lock was still attached. Meghan stood behind Nick.

"What are you doing here, Nick?" Violet spat.

"I came for my kids." Nick stayed calm—always calm.

"And you brought *her*?"

Out of the corner of her eye, Meghan could sense Violet's cold stare. She forced herself not to respond.

"She's not getting anywhere near these kids."

Meghan bit back words she didn't want her kids to hear.

"Mom, you had no right to do this."

"You're trying to get them away from her yourself, Nick."

"You don't understand. Let me in." Nick pushed against the door, cutting Meghan's view of the evil woman who stood behind it. "Where's Nadia?"

"She's fine."

"I'm warning you, Mom. Open the door or stand back. I'm coming inside to get my daughter."

"Don't you talk to me like that, Nicholas. I'm still your mother." Violet slammed the door. From inside, the old woman fumbled with the lock, then finally popped it open, revealing a black room behind her and no Nadia in sight.

"Where is she, Violet?" Meghan leaned into Nick, her palms sweaty, her stomach raw.

Violet's eyes blackened as she examined Meghan. "You think a drunk like you deserves these kids, Meghan Barber?"

"Don't talk to her like that, Mom."

"Oh, I'm just getting started." Violet walked inside the room, leaving the door open. Meghan glanced at Nick, then followed him inside.

Photos were scattered across the bed, along with a flash drive. Meghan's skin went cold as she realized what they were.

"*You* leaked the photos," Meghan said. She spun around and caught Violet's raised brow, her smug expression.

"I always knew they'd come in handy." She smiled.

Meghan's heart dropped to the floor.

"How could you do this, Mom?" Nick ran a hand through his hair, as if he could force the pain away.

"I told you from the beginning that this girl wasn't good enough for you. You just wouldn't listen." She crossed her arms. "I had to prove it."

Meghan stared at her feet, then scanned the room for Nadia. Violet stood in front of the closet—Nadia would be in there.

"You don't know what you're talking about," Nick said.

Violet stepped toward him. "You're so blind. Do you know how many times I had to go get your father from that very same bar? Usually wrapped in some woman's claws? This is not the life you want. Trust me."

"Where's Nadia?" Nick's tone remained steady. How long could he go without losing his temper?

"We're talking about *her.*" Violet thrust her finger at Meghan.

Meghan straightened and walked toward her ex-mother-in-law. A head taller than Violet, she held the upper hand. Nick put an arm on hers, but she shrugged him off.

"You don't know what you're talking about, Violet. You've had a hard life—a horrible life, but it's turned you into a bitter, mean, delusional woman." Meghan glared at her.

"When I saw my son was planning to hand the kids to you at will, I had to act fast. I am protecting my kids."

"*My* kids."

Violet's eyes darkened and she shook her head. "They stopped being yours the day you pushed them back here."

Meghan took a breath. "You're right. I messed up. But this isn't the way to handle any of it."

Violet's eyes narrowed.

Meghan stared at her. "Get away from the closet."

Violet raised an eyebrow. "Or what?"

Nick glared at his mother. "I can't believe I thought you'd changed. I thought after Dad died, you'd finally become the kind of mother you were supposed to be."

"Watch it, Nick," Violet seethed.

"Get away from that door." Meghan moved closer. She needed to get to her daughter. She glanced at Nick, who held on to his mother's gaze. Then, before she lost her nerve, Meghan rammed herself into Violet, knocking her to the ground.

The old woman screamed and yanked Meghan's hair, pulling her down.

Meghan blocked Violet, using the full weight of her body, but the woman fought back—hard.

Nick flung the closet door open. Nadia lay on the ground curled in a ball. Tears streamed down her face. Nick scooped her up and hugged her. "You're safe now, sweetheart."

Outside, red and blue lights flashed in the parking lot. They pulled Violet's attention, and she scooted away from Meghan, leaned against the wall and glared at her son.

"You called the cops?"

Nick stared at her. "You need help, Mom. Help I can't give you."

Meghan stood and went to Nadia, then brushed the little girl's hair off of her wet face.

"You okay, honey?" Meghan asked, her voice soothing.

Nadia nodded, then reached her hands toward Meghan, wrapped them around her neck and squeezed.

"Let's go." Nick heaved their daughter up over his shoulder and wound an arm around Meghan, pulling her close.

Nick nodded at the police officer who approached them. "She's in there," he said. "She probably needs a psych evaluation." Nick pressed his lips on Nadia's forehead, then glanced at Meghan.

"I'm sorry," she said. "I know how hard that was for you."

Nick rubbed his eyes. "Should've been done a long time ago."

He'd beat himself up for not realizing his mother hadn't changed—that she did every terrible thing to their children that she'd done to him.

From the other side of the parking lot, Finn ran toward them. Meghan welcomed his arms around her, kneeling to take the brunt of his hug. Jane stood in the distance, watching with a contented smile on her face.

An ambulance pulled in just as the police officer emerged from the room with Violet, hands cuffed behind her back. Meghan shielded Finn's eyes, but Nick watched intently.

"This isn't your fault," Meghan said.

He looked down at her, then brushed his lips against her forehead. "I wish I believed that."

Meghan knew that pain firsthand. The pain of feeling responsible for the out-of-control events that unraveled the cozy cocoon they lived in. She leaned into him and inhaled.

Maybe Mama was right—they really were all just a bunch of mistakes with feet.

Violet shouted obscenities and seethed venom, then turned and spotted Duncan standing next to James near their parked car.

"This is all your fault!" Violet pulled away from the police officer and marched toward Duncan. "You were more than happy to pay me for those photos and this is the thanks I get?" The officer pulled her away and shoved her into the squad car.

Meghan watched as Duncan tried to hide the stunned look on his face.

"Duncan?" Meghan tried to make sense of it—the way the photos had magically appeared, how Shandy Shore had gotten her hands on them the very day they were on her show. Duncan had known about the papers Nick filed and leaked those to Shandy too. He'd always said "any publicity is good publicity."

The air drained from her lungs like she'd just been punched in the stomach. "How could you?"

Duncan rushed over. "Meghan, this is not what it looks like. She was going to leak those photos regardless of what I did—I ensured that we had control over how it all happened."

"Get away from me, Duncan." Meghan couldn't even look at him.

"Meghan, we've been having a heck of a time finding anything on Nick, and this is exactly the sort of thing we've been waiting for. A kidnapping? We couldn't have asked for better dirt!" He tried to grab her arm, but Nick stepped in his way.

"She said go away."

"You can't do this, Meghan. I'm the reason you're a star. Don't forget that." He started walking toward the car. "You know this is how the game is played."

Meghan pulled her kids into a tight hug and kissed each of their foreheads. "I'm so glad you're both okay." She looked at Finn. "You were so brave."

"I'm a warrior." He grinned and squeezed her neck.

The EMT hopped out of the ambulance and walked in their direction. "We should check them both out," he said. "Just to be sure." Meghan nodded as the kids went with the man.

Nick stood outside the ambulance, watching. He'd protected them all so many times and in so many ways, yet a terrible thing had happened—in spite of his goodness.

Accidents really did happen.

Nick waved her over to the ambulance. "They're both fine. At least physically."

Nick closed his eyes and let out a deep sigh. When he opened them, they'd filled with tears. He knelt down in front of Finn. "Listen, buddy, now that we know about this, we're never going to let it happen to you again. Ever. Do you understand?"

Finn nodded.

"And you need to tell me if someone hurts you. I'm your dad. You can tell me anything."

"She said you'd be mad." Finn looked away.

"You didn't do anything wrong, okay, Finn?" Nick forced his attention. "Okay?"

He glanced at the squad car. His mom sat in the back. "I'm not going to press charges. I just want to make sure she gets the help she needs."

Meghan followed his gaze. Violet sat stock-still in the back of the car, her eyes fixed on something ahead of them. She'd likely never speak to Nick again. And he still insisted on helping her.

Meghan turned and saw Jane and Graham talking to a police officer.

Finn's words rushed back to her. *She saved me.*

When Meghan reached her, the police officer snapped his notebook shut. "I'll be in touch," he said. He walked away.

"I wanted to thank you." Meghan nearly choked on the words. "For coming along. I don't know what I would've done if—"

Jane put a hand on Meghan's arm as a kind smile warmed her face. "I know how much you love those kids."

Meghan surveyed the scene. The engine of the squad car started, and the officer slowly pulled across the gravel parking lot toward the highway. They stopped only feet from where Meghan stood. From the back seat, Violet slowly turned and looked at Meghan. Her eyes, dark and shadowed, shone ominous in the moonlight.

"I had no idea how disturbed Nick's mom is," Jane said.

"Yeah, I guess some people are really good at hiding their secrets." A shiver passed over her as she watched the car pull away. "I want you to know I think about Alex every day." Meghan stared into the blackness of the cornfield across the street.

Jane sniffled. "Me too."

Meghan looked at her. Tears streamed down Jane's face.

"But it was an accident," Jane said.

After a few seconds, Jane faced her. "I love you, Meghan. Nothing will change that."

Meghan broke at the sound of the words—the sound of forgiveness billowing toward her like clouds on a perfect summer day. "I love you too, Janie."

Jane took a step toward her and wrapped her arms around Meghan. And just like that, Meghan discovered how it felt to be forgiven.

FORTY-NINE

Meghan

After the police questioned everyone on the scene, Meghan and Nick loaded the kids into the truck and drove back to Sweethaven. With two tiny bodies draped over her, warmth and comfort nestled into Meghan like a newborn puppy into its mother. She leaned on the headrest and struggled to keep her eyes open.

The truck came to a stop and jolted Meghan awake. She sat up, her mind foggy.

"You fell asleep," Nick said.

"I guess so."

"Just stay there—let me get them one at a time." Nick pulled Nadia from the truck, leaving Meghan alone with her son. She studied his softly parted lips as he drew air in at steady intervals.

She'd missed so much already. She didn't want to miss out on another moment with her kids. "I'm going to do better, Finn," she whispered. "I promise."

Nick took the rest of the week off just to spend time with her and the kids. They didn't talk about what happened or about what would happen, but they didn't have to.

Nick slept on the couch every night, like the gentleman he was, and every morning, Meghan woke to the sounds of laughter filling the once empty lake house—and Meghan's once empty soul.

After a week of hiding out, Meghan awoke to find Nick sitting at the kitchen table, nursing a cup of coffee.

She walked into the kitchen, surprised to see Mama standing at the stove stirring eggs into a mixing bowl.

"What are you doing here?" Her words cut through the silence.

"I asked her to come." Nick stood.

"Just to keep an eye on the kids," Mama said. "So you two can have some alone time."

Meghan frowned. "I don't want to leave them."

"Just for an hour, Meg. So we can talk." He held out a cup. "I got you a latte."

She glanced at the drink, then at Mama.

"Meghan, I'm sorry," Mama said, setting the bowl down. "I don't know what I was thinking."

The memory of Jane's forgiveness rushed back—how it had made her feel. Is that what Mama needed too?

She couldn't explain the peace that washed over her, but she didn't want to be angry anymore—not at Mama or Nick or Jane or even herself. She wanted a fresh start. She reached out and pulled Mama into a hug. "I forgive you, Mama."

"For everything?"

Meghan laughed. "Yes. Now watch my kids like a hawk, okay?"

"Promise." Mama smiled through wet eyes.

Meghan took the drink from Nick and followed him outside. "Where are we going?"

"A walk?" He headed to where the yard turned to woods and offered an outstretched hand.

Across the lake, she could see the town in full gear for the Labor Day Festival, just over two weeks away. The Boardwalk had been decorated, and at sunset the entire shore would be covered with twinkling white lights. In the distance, she could see the lighthouse, standing tall through every storm, calling weary travelers home.

Not unlike Nick had done for her.

They walked out onto the dock and sat with their feet in the cool water, soaking in the morning air.

"Do you think the kids are okay?" she asked.

"I think they will be," Nick said.

Meghan stared at the morning sky, a half-moon still visible on the blue backdrop and surrounded by clouds.

She rested her chin on her knees. "What's next for you?"

Nick caught her eye and smiled. "I'm moving."

She sat upright. Her heart dropped. "Where to?"

"A little yellow cottage down by the lake."

Visions of the old cottage flashed in her mind. All that work he'd done—for himself?

"Finn can't wait. He's so excited to catch frogs in the creek out back." Nick's eyes sparkled in the morning light.

Meghan could picture it, but she couldn't ignore the pang of jealousy that scratched at her. "It'll be a good life for them," she said.

He didn't respond.

"I can't believe you bought that old house—why didn't you say anything when I was there?"

"I didn't buy it for me."

Meghan pulled her eyes from his. A sob got stuck in her throat. What was he saying?

His hand worked its way up her back to her shoulders and stayed there, comforting her.

Two sailboats caught her eye in the distance, leaving the marina for an early morning sail.

"You're so much stronger than you think you are, Meghan."

And for the first time in her life—she believed it.

*****

Jane

With only a couple more weeks left in Sweethaven, Jane had begun preparations to pack for home, a newly discovered peace accompanying her. They'd stay through Labor Day, but school started the day after. Real life waited for her.

And for the first time in years, she felt ready for it.

Jane picked up her prayer book for Meghan and hugged it to her chest. She'd given her friend space, but it had been over a week since the night Violet ran off with the kids, and Jane knew what she needed to do.

The car ride out to the edge of town gave her time to think. She'd turned a corner. She'd saved Meghan's son. She wouldn't fool herself into believing he wouldn't have been okay, but she'd played an integral part in getting him out of harm's way. If it had been any other child, it might not hold so much weight, but it was *Meghan's* son. And that meant something.

The driveway of the lake house curved up a hill, and Jane slowed the car. Finally, she was ready to heal—but there was one more thing to do.

Nick's truck sat in the driveway. This early in the morning?

Jane parked the car, as her thoughts tumbled around in her head.

The front door beckoned, and Jane tromped on, purse over her shoulder, scrapbook pressed against her chest, begging herself not to lose her nerve. The leaves overhead already had a hint of what was to come—a glorious change of color as Sweethaven welcomed autumn in just a few short weeks.

On the porch, she listened for sounds inside, but none came. What if they weren't even awake yet?

A noise in the yard stopped her raised hand from knocking. She walked to the edge of the porch and saw Meghan and Nick sitting at a table on the spacious brick patio, empty plates in front of them, the kids up in the tree house, laughing.

From a distance, Jane watched them, her mind whirling back years, images of her friend and the love of her life passing through like a slide show. Jane had been there for so much of Meghan and Nick—maybe this could be a do-over for them. A fresh start. A clean slate could work wonders for a marriage—she knew that firsthand.

The scrapbook could wait. The last thing Jane wanted was to interrupt their morning—especially one that seemed so peaceful. She turned, but before she moved she heard Meghan's voice.

"Jane!"

Her heart leaped as she saw Meghan waving. How she'd missed her!

Jane watched her feet as she approached them, willing away her uncertainty.

Face-to-face with Meghan, Jane stopped and took a deep breath. "I don't want to interrupt your morning."

Nick reached out and put an arm on Jane's shoulder. "You can interrupt whatever you want."

Jane met his eyes but quickly looked away.

"Thank you, Jane—and please thank Graham for me too. Actually, I'll do that myself. Should've done it already."

"What'll happen to your mom?" Jane asked.

Nick shrugged. "Time will tell. We aren't going to press charges if she can get help."

"I'm sorry." Jane felt crushed under the weight of his burden.

He stacked the plates one atop the other, then put all the silverware on the top plate. "I'm going to wash these."

Jane glanced at Meghan, who stared at Nick, an undeniable respect on her face. Once he moved out of earshot, Meghan motioned for Jane to sit.

"Remember when you came to see me in Cedar Rapids?" Meghan rested her head on the back of the chair and smiled. "I think it was your first concert."

"Well, the first one that wasn't held in a church."

Meghan laughed.

"I remember you called me the morning of and told me you had backstage passes for me. I almost didn't come."

Meghan sat up. "I'm so glad you did."

Jane smiled. "Me too."

Meghan held her stare for a brief moment.

Jane set the book on her lap and studied it. "I brought you something."

Meghan's eyebrows shot upward. "You did?"

Jane handed her the prayer journal.

Meghan ran a hand over the cover of the small album, then opened it to reveal the title page. Jane had stared at that page for an hour before adhering anything, wavering in her decision to make the book. How could she fill it with prayers for the one person she knew she could never forgive?

Finally, she wrote a prayer. Short. Heartfelt. All she could muster at that point. Later, she added embellishments and a photo—the two of them, eight years ago, sitting on the beach in Sweethaven.

Dear Lord,

Today I pray for my friend. I pray for her heart—for her spirit—heal them, Lord. And let her know she is loved.

Meghan read the words slowly, then swiped a freshly fallen tear from her cheek.

"It's a prayer book," Jane said. "My therapist thought it would help me."

Meghan smiled. "Did it help you to pray for the enemy?"

Jane stared at her folded hands in her lap. "You were never my enemy, Meghan."

Meghan flipped through the pages. In it, she would find longer prayers as Jane wrestled with her own anger, somber prayers as she'd been able to put herself in Meghan's shoes, assigned prayers she'd only written as therapy homework.

But all prayers she'd prayed. And all from the heart.

Jane glanced at the kids, their red heads showing through the window of the tree house.

"They're your gift, Meghan," Jane said. "Your chance at a happy, happy life."

Meghan pulled Jane's focus and their eyes met.

Jane took the book from her and flipped through the pages until she found the prayer she was looking for. She opened it and handed it back to Meghan.

Dear Lord,

Today I feel sad. Not only for the loss of my son, but also for the loss of my friend. I don't think she knows You love her. I don't think she understands that You aren't a prize to be won. I don't know if she realizes that nothing she does will make You love her more—You've already decided to love her, no matter what. I pray for Meghan today, that she'll find Your grace and Your peace—because none of us deserve it, but we all need it.

Let her see she is beautiful—even at rock bottom.

Let her call out to You when she is sad or broken or overwhelmed.

Let her know she doesn't have to earn it—Your love is a gift, freely given.

Help her receive.

As Meghan read the words, Jane watched them wind their way into her heart. Sitting next to her, she prayed that somehow God could get through to Meghan. Jane didn't have easy answers for her friend. Only the simple truth that had carried her through her darkest moments.

"His grace is big, Meghan. Bigger than any of us."

Meghan dipped her face out of Jane's sight, but Jane heard her quiet sobs escape. Slowly, Jane moved closer and put an arm around Meghan's shoulders.

Neither of them spoke another word. They simply sat together, Meghan's kids playing in the yard, as the lake lapped the shore in the distance and the sun moved slowly across the sky.

FIFTY

Meghan

In the wings of the outdoor theatre, Meghan paced, trying to remember her pre-performance rituals. Her band had already warmed up, finished the sound check, and then spent a good fifteen minutes making fun of her for being from such a small town.

She laughed it off, thankful to have them backing her up.

No other venue would be as difficult—or as wonderful—as this one.

The Labor Day Festival had started with a bang—fireworks down on the Boardwalk, and Meghan had taken them in surrounded by her family and her friends. She hated that this festival signified the end of summer, but she wasn't about to let a moment of it pass her by.

Nick had been working around the clock to get the cottage ready for him and the kids, and he wouldn't let anyone see his work until he finished. He hadn't said another word to her about it since their walk in the woods a couple weeks ago. He continued to camp out on her couch, and while she told herself there were reasons they hadn't worked out, the more time they spent together, the less she could remember what they were.

Posters with her face on them had been plastered all over town, and the concert had sold out in hours. Paparazzi invaded the tiny Michigan town for a shot at capturing another one of Meghan's breakdowns, but this time she wouldn't give them what they wanted.

Instead, she'd focus on being the kind of singer she'd always intended to be.

One with a family that loved her. Whether she deserved it or not.

Meghan tried to shake the nerves that always accompanied a live show.

"There you are."

She turned and found Nick walking toward her. "Kids are with your mom in the front row, but I wanted to show you something." He handed her his phone, and she saw a news article he'd pulled up.

For redeemed country singer Meghan Rhodes, it wasn't enough to save her children from their grandmother's abusive clutches, now, she has to save her hometown as well.

Meghan's eyes filled with tears. "It's awfully dramatic."

Nick grinned. "But they love you. I know you don't have time, but there's at least a dozen more like this. Everyone's cheering for you, Meg." He pulled her into a warm hug. "You're home."

The stage manager appeared in the wings. "Five minutes."

She nodded, then turned her attention to Nick. "Thanks for this."

He smiled. "Break a leg."

As she took her place on the stage behind the curtain, Meghan's heart filled with gratitude. Duncan said she'd used up all her chances, but he'd been so wrong. About everything. And now, without even trying, the spotlight shining on her highlighted the good things she'd done—not the shameful things.

The announcer's voice bellowed through the speakers, and Meghan nodded at each of her band members. They'd done this hundreds of times, but never here. Never at home.

"Ladies and gentlemen, please welcome to the stage, performing a concert to benefit her hometown and yours, country music superstar and Sweethaven's sweetheart . . . Meghan Rhodes!"

The curtain shot up just as the lights flashed and the band started, a high-energy song that got the crowd shouting and screaming. Adrenaline coursed through Meghan's veins and she moved toward the microphone. As she sang the first line, the crowd cheered again, and Meghan peered out over the crowd. Signs bobbed up and down in the audience. *Sweethaven Loves You, Meghan!* And *Welcome Home, M.R.!*

From deep down, something started bubbling, something inexplicable and unfamiliar.

Joy.

Her voice cracked with laughter—the forgivable kind. The kind that told the audience that because of them, she exploded with joy.

Joy that came with the grace of being forgiven.

Nick stood in the wings, watching her, a proud smile on his face. Like sailors had for so many years, Meghan had followed her own lighthouse, and it had led her right where she needed to be.

Home.

FIFTY-ONE

Meghan

The day after the benefit concert, Meghan strolled down Elm Street toward Mama's house, where she'd meet her friends to finally work on their new scrapbook. Dressed in old blue jeans and a simple white button-down, she fit right in to the Sweethaven background. The trees had turned, and the crisp air said autumn waited in the wings.

Meghan loved autumn more than any other season, otherwise she might not have made the walk from the café downtown to Mama's house.

Rather than gawk at her, the people of Sweethaven smiled and waved. Some stopped her to say things like "Great job last night, Meghan." Or "Thank you so much for what you did for Sweethaven."

One woman stopped her just before she turned onto Elm Street. "We're all so happy you came home," she said.

The words warmed Meghan, who didn't have the heart to tell her that in less than a week she'd be back in Nashville.

Or maybe she didn't have the heart to tell herself.

Mama's cottage came into view and Meghan stopped for a moment to take it in. It was hardly fancy and had none of the frills she was accustomed to. Mama's decorations were at least fifteen years old and she had one too many flower arrangements for Meghan's taste, and yet, she couldn't think of a more comfortable place in the world.

Meghan found Jane alone on Mama's slip-covered couch in the living room, the makings of a new scrapbook spread out on the coffee table in front of her. They'd decided they'd all bring their photos and supplies. Mama would provide the food, and they'd spend two full days capturing their summer memories, laughing over their struggles and whispering prayers of thanks that God had brought them together again.

Maybe one day her own kids would cherish this new scrapbook the way Campbell cherished theirs.

"We're the first two here," Jane said. "Well, Campbell's around somewhere. I think she's talking with your brother."

Meghan grinned. "They're so cute it almost makes me nauseous."

The new scrapbook sat at the center of the table, and Meghan patted the messenger bag over her shoulder. In it was her contribution to that album—and what it would take to make it complete.

Jane laughed. "You look good."

Meghan smiled. After a month in Sweethaven, Meghan had begun to feel like herself again—a version of herself she thought she'd lost. "I feel good."

"I'm sad we have to go back to Iowa," Jane said.

"I'd be sad if I had to go back to Iowa too." Meghan waited a moment and then laughed, but her thoughts turned to the yellow cottage where Nick worked, day in and day out—like a man on a mission. He'd begun creating a home for them—though he'd never said so. How could she walk away now?

Jane eyed her, and a glimmer of suspicion flashed. "What's going on with you and Nick?"

Meghan pursed her lips and sighed. She started to speak, but then shook her head.

Jane put her hands over Meghan's. "You two were made for each other. You know that, right?"

"I guess I'm scared," Meghan said. "I don't want to mess it up again."

Jane smiled. "Then don't."

The front door opened and Lila appeared in the doorway, clinging to her oversized purse as if she needed it to stand.

"What happened to you?" Meghan asked as Lila slumped into an empty wingback chair.

Campbell emerged from the kitchen, her face beaming, Meghan was sure, from a stolen moment with her brother.

When Luke appeared seconds later, he confirmed Meghan's suspicions. She caught his eye and the playful look of guilt he wore. She raised her eyebrows and he shrugged.

Meghan grinned. Stolen kisses were the best kind. She scooted over to make room for Campbell on the love seat beside her.

"Lila, are you going to tell us what's wrong?" Jane used her mom voice.

Lila leaned her head back on the seat, her perfect posture a thing of the past. "I feel terrible." She rubbed her forehead.

"Why did you come?" Campbell asked.

"Because it's the new Circle. A new scrapbook. A new us. I didn't want you all doing that without me." Lila rubbed her temples.

"You're afraid we'd forget you, or what?" Meghan shook her head. "You're going to get us all sick."

Even in her current state and without makeup, Lila resembled a beauty queen, her Southern charm carrying her through this illness with an ever-present grace.

"Did you catch a cold or something?" Campbell leaned away from Lila, as if that could keep the germs away.

"I don't know. I've been feeling like this every day this week. I'll be fine this afternoon—it comes and goes."

Jane frowned and met Meghan's eyes.

"So, it's a morning thing?" Meghan asked.

Lila sat, her elbows propped on the arm of the chair, head in her hand. "I'll be right back." She rushed to the bathroom, leaving Campbell, Jane and Meghan to speculate about what "illness" their friend had "caught."

Seconds later Mama rushed in through the back door, her arms full of bags. "I'm sorry I'm late, y'all. I picked up some scrapbooking things for everyone." She grinned. "I've been over at the Commons getting things ready for the Labor Day arts and crafts show." She looked at Meghan. "Though, we don't really need to make any money thanks to your concert." Mama smiled at Meghan. "Thank you for that, darlin'."

"Thank Lila, it's her brilliant idea."

"Where is she?"

"Bathroom," Jane said. "Sick."

Mama grimaced. "She can go back to bed. I don't want to catch it—whatever it is." Mama set a little velvet box on the table in front of her. "Meghan, I brought this for you."

"What is it?"

"Just open it." Mama's smile turned apologetic.

She pried the box open and stared at the turquoise charm on a silver chain. Mama's favorite necklace. She'd always said one day she'd pass it on to Meghan—but somehow, the timing had never been right. "Your daddy—Teddy—gave that to me, but now, I think he'd want you to have it . . . " Adele folded her hands in her lap. "He loved you and Luke more than anything."

Meghan turned the little charm over in her hand. "Thank you, Mama," she whispered. All that time she'd been so upset her father didn't love her, she'd forgotten that her daddy did. If only she could thank him for that. Mama's eyes filled with tears. "It looks just beautiful on you." She pulled Meghan into a tight hug.

"You're crushing me, Mama," Meghan said, laughing.

"I have a lot of years of hugs to give you, little girl." She pulled away and patted her cheeks dry.

"I wish my mom was here for this," Campbell said.

Adele pulled the younger woman close. "Me too."

Jane sat in silence across the table. Meghan hoped she didn't regret offering her forgiveness—it had given her hope. Every night before bed, Meghan read one of the prayers Jane had written for her. Knowing someone had taken the time to do that for her, to wish those things for her—Meghan had come to believe it had single-handedly saved her life.

"Oh my stars and bananas," Mama said. "You weren't kidding."

They all followed Mama's gaze to the bathroom, where Lila had just emerged, looking green. She sank back into the empty chair, looking dazed.

"Lila, I don't want to alarm you, but have you considered . . ." Jane stopped.

"What?" Lila stared at her.

"You're pregnant," Meghan said.

Adele and Campbell both gasped.

Lila sat up straighter in her chair. "How is that even possible?"

"When a man and a woman love each other very much—"

Lila cut Meghan off with an upheld hand. "Don't be a smart aleck. You know what I mean. I'm forty-two."

"My mom worked with a woman who got pregnant at forty-five," Campbell said.

Lila groaned. "No way."

"Are you and Tom back together?" Jane's eyes were wide, waiting for the answer they all wanted.

"I've seen you two together," Meghan said. "It's possible."

Lila laughed. "We have had a bit of a rebirth in that area." She looked at Campbell. "Sorry, hon."

"I'm pretending you're not talking about my father."

They laughed, and then Lila's face went pale.

"Are you going to throw up again?" Meghan backed away.

"No, no. I'm just trying to understand this—do you really think?"

"Only one way to find out," Jane said. "Go get a test."

"And what? Do it here? In the bathroom?" Lila brushed her off.

"Why not?" Meghan smiled. "You know you're dying to find out."

"Correction. *We're* dying to find out," Jane said.

"I'll go buy you one myself," Mama said. She stood up and before anyone could stop her, she was out the door.

"Well, that's that," Meghan said. "I wonder what the cashier at the drug store will think when Mama shows up at the counter with a pregnancy test."

"Oh, the rumors that will spread . . ." Jane laughed.

In record time, Mama returned and waved a little white plastic bag in Lila's direction. "I got it!" She held the bag out to Lila, who stared at it, unmoving.

"You okay?" Jane put a hand on Lila's shoulder.

"I'm terrified," Lila said. "I don't want to get my hopes up. I've accepted that I'll never have a child."

"Hon, you'd given up all hope of having a great marriage too, and look how that's turned around," Jane said.

Lila met her eyes and then stood. "You're right."

They all watched her return to the tiny bathroom under Adele's stairs, eyes full of anticipation for a full two and a half minutes. No one said a word, with the exception of the occasional "Should we check on her?" and "What's taking so long?"

Finally, Lila emerged from the bathroom, emotionless.

They let out a collective sigh and prepared for the worst, but the closer Lila got to the table, the bigger her smile grew.

"It's positive," she said. "I can't believe it, but it's positive."

Excitement erupted as they all screamed. Jane cheered and hugged their friend and they all congratulated her, but Lila's face had gone blank.

She dropped into the chair and stared at the table. "You guys, what if I lose this one too?" She met Jane's eyes. By some invisible thread, Jane held her steady. "I can't lose another baby."

Meghan watched as Jane comforted her, thankful she'd returned to Sweethaven, thankful she'd found forgiveness and these women—her best friends—had welcomed her back with open arms.

"We're going to bathe that baby in prayer," Jane said.

"You have to say that, Jane. You're married to a pastor." Lila cocked her head and stared at her friend. "You know God and I aren't exactly close."

Meghan fished inside her bag until she found the spiral-bound journal Jane had given her. She reached across the table and handed it to Lila. "Here," she said.

Jane met her eyes.

"Now, I'm going to want this back, but you should have it. At least for a little while." Meghan smiled. "There are words in there that almost seem . . . alive."

Lila opened the book and flipped through the pages. "Prayers?"

"Good ones." Meghan smiled at Jane, who held her gaze for a few beats and then glanced at the book.

"Thank you," Lila said.

Adele clapped her hands together. "Girls. I hope you're ready because I've got a full weekend planned, and I can't wait to get started."

They all pulled photos from their bags and started organizing them by event.

Meghan stopped for a moment, staring at them, and when Mama glanced at her, she frowned. "You okay?"

Meghan smiled. "I'm better than okay, Mama. I'm home."

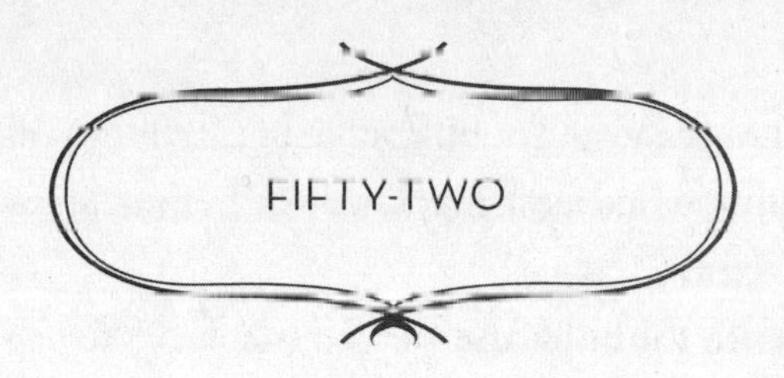

FIFTY-TWO

Meghan

Sunday afternoon, after spending two full days of eating far too many baked goods and capturing so many memories on the pages of their new album, Meghan headed home, sad that tomorrow—Labor Day—she'd need to return to her real life. Find a new manager. Promote her album.

Figure out how to be apart from the kids, even for a little while.

Before she reached the lake house, Nick texted and asked her to meet him at the little yellow cottage—the house he'd bought and restored. Not for himself, he said.

But for who?

Maybe he'd done it for the kids—not for her as she'd hopefully assumed.

Meghan reached the cottage and parked the car, surprised Nick's was the only vehicle in the driveway.

She stopped when she saw him leaning against the beams on the front porch, watching her.

"You taking the day off?" She shielded her eyes from the sun.

"Just enjoying the view." With his hands stuffed in his jean pockets, he reminded her of the boy she'd fallen in love with so many years ago.

"It is pretty out here."

"That's not the view I'm talking about." His eyes stayed intently on her, and she smiled as she reached the bottom steps.

"Is that right?"

Their relationship had settled into a nice friendship, and she had to admit she loved having him back in her life. Did they dare mess with that now? Maybe she should be thankful for what they did have and leave it alone?

"It's finished," he said with a quick glance toward the house.

She grinned. "You gonna show me?" Nick had been so secretive about the renovations. He'd refused to take her through it until he was completely finished.

Without a word, he opened the front door and led her inside, and what she saw took her breath away. Without the tools and cast-off pieces of wood and trim, the home had taken on a new look. He'd remodeled the cottage in its original style—keeping all of its integrity but adding details and charm to make it unique. The house had been expanded, the master suite made larger and a third bedroom had been added to the upstairs.

Meghan took it all in. The white molding. The window seat. The screened-in sleeping porch out back. Meghan's eyes filled with tears.

"What's wrong?" Nick watched her.

"That summer we stayed here—before Alex . . ."

He reached out and wiped a tear from her face. "You told me what you'd do to make this place yours."

"And you remembered?"

"Every word."

Meghan followed him up a set of stairs that seemed to land them over the garage.

"This is what I really wanted to show you," he said.

She stared across the bonus room. As if the roof had been removed, raised and replaced, the pitched ceiling offered a perfect loft space.

"Luke helped me design it," Nick said.

A long table with two computers on it sat across the back wall. A boom stand and microphone were situated off to the side, along with a mixing board and a keyboard. "Nick . . ."

She tried to take it all in, but the magnitude of what he'd done for her stole her words.

"It's a recording studio. I know it's not state of the art, but I figured for writing—for demos and that sort of thing."

He leaned against the wall, avoiding her eyes.

She inspected the equipment—almost a mirror image of what she had back home in Nashville. It made sense—he'd built her that studio too. She used it to record her ideas before actually buying studio time—it let her work from home most of the time.

"You went to so much trouble." She turned around and stared at him. He finally met her eyes. They begged her to stay.

He walked toward her and took her hand. Still holding her gaze, he slipped a ring onto her left-hand ring finger. "It's time to come home, Meghan."

She turned her hand over. Her wedding ring—the thin silver band he'd given her before they had a dime—stared back at her, welcoming her like a long lost friend.

"Will you?" His eyes danced across her face and she studied them with a newfound appreciation for his love. Unconditional and unfailing, he'd loved her so wholly it threatened to take her breath away.

She didn't deserve it, but could she accept it?

He stepped toward her and took her face in his hands. She stared up at him.

"You're all I've ever wanted," he said.

She closed her eyes. "It's always been you."

A tear fell down her cheek and he wiped it away with his thumb.

Without another word, his lips found hers. She closed her eyes and savored the way they pressed into hers, unhurried like he wanted to drink her in—body and soul. Passion enveloped his kiss and in a flash, she remembered every intimate moment they'd spent together—every night falling asleep in his arms, every morning she awoke, savoring the way his skin smelled, the way his hands caressed her with such care. She'd missed everything about him.

He pulled away and stared at her.

Meghan wrapped her arms around his neck and leaned into him. "Nick Rhodes, every love song I write is for you."

As she melted into his kiss, Meghan kept hearing the words and melody of a new song . . .

Home is like the open arms, the kiss after a fight

Home will leave the light on for ya, when the world has said good night.

No matter how dark your day, there's still one place to go

When the big, wide world gets the best of you . . .

You can always go . . . back home.

FIFTY-THREE

Meghan

Three weeks later, with autumn in all its splendor, Meghan stood at the back of the Sweethaven Chapel staring out the window. Luke and Nick had set up chairs underneath white lanterns that hung from trees so vibrantly red and orange they looked like they'd been plugged into an electrical outlet.

The contrast of color made her smile, but seeing her friends and family gathering for their wedding filled her soul.

"Meg?" Jane's voice pulled her out of her daydream. "You ready?"

Meghan nodded as Luke appeared in the doorway. "The cowboy boots are a nice touch," he said, glancing at her feet.

"They look great with my white sundress, don't you think?"

Luke studied her. "Better than the first time we did this. That dress made you look like a Stay Puft marshmallow."

Meghan shot him a look.

He grinned. "Let's get this over with already." Outside, he offered her his arm and then stood at the back of the makeshift aisle lined with sprays of cream roses.

Nick stood, hands clasped in front of him, eyes focused on Meghan—inviting her to join him and stay with him for as long as they both should live.

Meghan smiled at him, took Luke's arm and followed the twins down the aisle, accompanied by an instrumental version of "My One and Only."

When she reached Nick, he took her hand and kissed it, then led her to the end of the aisle where they stood in front of Graham, who waited, Bible in hand, to start the ceremony.

On a hill overlooking Lake Michigan surrounded by friends and family, Meghan handed herself over to the love of her life with no intention of taking herself away from him ever again.

"Ladies and gentlemen, I'm pleased to present Mr. and Mrs. Nicholas Rhodes," Graham said.

Meghan and Nick turned and faced the tiny crowd, and everyone erupted in cheers. It was as if they'd all been waiting for this day to finally come right alongside them—and now, thankfully, they were right back where they were supposed to be.

As Nick brushed her long hair away from her face and leaned in to kiss her, the promise of a lifetime of kisses filled her mind.

Nick held her face in his hands as their kiss ended. "I promise, Meghan, I'm going to love you and protect you for as long as we both live."

She smiled. "And I promise, Nick, I'm ready to let you. Thank you for never giving up on me."

"It's time to become the family we were always meant to be."

Meghan had been on many stages in her lifetime. She'd won awards and received standing ovations more times than she could remember. Still, nothing she'd ever done compared to the kind of joy she felt in that moment. As Nick leaned in to kiss her, she felt a little hand slip into her own. She glanced down and saw Nadia peering up at her.

"I'm glad you're coming home, Mommy."

Tears sprang to her eyes and Meghan smiled. "Me too, Nadia. I'm so glad to be home for good."

Dear Reader,

I've always been a homebody. When I was a kid, I never spent the night anywhere because I had a terrible case of homesickness every time I tried. I was fortunate to grow up in a loving home with two wonderful parents and two (usually) wonderful siblings, and I suppose these are the reasons coming home has such appeal to me.

After the release of my first novel, *A Sweethaven Summer*, I boarded a plane and went back to Illinois to celebrate with my friends and family. It was there I discovered how important the rich support of a community can be. I don't think I realized when I wrote the first book how my own special friendships played into the creation of my characters, and I certainly didn't fully grasp the magnitude of their support until after that weekend.

We're all searching for that place, aren't we? That place where we can come as we are, be accepted for who we are, whether we're celebrating, healing, recovering, or regrouping. In each of us is that need to belong, and that's what I wanted to capture in this book. It's a universal need we all have. For you, as with me, it may start with your childhood home, your hometown, the place you've created for your own family. But for others, it may feel far away and unreachable.

I hope that through Meghan's story, you're able to uncover the reality that no matter where you live or what kind of memories you have when you think of "home," there is a place you can go where you're always loved and accepted just as you are.

See, there's something else that's universal—the love of the One who made you—and I don't think it's an accident that He's created in each of us a need that only He can fill.

Every day is a journey moving us closer to Him. I'd love for you to join me on my journey by connecting with me on my Web site (www.courtneywalshwrites.com) or my blog (www.courtneywalsh .typepad.com).

And I want to sincerely thank you for taking the time to visit Sweethaven. It means so much to me.

Sincerely,
Courtney Walsh

ABOUT THE AUTHOR

Courtney Walsh is a published author, scrapbooking expert, theater director, and playwright. She has written two papercrafting books, *Scrapbooking Your Faith* and *The Busy Scrapper,* and is currently working on her third. She has been a contributing editor for *Memory Makers Magazine* and *Children's Ministry Magazine.* She has also written several full-length musicals, including her most recent, *The Great American Tall Tales,* and *Hercules* for Christian Youth Theater, Chicago. *A Sweethaven Summer* is her debut novel. *A Sweethaven Homecoming* is the second book in the series, and *A Sweethaven Christmas* will release in the fall of 2012.

Courtney recently moved from Colorado back to her home state of Illinois with her husband and three children. She loves to make new friends, so feel free to contact her via her Web site, www.courtneywalshwrites.com, or through her blog, www.courtneywalsh.typepad.com.

We hope you enjoy *A Sweethaven Homecoming,* created by Guideposts Books and Inspirational Media. In all of our books, magazines and outreach efforts, we aim to deliver inspiration and encouragement, help you grow in your faith, and celebrate God's love in every aspect of your daily life.

Thank you for making a difference with your purchase of this book, which helps fund our many outreach programs to the military, prisons, hospitals, nursing homes and schools. To learn more, visit GuidepostsFoundation.org.

We also maintain many useful and uplifting online resources. Visit Guideposts.org to read true stories of hope and inspiration, access OurPrayer network, sign up for free newsletters, join our Facebook community, and follow our stimulating blogs.

To order your favorite Guideposts publications, go to ShopGuideposts.org, call (800) 932-2145 or write to Guideposts, PO Box 5815, Harlan, Iowa 51593.